every

moment

after

By Joseph Moldover

Houghton Mifflin Harcourt
Boston   New York

hmhco.com

The text was set in Adobe Garamond Pro.

Library of Congress Cataloging-in-Publication Data
Names: Moldover, Joseph, author.
Title: Every moment after / by Joseph Moldover.
Description: Boston ; New York : Houghton Mifflin Harcourt, [2019] |
Summary: After high school graduation, best friends Matt and Cole
strive to put behind them the school shooting they survived in first grade
and really begin to live. Told in two voices.
Identifiers: LCCN 2018014689 | ISBN 9781328547279
Subjects: | CYAC: Best friends—Fiction. | Friendship—Fiction. |
Community life—New Jersey—Fiction. | School shootings—Fiction. | High
schools—Fiction. | Schools—Fiction. | New Jersey—Fiction.
Classification: LCC PZ7.1.M63965 Eve 2019 |
DDC [Fic]—dc23
LC record available at https://lccn.loc.gov/2018014689

Manufactured in the United States of America
DOC 10 9 8 7 6 5 4 3 2 1
4500750743

For Leah, with all the love in my heart

One

— Cole —

People want to forget. No one would ever say it, but I think this town will be glad to see our class leave. They put up all the memorials you'd expect, but there was no need: we're living reminders. Year after year, walking the streets, sitting in the diner, popping up in marching band and on the baseball team.

Teachers retired right before we got to them. Like we were a wave slowly sweeping from grade two to twelve, washing away all the old and tired ones, the ones who were sick of telling people they taught school in East Ridge, New Jersey, and getting that horrible look back. The ones who couldn't deal with staring out at our faces for a whole year. And now those who made it all the way to this afternoon have convinced themselves that they need to get through only a few more hours, as if they'll be able to forget us after we're gone.

Even the weather knows the script today. Low gray clouds, black in the distance. A warm wind, midsixties. It will rain later, but it will hold off until after we've all gone home for quick parties with our parents before coming back to be bused off for Project Graduation. It will rain on empty chairs, eighteen of them still draped in black, and it will turn this field into mud.

There are lots of people here now, though. Teachers, some parents, and other students who are helping to set up. Mom is toward the back, unfolding chairs from a cart. The principal and superintendent are going over paperwork together, probably making sure the superintendent knows how to pronounce all the last names. Lots of police, not surprisingly, some of them leaning against the back wall of the school and some in the parking lot, holding the press at bay. It's a few minutes past one; we're supposed to line up in half an hour.

I'm trying to stay busy and starting to get frustrated with this uncooperative row of chairs. It's the tenth row back, left-hand side. I can get every chair to align with the one next to it, but somehow when I get to the center aisle, the line in its entirety is veering off on a slant. I start back to try again when I hear someone calling my name and see Mrs. Kennedy, my tenth-grade history teacher, waving to me from the front. I look around to see whether anyone's watching, push my sunglasses up the bridge of my nose, and make my way down to her.

The black draperies aren't staying on in the wind. "Help me with this, Cole," she says. "I don't want poor Mrs. Maiden to have to." The fabric is a weird sort of material, heavier than a bedsheet, kind of glossy. It's draped over the same flimsy chairs that we all have to sit in and it's taped in a few key spots so that it folds right, but the tape isn't holding. I study the third chair in from the aisle. If they were arranged alphabetically, whose seat would this be? Abrams, Clemson, Edwards. Susie Edwards. Unless Principal Schultz got the aisle, in which case everybody would be pushed in by one. Poor guy, having to show up for a high school graduation ceremony eleven years after his death. We should let him rest in peace. So let's just say that this one belongs to Susie. She was a funny little girl with pigtails. We played tag together. When we went out for recess that last winter, she used to ask me for help getting her snow boots on the right feet. I go in search of stronger tape so that her chair will look good.

Mrs. Maiden is collating programs at the edge of the risers, and she pauses what she's doing to smile at me and squeeze my arm as I pass. I smile back and then instinctively look down. Some of the parents are coming today and some aren't, but I think Mrs. Maiden is the only one who's actually volunteering with setup, as though she had a living child getting ready to walk. I move past her as quickly as I can.

Families are filtering in, setting bags and umbrellas down to reserve long lines of seats. The media is back behind the police line on the far side of the parking lot. They've been around all week doing retrospectives, just like they were at the first and the fifth and, to a lesser extent, the tenth anniversary. We've been told to notify one of the police officers if we see someone suspicious taking pictures, although I don't know how you enforce that at a graduation, since everyone's going to be taking pictures of everything. Anyway, I think that most people they'd want to interview have already said no. I don't think that's right. There's a responsibility that comes with being a survivor.

Someone nudges me hard, and I turn. "What's up, bro?" Eddie Deangelo asks, swinging his hand around in a wide arc to grab mine. Awkward. I never know how to respond when someone calls me *bro*. Like, do I have to call him *bro* back, or is it a one-way street? And the sideways handshake, the hand clasp, I can never get the angle right. Are we shaking hands? Is it a high-five? Are we supposed to do something afterward, like a secret handshake? I manage to grab his hand and mumble a greeting that may or may not include the word *bro,* not that Eddie seems to notice. He slaps me hard on the shoulder. Eddie is the only other person who's wearing sunglasses under the overcast sky, and seeing him makes me realize that mine must make me more noticeable, not less. I push them up on my forehead.

"We good?" he asks. Eddie's somehow managed to rumple and stain his gown, even though this is the only time he's worn it. Probably will be the only time he ever wears a graduation gown, I think. Even with the wind, he reeks of pot. Eddie's one of the select few not going off to college in the fall. Me and Eddie Deangelo: Who would have thought?

"We're good," I say.

"Your boy had some cash-flow problems, huh?"

"What boy?"

"Your bro, Matt!" Eddie must live in a world of people who

are all *bro*s. "Don't sweat it," he continues. "We got it all worked out. I'm looking forward to seeing what you got." He slaps my shoulder again, wags his finger in my face, and turns away, leaving me to wonder what the hell he was talking about.

Matt Simpson and I made an arrangement with Eddie, one I'm counting on, but Matt didn't tell me about any problems with money. If there's one thing you can usually count on Matt for, it's having cash. I scan the crowd, looking for him. If there's something you can absolutely *always* count on him for, it's turning up at the last minute.

Over on the other side of the field, Mom has finished setting up the chairs and is talking with some other parents. People are milling around. There's a family standing nearby, and the mother is whispering to the grandmother. They both look in my direction. I freeze for a moment, the way I always do, feeling like a bug under a microscope. *Is she pointing me out? Are they looking at me?* The Boy in the Picture, all grown up. That photo won a Pulitzer for the reporter and a lifetime of wearing sunglasses for me. I pull them back down over my eyes and hurry toward the school.

There was a lot of discussion about how the ceremony was going to go. First, the governor was going to come and speak, but that got scrapped. We have a Republican governor for a change, and I read that it was because he hasn't been great on gun control. So, you know, awkward to be facing all those empty chairs. Then the senator was going to come. He's the opposite of the governor; every year on the anniversary, he puts enlarged photos of everyone who died up on the floor of Congress and asks why they still haven't done anything about guns. But now the senator's not coming either. The same article I read about the governor said that the senator didn't want to be seen as making it political after all this time.

I don't pay much attention to politicians, but one thing I do notice: for a while it was too soon for them to talk about it or do anything, and then right after that, it was too late, like they were dredging up the past. I don't know when it would have been the right time for someone to do something. I don't know what anyone could have done, though I do think they should have gotten rid of the big guns. A crazy dude isn't going to kill seventeen first-graders and their principal with a knife. Probably not with a pistol. Not even with a hunting rifle, people said, though I'm not a gun person and I've never checked one out. But there's one thing I do know: an assault rifle made it pretty fucking easy.

I make my way up the center aisle and step to the side to let Chris Thayer's wheelchair roll by, narrowly avoiding getting my feet run over in the process. He can basically move one arm, and even that's hard for him, so he steers the thing with a joystick. Chris knows everyone, and everyone loves him. It was no surprise when he was elected our senior class president.

"Hey, Cole," he says, pausing and turning toward me, "how're you doing?" His voice is always soft and unsteady, like he can't quite control it.

"I'm okay, Chris. How are you?"

He shakes his head. "Can you believe all the reporters?"

I shrug. "We're still a story."

"A few of them tried to take a picture of me, but my mom blocked them."

"Crazy."

"You know what I think, though?" he asks, dropping his voice. I lean in to hear him. "I think it would have been more terrible if they didn't show up. You know?"

"Maybe it would have been," I say. "Maybe they'll forget about us after this, and then we'll know whether it's worse than being remembered."

"That's a good line. I should use it." Chris gets to give a speech as class president.

"It's all yours."

He considers for a moment. "Nah, I'm trying to be upbeat. I'll see you, Cole."

"Good luck, Chris."

Chris moves along, and I go in the opposite direction. A few parents greet me, and one gives me a hug. She looks teary. I can't remember whose mother she is, but I half hug her back without fully stopping. I don't like big crowds, and this one is getting bigger by the minute. I zigzag back and forth, feeling my tension rising, sort of looking for the custodian but mostly looking for someone else. I wind up momentarily wedged against the back wall of the school as an old man with a cane is being helped along by a woman with three toddlers trailing behind her, and I take this moment to look for Viola.

This is how I've walked through most of senior year. No matter what else was happening, no matter what I was doing, a very significant part of my brain was devoted to Viola Grey. I'm constantly thinking about where she might be, what she might be doing, who she's with, and what I can say if and when I see her. It's amazing how much time I spend thinking about her. It's amazing how many things I think of to say, and it's even more amazing how few of them ever actually wind up coming out of my mouth.

The family finally trickles past, and I'm able to make my way around the bleachers and into the school through one of the rear doors. I find the custodian in the gym; he's pushing his mop around, which seems stupid, given that no one's coming in here and he has the whole summer to clean the place up. He tells me where the tape is, and I notice that he seems uncomfortable. A lot of people are around me. Like I said, people want to forget. So here we are, hours away from being gone forever, and I know it will be a relief for the custodian and for lots of other people. I get the tape from his closet and head back out to the field, weaving through the thickening crowd, making for the empty black chairs. I spot a few other survivors, scattered like islands.

Mrs. Kennedy thanks me for the tape and, apparently recognizing that it's not at all the sort of thing I'm good at, starts fixing the chairs herself. I feel eyes on me and don't want to stay down front, so I go back to the tenth row and start over, keeping my head down. It's like there's some microscopic problem I'm having in lining this up, and it's so small that I can't see it when I look at one seat next to another, but when it's amplified over a whole row, it looks like it was done by a toddler. How does everyone else's look better?

"Cole, say hello to the Gerbers."

Mom has snuck up on me with Frank and Ruth Gerber, and their son, Paul. Frank and Ruth size me up the way they always do, looking me up and down with sad, surprised smiles. There used to be three of us: me, Matt, and Andy Gerber. Always together. Seeing me must make them remember how long Andy's been gone.

"My God, Cole," Mr. Gerber says, "look at the size of you."

I shake his hand, and then Mrs. Gerber's, and then look awkwardly to Paul, who, as usual, isn't acknowledging anyone around him.

"You're looking good, kid," Mr. Gerber says, and I smile and nod. I glance at Paul again. He has his gown on, but it's misbuttoned. He's shifting his weight from one foot to another, staring down at his shoes in the grass, making a sort of high-pitched humming noise. "Paulie," Mr. Gerber says, "Paulie, say hi to Cole." Paul doesn't respond, just keeps shifting his weight and humming.

"You look good, Paul," I offer. He does, relatively speaking. He's lost about a hundred pounds since they took him off the medicine he was on. I mean that: a literal hundred pounds.

Sophomore year, Paul Gerber blew up like an absolute blimp. Not that it was his fault; it wasn't anyone's fault, except maybe the doctor who was prescribing for him. I guess he needed the meds—he was getting out of control and all—but it was sad because when he was younger, he looked just like Andy, although you would never confuse them. Paul was always flapping his hands and spinning in circles, staring at the ceiling fan in their kitchen, not talking. It's a weird thing, but it's true: you can have identical twins where one has autism and one doesn't. Same genes, same family, different random quirks of the brain.

"Cole," Mrs. Gerber says, "when everyone lines up, can you help make sure Paul's in the right spot for us?"

Gerber is a few places before *Hewitt*. I promise I will and then stand looking at the grass while my mom makes small talk. She seems well, for the moment. She has makeup on and is chatty and lively.

There's a family taking a picture off to my left. I can see them from the corner of my eye, and for a moment I think they're trying to get a photo of me. Then I tell myself that's ridiculous and that I'm being paranoid. I'm a curiosity, not a celebrity. I kick at a small tuft of tickseed.

Coreopsis, I think automatically. *Coreopsis . . . lanceolata.* That's it. *C. lanceolata.* As always, the scientific name comes to me in Dad's voice. As always, it calms me.

I tell Mom I have to keep helping with the chairs. I say goodbye to the Gerbers, and a few moments later, I'm alone again, jealously contemplating the architectural precision with which Rosie Horowitz has set up rows eleven through fourteen. I am seriously considering moving at least a few of her chairs off-kilter when I hear a voice behind me. It's the one I've been waiting all day to hear: light English accent, slower paced than we talk in Jersey. Excellent diction, the last consonant in my last name snapped off clean. Maybe just a hint of a tease, though I might only be kidding myself.

"Cole Anthony Hewitt."

I turn around, and there is Viola, standing just a few feet away. She's holding a program and her cap. The wind picks up a little bit and ruffles both our gowns, blowing a strand of hair over her face. She reaches up to loop it back over an ear.

She is beautiful. Her chestnut-brown hair is up in a twist, and if the sun were out, her eyes would be a bright green, but with the clouds, they've faded to a sort of steel blue. I could go on all day about Viola's eyes, by the way. Green can be described by all sorts of things: emeralds, the ocean, budding leaves in early spring. I think I've used them all; I have notebooks full of poems at home, lined up on a shelf in chronological order. If you went back a few years and read forward, you'd find me writing about nature, about the lake, about kids at school. As you went along, you'd find a few minor crushes, and then you'd find my dad getting sick. It would get heavy fast. And then you'd start to read my poems about Viola, and you'd find every way the English language offers to describe green eyes.

She looks me up and down with a crooked smile, and I can't help but grin back, even though my mind has gone completely blank. I spend so much time thinking about her when she's not around that I'm always shocked when I come face-to-face with the real person.

"You look good in black," she says.

"It suits you, too," I say. I resist the impulse to comment that I've already worn too much black this year; it's the kind of self-pitying crap I'm prone to, and I know it's no way to make a girl fall for you. Viola knows that my father died.

"Seen your best friend around?" she asks. "I have a funny story for him."

"Matt? No, I haven't seen him. Haven't seen him since yesterday. No idea where he is." I glance over her shoulder to where Matt is walking across the parking lot as we speak, black gown streaming behind him like a cape, cap held in one hand, the other held aloft with the middle finger extended toward the crowd of reporters. We've been told not to acknowledge them; reference to the shooting is to be confined to one moment of silence, followed by a reading of the names, and to the silent tribute of the black, empty chairs. No one, in other words, is to turn to the crowd after taking their diploma and shout, "Fuck Sam Keeley!" Or do the sort of thing that Matt is doing right now.

"What's the funny story?" I ask.

"Oh, it's about someone I don't think you know. She's a junior on the volleyball team. She had a thing for Matt." She shrugs, apparently resigned to talking to me instead of my friend. "You didn't play any sports, did you?"

"No. No sports."

"Were you in any clubs?"

"No clubs."

She gives me a quizzical smile. "What exactly *did* you do in high school, Cole?"

Think about you, I want to tell her. "Mostly wait for it to be over," I say.

She pauses for a moment and then bursts out laughing. I love the way she throws her head back but keeps her eyes on me, as if she's watching to make sure I don't pull something on her in this moment of vulnerability. I want to surprise her and make her laugh so hard that she closes her eyes.

Viola moved to town midway through the ninth grade. She came from England, and everything about her has always been different. She did lots of things in high school: field hockey; the fall play a couple of times; speech and debate. She had a fair number of friends, but she always seemed like she was watching us from a little bit of a distance.

"I was just talking to Paul Gerber's parents," I say, trying to keep her talking. "You know, about helping him line up."

"I don't think he's actually graduating, is he?" she asks.

"I think that kids like him get a blank diploma and then come back to school next year to do life skills."

"Do you think he understands that all the rest of us are done with school? I'm just imagining when he gets home and takes his piece of paper out of the tube, unrolls it, and finds that it's blank. Will he feel left behind? Does he know we're all leaving?" She must see a look on my face, because she quickly adds: "I mean, you're going too, Cole. Eventually, right?"

"Right," I say. "Right. Next year. That's heavy, about Paul. I don't know." I can't remember any of the thoughtful, reflective lines I came up with for a serious moment.

Matt has reached the field, but Viola still hasn't turned and seen him.

"So," I say, "are you supposed to be giving a speech today? Going to quote some Eliot? Tell us not to live out our lives in coffee spoons?"

"*Measure out* our lives *with* coffee spoons, not *in* them. And the salutatorian doesn't get to speak, Cole; only the valedictorian. There's no silver medal, and if there were, I wouldn't want it."

"Right. Uh, right. Well, it was so close, I thought they might put you in anyway. What were you off by, a thousandth of a GPA point or something?" I laugh. She doesn't. This is pretty much why I talk to her only a fraction as much as I plan to: I will inevitably say something agonizingly stupid.

I quickly start blathering on about summer plans and whatever else comes to mind, which honestly is not much. I haven't met many British people, but Viola is listening and nodding with one raised eyebrow in what I interpret as a classic posture of resigned English indulgence. I love that she can raise one eyebrow like that.

Matt has disappeared into the crowd, and I soon run out of things to talk about. Viola's family is nearby, and she excuses herself to go and join them. I ache as I watch her walk away. Things have to work out this summer. I don't know what will happen to me if I have to watch her walk away for good in August.

I look around, wanting something to stay busy with. Mom has found a seat with the Gerbers. Paul is with one of his special-education teachers and seems to be all right. The clouds are a little bit darker. A bunch of younger kids are milling around, looking bored.

Something stirs down front, near the podium. There's a change in tone, a little murmur, people looking and then quickly looking away. Maybe someone is having a breakdown, I think. Maybe seeing those black-draped chairs was too much. Maybe the school shouldn't have done that. We couldn't have done *nothing,* though. There's never a right thing to do or not to do. Say something, don't say something—it doesn't change it. I start to make my way down to get a look. Whatever's happening can't be too serious, or else the police would be getting involved. I get a little closer, craning my head to look in the direction where Mrs. Maiden had been standing; for some reason, I think the most likely thing is that she's collapsed. There are a few parents by the risers, arms crossed on their chests, speaking quietly to one another. One of them turns and looks over her shoulder. I follow her eyes, and I see him.

Matt is sitting in one of the chairs. Right there, in the front row, all alone. He's set himself down in one of the black-draped seats and he's just sitting, staring at the stage, rubbing his right elbow. I stop and watch for a moment, but no one is doing anything, so I go over and stand in front of him. He looks right through me.

Matt Simpson has always had a special status. I don't mind saying he's handsome: over six feet tall, big and athletic, sandy blond hair. The guy's going off to college on a Division I baseball scholarship, and he looks the part: all American. He even has the square jaw. Right now, though, he just looks lost.

No one else is coming over. For the last eleven years, the school has always made a big deal out of providing counselors for everything, and now here we are at the finish line, and there's no one to be seen.

"Matt," I say. He doesn't look at me. "Matt, get the fuck up."

He just sits, holding his elbow.

"I thought your arm was getting better."

"It was."

"Is your blood sugar low?" I ask. "Do you need some juice?"

He doesn't respond, but he doesn't look like that's the problem. He usually gets all sweaty when his sugar's low.

"Do you smell something?" Matt asks.

I sniff the air. "No."

"It's some sort of chemical or something."

I shake my head. He has to get up. "Matt," I say, "you're being disrespectful. These chairs are supposed to be empty. They're memorials, you know? You can't just sit in them. It's wrong. It's like you're taking a leak in a reflecting pool."

"Why are they empty?" he asks. "Why do you think they're supposed to be empty?"

What a stupid question. "Because they're gone," I say. "Because they're never coming back and . . . and they've left a gap here. It's symbolic. The holes never closed up, you know?" I shouldn't have to explain it to him. My eyes turn toward the press on the far side of the parking lot, and I wonder whether that's what he's upset about, whether he thinks the chairs are some sort of media stunt. That's the sort of thing that would drive him nuts. Matt's always had a hard time with the tributes and memorials. I don't think he's ever gotten over not being at school that day.

"Think of Andy," I say. "That chair is for Andy. You have to get out of it. I know you hate shit like this, but you have to go along with it. This is the last time."

He shakes his head. "You remember that movie Andy liked?" he asks. "The cartoon one with the spaceman?"

"Yeah?

"What was the stupid line he liked to say? I've been trying to remember."

"Get up and I'll tell you."

"He said it all the time. I can't remember."

17

"I remember. Get up and I'll tell you."

He gazes off to his left, down the long line of black seats. "I don't know, Cole," he finally says. "Maybe this is where I was meant to be sitting." Before I can think of a response, he looks up and really focuses on me for the first time. "You want to hear something crazy?"

I'm not sure I do, but I nod. It's something you do for your best friend. You listen to the crazy stuff. He's always done it for me.

"I don't think I can remember what Andy even looked like anymore."

I remember. Andy had curly black hair and dark eyes and a dimple in his chin. He looked like his dad and, of course, like Paul. "I have some photos," I say. "I can show you."

He shakes his head. "I don't want to remember." He gets up and turns to stand next to me, gazing out over the crowd like nothing happened. I look up at the sky: not a hint of blue. It's time to start lining up. I put my hand on Matt's shoulder, and he lets me guide him back to the center aisle and to the rear of the field, where people are taking their positions in line. Matt heads toward the *S*'s. I remember to look for Paul and make sure he's in the right spot, and then I stand and wait for the ceremony to begin.

It's only when we start walking that I realize Matt forgot to ask me what Andy used to say, and that I forgot to tell him.

Two

— Matt —

The lake is there, whenever I close my eyes. I see it from the beach where Andy, Cole, and I used to make sand castles, and where they'd gobble their double-scoop ice cream cones while Mom weighed my serving and prepped an insulin injection. I see the water, green and cold and deeper than anyone knows, stretching out to the far shore. For months, it's the only thing I've been able to dream about, and now it's where I have to go.

But first, I have to get Cole off this motherfucking bus.

I'm scanning the school parking lot as soon as we pull in. They should have cops here, but they don't. A reporter could step right up to him, take a photo, stick a microphone in his face. The Boy in the Picture, eleven years later.

The brakes squeal, the bus stops, and I'm out of my seat before anyone else. I push my way down the aisle to the door, and I'm the first one off. It's completely still. The sun is just beginning to rise, but there are plenty of shadows where someone could hide. I walk along the edge of the lot, looking in between cars, examining the trees that separate it from the town dump. Nothing.

"Captain!"

I turn and see Luther Schmidt coming toward me, duffel thrown over his shoulder, the usual grin on his big, wide face. He slaps me on the arm, hard. Luther does everything hard. He sees me flinch.

"Still sore?" he asks.

"Yeah. A little." My elbow is throbbing, the injury that almost ended my season stubbornly refusing to heal.

"It's not gonna be a problem in the fall, is it?"

"Nah. I've got some meds, and I'm doing PT all summer. I'll be ready."

"Good." He walks over to his pickup, flips the gate down, and sits. I pull myself up next to him. "So what're you now?" he asks. "You're a moose, right?"

"A bison. They're the Bucknell Bisons." Luther is the only person I know who's even worse with names than I am.

"Huh. Anyone famous ever play for them?"

"Christy Mathewson."

"Never heard of him." Luther opens his bag, takes out a two-liter Sprite bottle, and has a long sip. He hands it to me, but I push it away. I don't feel like vodka. We sit and watch the rest of our class streaming off the bus. People are milling around, some heading for their cars, some signing yearbooks. I spot Cole, finally talking to Viola. She's yawning and clearly wants to go home. It's fair; we've been up all night. Cole's never been good at picking up on other people's signals, and he's never known how easy his own are to read.

"You do laser tag?" Luther asks.

"No."

"What about the zipline?"

"No."

"Skating?"

"I didn't make it to the rink."

"So what'd you do?"

The truth is, not much. Project Graduation is always at a mystery destination. They keep us there all night so that some kid doesn't get drunk and drive into a tree. It turned out to be at this massive indoor sports place up the Turnpike: tennis, ice skating, laser tag; they had everything, and I wanted to do it all. I wanted to try to shake this feeling off, this thing that's been in my head for weeks now, maybe months. I wanted to try to have some fun.

Even more than that, though, I wanted Cole to actually talk to Viola. He barely ever talks to her. I mean, he talks to me *about* her. All the time, he talks to me. He's crazy about her. Cole thought she was going to NYU; he didn't come to school for three days when she decided on UC Berkeley.

Still, he wouldn't do it. He can be so pathetic sometimes, and the closer I get to leaving, the less I can stand it. So I tried to do it for him. I went up to her and started a conversation, and then I tried to hand it off, but he just did his Cole thing, staring down and mumbling and turning red and basically looking like he wished he wasn't there.

Which left me to listen to Viola go on and on about the government and the job market and God knows what else. I mean, she's cute and all, but I honestly don't know what Cole sees in her. Talking to her was like listening to my dad at a dinner party, all plans and opinions and breaking details down into more details, when I should have been playing laser tag.

I remember when Cole first started talking about her. He was so excited that she knew some poem he liked. He was all, "She actually knows it by heart!" and I'm pretty sure he was in love from that moment on. I don't see it, but I just want him to be happy. Which is why I wanted him to talk to her, and why I tried so hard to be nice to her when he wouldn't.

And now, when I'm ready to go, when she's half-asleep on her feet, Cole picks *now* to try to get something going.

A couple of girls stop on the way to their cars and start talking to Luther. He elbows me in the side. "Simpson. Wake up." All three of them are looking at me. I have no idea what they just said. "Are you?" Luther asks.

"Am I what?"

"Dude, are you coming over to my place on the Fourth? My parents are out of town. I have it all to myself."

"Oh, yeah. Yeah, I'll be there."

"Yeah, you will." Luther passes the bottle to the girls, and they look over their shoulders for the chaperones and then each have a drink. One of them holds it to out to me, but I shake my head. They chat with Luther for another moment, and then they leave. Cole is still talking at Viola, and now she's openly staring off toward her car. He's hopeless. I love him, but he's hopeless.

"Crazy, man," Luther says.

"What's crazy?"

"Everything. You see the press yesterday? There haven't been that many since I don't know when."

"The fifth anniversary."

"Yeah, probably."

"I fucking hate them."

He shrugs. "They're doing their jobs, I guess. Did you think they were gonna skip it?"

I didn't. I look past the bus, toward the school. The risers are still up, but the chairs have been put away.

"Luther, do you ever think about it?"

He pauses, bottle halfway to his mouth. "Nah."

"Really? Never?"

He shifts his weight and squints into the bottle. "I was in Mr. Davis's class."

"Yeah, but you could've been in our class."

Luther takes another drink. "My mom said it wasn't my time," he finally says. "Like, I was meant to live, right? I was meant to live so that I could do something good. That's why I'm gonna be a teacher, to do something good in the world."

"You're going to be a teacher?"

"Yeah, a gym teacher. Teach little kids to play ball and cooperate and shit like that."

"I didn't know you wanted to be a teacher." I slide down off the tailgate, stretch, and then I turn, take the bottle from his hand, and pour the remainder out onto the ground.

"I wasn't done with that, Captain!"

"I'm not team captain anymore. High school's over. Anyway, it's part of your plan. You're not supposed to drive off the road."

"I can drive buzzed."

"Time to go home, Luther."

"See you on the Fourth?"

"Sure. See you." I start to walk away.

"Simpson."

I turn back. He's still sitting in his truck, looking at me. "What about you?" he asks. "Why were you meant to live?"

I look at the puddle of vodka below Luther's dangling feet, mixing with oil and the first light from the sunrise.

"I'm not sure I was."

I turn my back on him again without waiting for a response. Luther's not a bad guy. He was a solid first baseman, and he'll be a hell of a gym teacher.

"Cole!" I call. He stops talking and looks around. I walk toward him. "Cole!" Now he sees me, and I wave him over. He turns back to Viola, says a few more words, and then trots toward me. I turn and head for my car, Cole falling into step alongside. "Let's go."

24

"We were talking," he says.

"You had all night to talk," I tell him. "She's tired. She wants to go home."

"I talked to her last night."

"Sort of."

"I can never think of the right thing to say."

"You think too much, Cole. That's always been your problem."

We pass Rosie Horowitz and two of her friends, sitting on the hood of her dad's Mercedes. They watch me without saying anything.

"So long, Rosie," I call to her. "Take care." There's no point in being an asshole.

She doesn't say anything. "Take care, Matt," one of her friends sings to my back after we've passed. *Fuck them.* We reach my truck, and I throw my backpack into the back.

"You going to check your sugar?" Cole is a mini version of my mom sometimes.

"I'm fine," I tell him as I get behind the wheel and start the engine. He stands by the open passenger-side door, looking at me.

"I can drive if you want," he says.

"I'm fine. I've been diabetic since before I could talk. You think I can't tell when my sugar's low?"

Cole keeps staring at me. I hate it when he does this. I stare right back. The sun is behind him, and for a moment he looks so much like he did in the picture, I can't stand it. His eyes have the same look: sad, accusing, like he's thinking something that he's not going to tell you. I shrug and check my phone. "Now you're going to have to wait," I tell him. "It needs a blood calibration." I get out of the truck, retrieve my backpack, and get my kit out. Cole watches as I prick my finger and catch the drop of blood on a plastic strip sticking out of the glucometer. After a moment, the meter beeps and then reads eighty-seven. Totally normal. "There," I say, holding it out for him to read. "Happy?"

"Thrilled."

We both get in and sit, the engine running, watching as the rest of our class scatters. Luther in his pickup, Rosie in her Mercedes, Chris Thayer driven by his mom in their special handicap van, Eddie Deangelo in a rusted-out hatchback.

"Eddie said something about a problem with cash," Cole says.

Fucking Eddie. I didn't want to talk about this today.

"Don't worry," I tell him. "It'll work out."

"Are you out of money?"

"I have the money; it's just that my parents are watching my account. I can't get it."

Cole takes a deep breath and lets it out slow.

"Don't start," I tell him. "This is why I didn't tell you right away."

"What happened?"

"I screwed up, okay? A few months ago, I took too much out all at once. A present for Rosie; this really nice necklace. Stupid. I didn't even know they pay attention to the account, but they do. They track it, and we had this big talk, and . . . I don't think I can pull what Eddie's asking for."

He shakes his head. "I just feel bad that it's not going to work out."

"Christ, Cole, show a little spine, will you? Of course it's going to work out. Eddie and I set something up. A trade."

"For what?"

"Okay, so, the fridge in your living room, with your dad's stuff in it . . ."

"His meds?"

"Yeah."

"Dad's old pain meds?"

"And weed, right?"

"We're giving Eddie drugs?"

"Well, what else are you going to do with it all?" I feel bad saying it, but it's true. Cole's dad has been gone for almost a year now, but his house hasn't changed. The hospital bed is still set up in the living room; there are piles of boxes with medical supplies. Mail is piling up. It's not a good situation.

"There's not too much left," Cole says.

"How much?"

"I don't know; I mean, he used a lot . . . he used a lot of meds, at the end."

"I told Eddie we have a whole refrigerator full."

"We don't."

"Oh."

I had told Cole to make a plan. A month ago, when he was coming to school every day looking like the world was ending. When he was sitting up all night writing poetry that doesn't even rhyme. It was all because Viola is going off to the West Coast and he's staying here to take care of his mother and he had no idea, absolutely no fucking idea, what to do about it. So I told him that he's the most creative guy I know and that he should come up with the craziest, most incredible, best plan he could to win her heart and that I would make it happen. I'd set it up.

And he did it. Cole made a plan. A great plan, which turns out to require help from Eddie Deangelo, and Eddie doesn't work for free.

"It'll be fine," I tell him, slapping him on the knee. The parking lot has emptied out while we've been sitting here. I shift into drive. "I want to go somewhere."

"Where?"

"I want to go out to the lake."

"I should get home."

"It won't take too long." I pull out of the lot and onto Knickerbocker Road. "I've been meaning to ask you something. You want to drive this in the fall?"

"Your truck?"

"Yeah. It'll be better than your car in the snow."

"Anything would be. You're not taking it with you?"

"Freshmen don't get parking spaces." My dad could buy me a

permit, but I'll be damned if I'm going to be that guy who gets to have a car on campus just because his parents have money.

"Sure. Sweet. Thanks."

"You got it." We pull out onto Route 21 and speed up. It always makes me feel good to do something for Cole. I turn the radio on, lean back, and take a deep breath. We drive quietly until we get to the lake. I park on the far side of the lot, underneath the trees so it would be hard to see the truck from the road, and we get out. My phone beeps, and I glance at the screen. My blood sugar is falling: sixty-nine, with an arrow pointing down. I take an apple from my backpack. Cole comes around to stand next to me.

"What are we doing here?"

"There's something I want to do." An owl hoots once from the woods, then again, and then is silent. We stand very still, looking across the lot, across the beach, down to the water. "I want to go for a swim."

"Funny."

"Come on."

We cross the lot and step onto the sand, pass the shuttered and locked Snack Shack, and head down to the water's edge. They don't open until ten, but who knows when the staff starts to show up? I set my bag on the overturned lifeguard boat and start to undress.

"You have to be kidding me."

I stand in my boxers and look across to the far shore. Each bite of the apple seems very loud on the empty water. Cole's dad used to row us around out here when we were kids. He knew the scientific names for everything we saw: fish, bugs, plants, whatever.

I finish and throw the apple core high into the air, far over the lake, and pain shoots through my elbow and down to my fingertips. "You know what I want to do?" I ask, shaking my arm.

"Go skinny-dipping with your best friend the morning after graduation?"

"I want to swim this motherfucking lake. I want to swim straight across it, across the middle, across the deepest part."

"Why?"

I step into the water. It's surprisingly cold. I trudge out until it reaches my knees.

"This seems like a really bad idea," Cole says to my back. "Was that a glucose alert before?"

Cole worries about my blood sugar more than anyone other than my mom. "I'll be fine with the apple."

"You should wait and retest. What am I supposed to do, swim out if you get into trouble?"

I'm up to my thighs.

"Whatever you do, don't you dare call 911." I've had enough of that for three lifetimes. The East Ridge ambulance probably had a special hotline for my mother when I was a kid. She used to call if my sugar was even a little bit out of whack.

"I don't think I could launch the boat by myself," Cole says. Of course he couldn't; the thing must weigh at least twice what he does.

Upper thighs. I don't know what he would do.

"I'm going to check you on your phone while you swim," he says.

"The hell you are."

"Matt, tell me the password to your phone. I'm going to track you."

"It's one, two, three, screw you."

"If you don't let me, I'm calling your mom right now."

He'd do it. It would be out of love, but he'd do it. I tell him the password.

"You're going to stop when it gets to your balls," he says.

I throw myself forward into the water, the cold striking me all at once, eyes closed, kicking first and then starting to pull with my arms.

We learned about the lake in fourth grade, when we studied the Native Americans who used to live in New Jersey. They had a name for it, which I forget, and a legend, which I half remember. It was something about a girl, some sort of princess, who lost the love of her life. The lake was made of her tears, and when it was full, she swam out into it and was never seen again. They said it didn't have a bottom, just like her sorrow; that it went all the way to the center of the earth. That's obviously not true, but it is supposed to be really fucking deep.

"Sixty-one!" Cole calls. I glance over and see him, walking along the shore, climbing over some rocks, my phone in his hand.

I have an app that's synced with a little sensor that I wear on my side. It tracks my sugar, which is handy in a baseball game; one of the coaches watches it on the bench and gives me OJ before I even need it. Sixty-one is low, too low to be swimming, but the sugar from the apple will kick in soon. The sensor has a little delay.

I'm pulling hard now. I feel good. I'm not scared, just focused, swimming in a straight line, farther and farther away from the beach. This is the way it's supposed to be. No one's going to bring me juice out here. It's just me, alone.

Maybe my elbow is starting to ache, though. I try to angle my arm so that I'm not flexing it so much, but I think it's the cold. I'm getting pins and needles in the fingertips on my right hand.

"Fifty-eight!" Cole shouts, his voice carrying across the water. Either I'm going to make it or I'm not; he doesn't have to narrate the whole damn thing.

My hand is going numb, and I roll over onto my back, kicking and waving my arms by my side so that I don't have to bend at the elbow. The sky is lightening above me, but it's still cloudy. There's a sound in the distance that could be thunder, though it's hard to tell with my ears underwater. Cole's going to be shitting a brick if it is. Floating in the middle of a big lake in a thunderstorm. I smile at the sky and kick harder.

After another minute I roll over, treading water, raising my head to make sure I'm not veering off from the center of the lake and taking a shorter path. I'm not. I'm dead center, and I've been making better time than I thought. The far shore is about two hundred yards off now, maybe a bit more. "Fifty-two," Cole calls from the shore off to my right. He sounds worried. I nod and wave at him. Fifty-two micrograms of glucose per deciliter of blood. The apple wasn't enough. I should have waited. "You all right?" Cole calls. I ignore him and start swimming again.

I can feel my limbs starting to quiver. I glance up without stopping. Not too far now. I don't see Cole as I turn my head to breathe. *One, two, one, two, breathe. One, two, one, two . . .* My head is starting to spin. I feel hollow inside. I swim hard, with everything I have left.

I feel my fingertips brush the bottom. I try to put my feet down, and I do, but I can't seem to take my own weight. I stumble forward one step, then two, then drop to my knees and pitch forward, my face plunging back into the lake, my arms nowhere to be found. For the first time, I panic. I'm going to drown on my knees in two feet of water.

And then I hear the splash of running footsteps and feel hands under my arms, and I'm being pulled up. Cole has me, and all hundred and fifty pounds of him is hoisting me out of the water and pulling me toward the shore. I suck air and cough. *No, no, no, this isn't how it's supposed to be.* Even as I'm thinking it, I'm wrapping an arm around his neck and stumbling along beside him.

Cole sets me down on the ground, hard. A moment later he's holding something to my mouth. Warm orange juice. He must have taken it from my bag when I started swimming. He holds it up and I greedily suck it down, unable to raise my hand and take it from him. He feeds me like a baby with a bottle. When I've drunk it all, I let my head sink to my knees and feel the molecules of sugar spreading throughout my body, my organs coming back to life. And when I'm finally able, I raise my head and look at him.

"You shouldn't have done that," I say. "I was gonna be all right."

He crouches and looks at me in the early-morning light. His shoes are soaking wet. So are his pants, all the way up to his knees. "I think you need more juice, asshole."

I study the clouds, thickening over the water, and lick my lips, absorbing every last bit of sugar.

"What the hell did you think you were doing?" Cole asks. "Are you suicidal?"

I'm not. I shake my head. "I just wanted to see if I could."

Cole sits down next to me and looks out at the lake. "Well, you did it," he says. "Pure stupidity, but you did it."

"Sort of."

"You did."

I shrug. "The last couple of feet count."

He snorts and doesn't respond.

Cole won't understand. He was there that day; he doesn't remember a thing about it, but he was there. And I was home, reading comics in bed while my mom made tiny adjustments to my insulin levels.

"I wanted to see if I was supposed to."

"What do you mean, 'supposed to'?"

"Like . . . just if that's the way it's supposed to be."

"The way what's supposed to be?"

"I don't know, Cole. I can't explain it." I climb to my feet, push my hair off my face, and look down at him. He's still staring out at the water, frowning, chewing on his lower lip. Like he's trying to figure something out. A classic Cole expression.

"Hey."

He looks up.

"Thank you."

"Yeah. No problem. Happy to do it."

I reach down, and he takes my hand and lets me pull him to his feet. He's so light; I can't believe he carried me.

"You have my clothes?"

He stares for a moment, then bursts out laughing.

"You're kidding."

He shakes his head. "I ran to get the juice."

I can't help but grin. "All right. Let's go."

There's a path that runs through the woods along the side of the lake, a bit farther back from the shore. We take it, me wearing nothing but my dripping wet boxers, Cole with his soaked shoes held in his hands and his jeans rolled up his calves. The sun is totally covered by clouds now, and the trees close in over us, the lake glinting through the trunks. We walk in silence, the birds chirping overhead. Stuff I don't usually notice, unless I'm with Cole and I'm imagining him writing some poem about it.

After five minutes, we come to a fork in the path where it breaks off to the right, toward the beach and the parking lot, and to the left, deeper into the woods. There's a birch tree growing at the split. We both pause. "Let's go back, just for a minute," I say. We turn left.

The path gets smaller, so we have to walk single file. It twists back and forth. It's narrower than I remember it, more overgrown. A single raindrop lands on my forehead. We round a turn, and then we're there, in the clearing.

I don't know who started calling it the Monument. Probably no one knows. It's been a while since I've been out here, but it's just the same as it ever was. There are big red block letters painted onto the surface of the rock face: FUCK SAM KEELEY. Each letter almost as tall as a person, the three words laid out vertically, the first one high up above anyone's head. They look like they're glittering, almost like the paint is still wet. And there, lower down, alongside KEELEY, are the two smaller rows of names, one on each side, nine in each. STEVEN ABRAMS, PATRICK CLEMSON, SUSAN EDWARDS, and so on. There, at the end of the second list, out of alphabetical order: PRINCIPAL SCHULTZ.

Cole stands beside me. "I haven't been out here in forever."

"Me neither."

There are memorials all over town; for a few years people

couldn't seem to stop putting them up. But this is the only one that really matters to us. I study the names. Cole walks over to the base of the rock. There are a few old teddy bears, some notes, and birthday cards left in clear plastic bags. He picks up a crumpled beer can. I can't imagine the asshole who would have left it here.

The air is very still, though the tops of the trees are waving a bit. My skin is dry now, and I feel cold. A few more raindrops rustle the leaves overhead.

"I don't even know who takes care of this place," Cole says.

"I guess people just do it."

"It's the only one I don't mind," he says. "The only one that doesn't make me feel strange." I know what he means. "Do you remember," he continues, "the first one they did? The little park, and there was a flagstone with each of their names? And we all had to come when they opened it."

"Even Chris. He was out of the hospital by then, right? I remember they wheeled him in."

"Right."

I hated it. I hated being there. They made me stand up with all the other kids who had been in that class, with all the survivors. I hate being called a survivor. Chris was a survivor; he got shot and lived. Cole was a survivor; the kids on both sides of him died and he didn't. He's *the* survivor, really. The famous one. Photographed as he was carried out of the school, wrapped in Officer Greg Jessup's big cop arms, his face spattered in blood, staring straight into the camera with that look in his eyes. It's the photo that literally everyone in the world has seen.

Me, I was at home eating low-carb soup. I've never survived anything.

I turn away from the Monument. I don't know why I wanted to come, but now I don't want to be here. "Let's go."

I lead the way back down the path and onto the trail. We get back to the beach, I pull my clothes on, and we head to the truck. The parking lot is still empty.

"I'll run you home; then I have to get to work," I say.

"You didn't take the day off?"

"Nah. I have to drive Chris to PT later. And Finn needs me."

"To keep up with his two customers?"

I shrug. Cole's been working at Finn's Grocery for a couple of years now, but I just started in the spring. It's the first real job I've had, and I'm trying to take it seriously. He's right, though. Ever since they put in the Stop & Shop, fewer and fewer people go to the old store.

I pull out of the parking lot. The radio is on and the windows are down. It's like coming back to the real world. Cole is sitting next to me, examining his waterlogged sneakers.

"Hey," I say. "Listen."

"What?"

"We'll take care of this thing with Eddie. It's going to work out."

"Yeah."

"I'll think of something."

"Sure. Thanks."

I will. I'm not going off to school and leaving him behind in the miserable state he's been in.

We don't talk anymore, the whole way back into town.

I drop Cole off, drive downtown, and let myself in the back door of the grocery store ten minutes early. I put my apron on and punch my card in the clock bolted to the wall. It sits in a slot above Cole's. His has a lot more time on it.

Mr. Finn comes into the storeroom a few minutes later, while I'm opening crates of produce. He congratulates me on graduating, slapping me on the back and winking when he asks if I had a good time. I don't think there was any Project Graduation in his day, and he probably thinks that last night was a lot wilder than it was. I smile and shrug, and he lets me get back to work.

Lifting the crates makes my elbow hurt, but I ignore it. It would drive my dad nuts, stressing it like this. He's invested thousands of hours and thousands of dollars, tens of thousands of dollars, in my arm. I've done everything, camps and clinics, one-on-one coaching with former big-league players. I'm Dad's biggest trophy. I told him I don't have to lift anything heavy here at the store, and he believed me because he's never had a job like this. A non-bullshit job, one where you have to work with your hands. Dad pushes paper around and worries about other people's money for a living.

Eight o'clock comes, and I hear the bells by the front door as the first customers of the day come in and Mr. Finn calls out a hello. A moment later there's a loud crash and a shout. I hustle up to the front, and there's Paul Gerber and his mother standing in the middle of an avalanche of soup cans that had been stacked in a giant pyramid. Paul's fists are balled up and his face is flushed. His mom stands in front of him with her eyes closed. She's breathing slowly. It looks like she's counting to ten in her head. Mr. Finn has come over from the checkout area, and he looks unhappy.

"Now, Paul," he says, "let's —"

"No!"

Mrs. Gerber takes one more deep breath, and although she looks as if she would really rather not, she opens her eyes. Before she can say anything, I have an idea.

"Hey, Paulie," I say, "I need you to help me with something." Paul looks at me, but he doesn't say anything. I pause, and then I reach out and put a hand on his shoulder. I take him a quarter of the way down an aisle, and we stop in front of a shelf full of more cans. Beans, all sorts of beans, all different brands. It seems stupid for a store this size to carry so many different kinds of beans. How much cash has Finn sunk into canned goods? What could the demand for beans be in a town like East Ridge?

"Help me with this, Paul," I say, taking cans down off the shelf, stacking them on the floor, and opening up a space until

40

there is a long gap. Mr. Finn and Mrs. Gerber watch from the end of the aisle. "Okay," I finally say, "let's put them away right." I start to restack the cans, ignoring the actual type of bean and just focusing on the label color. All the red ones to the far left, then blue. Paul watches for a moment, then understands and joins in, sorting the cans by color and placing them on the shelf. He quickly finishes reshelving the cans I had placed on the floor and then continues along, pulling cans off and rearranging them, sorting and shifting, completely focused. I go back to the front of the store and begin to rebuild the soup pyramid.

"Thank you, Matt," Mrs. Gerber says. "You've always been wonderful with him."

I wonder whether this is true. I don't remember spending much time with Paul at all; I think Cole was the one who usually tried to include him. I smile at Mrs. Gerber anyway and tell her that I'll keep an eye on Paul while she shops, and she thanks me again and hurries off with her list. I stack soup and watch as the aisle in front of me gets color-coded.

"He's going to rearrange the whole place," Mr. Finn says quietly.

"I'll fix it when they're gone."

Mr. Finn goes off to see about his paperwork, and I slowly stack the spilled cans, higher and higher, rebuilding a pyramid that should somehow get customers to spend hot summer evenings eating chicken noodle soup. I watch Paul, fascinated, staring at his face as he studies the shelves. He's moved on to cans of tomato sauce. I feel sort of proud for having settled him down, but also guilty for having given him such a random thing to do. It seems to be making him happy, though, or at least keeping him quiet.

I finish stacking, and Mrs. Gerber finishes shopping. Mr. Finn checks her out, and she thanks me one more time. I nod and tell her that I'll come by over the summer to check in on Paul, even though I haven't thought of that until the very moment when I say it. She seems so happy, though, that I'm not sorry I did.

I go back to unboxing the fruit.

Half an hour later, I'm feeling the lack of sleep and the burn-off of the adrenaline from the swim. Fluorescent lights shining on aisles of cracked white linoleum, the smell of cardboard and plastic and lettuce. I don't know how Mr. Finn has taken decades of this. I don't know if I'll make it through the summer. I'd tell him I have to go home and get some sleep if I weren't supposed to get Chris for PT at lunchtime. Our moms set it up so that we'd have it at the same time.

"Excuse me?"

I turn. The woman has come up behind me while I was spacing out, and I have the sense that she's already tried to get my attention.

"Sorry, what? I mean, can I help you?"

"I asked if you have strawberries today."

"Strawberries . . ." I scan the produce, stare into the empty box at my feet, and then look back at her. I'm dazed, like I've just woken up on my feet. "I don't see them."

"I don't see them either. That's why I'm asking."

"Right." She has black hair, tied straight back in a ponytail with a white ribbon. One small strand's come free, and the tips of a few hairs cling to the corner of her mouth. "Do you want a cantaloupe?" I ask.

She blinks. "A cantaloupe?"

I nod.

"No, not really."

"They're good for you."

She steps away, watching me carefully. "I'm good, thanks. I'll just look around a little." She moves off into the produce section, two rows away from me, running her hands over some watermelon. I break down an empty box, stomping it onto a pile of stained cardboard, trying not to stare at her.

It's been a long time since I've seen Sarah Jessup, a really long time, and I doubt that she remembers me. The last time we were together, I was an obnoxious kid playing a prank on my friend's babysitter at a sleepover, and she was a high school senior just trying to make a few bucks by watching us for the night. When Luther's parents got home, they woke us both up and made us come outside and put air back in her bike tires.

She was Officer Jessup's daughter; he was famous for being the cop carrying Cole in the photo, which made her a little bit famous too. And then later on, when he died of an aneurysm in his cop car while sitting in a speed trap, it reminded everybody of who he had been and of who she was.

"Hey."

I look up. She's standing by the bananas, holding up a box of strawberries, eyebrows raised.

"Well, will you look at that?" I say.

She shakes her head. "Half of these are past; they should be taken off the shelf."

"Sorry. I'm new here."

She nods, doesn't look up.

"I'm Matt. Matt Simpson."

"I know. I'm Sarah."

"Yeah, I know too." I grin. She doesn't look up from the fruit. She's dressed for work, like at an office.

"You might want to study up on produce, Matt."

"I'm open to all comments and suggestions."

She doesn't soften one bit. "Thanks for your help." She starts to turn away, consulting a list in her hand like I've disappeared into thin air.

"Do you always come in now? Like, around now? I can set some strawberries aside for you."

"Don't worry about it."

"I'll be here. This time, I mean. I just graduated. From high school, I just graduated from high school."

"Congratulations."

I don't want her to go, but for once in my life, I can't think of anything to say.

"Are you going to need help with your bags?"

"I think I can handle them. I work just up the street."

"Oh. Okay. Where?"

"Where?"

She thinks I'm a stalker, but my mouth is still going. "Yeah, where do you work?"

She finally blows the strand of hair out of her face and looks unsure. "You ask a lot of questions, Matt."

"Sorry. It gets boring, unpacking boxes all day."

"Try working in insurance." She turns and walks away.

"Hey," I call after her, "I'll talk to Mr. Finn. About the produce. We want to keep your business."

"Sure," she says without looking back. "Let him know." She reaches the end of the aisle. "You can also let him know that his stock boy isn't as cute as he thinks he is." She disappears around the endcap, leaving me alone with my pile of empty fruit boxes.

Lunchtime finally comes. Mr. Finn has given me extra time for PT, and I drive out to get Chris Thayer.

The Thayers' house is a little bit of a dump. They had to do all kinds of things to it so that his wheelchair could get in, move doorways and stuff, and it wound up looking stuck together and lopsided. There's a long metal ramp leading up to the front door.

I park my truck by the curb and get out. Chris is waiting in the driveway, next to the special van. I already know how to use it; his mom came over last weekend and showed me all the features.

At school, Chris always wore khakis with a perfect crease down the front and button-down shirts, but today he's in sweats for PT. His blond hair is still perfectly parted and his rimless glasses are spotless. He looks up at me from his chair as I approach.

"What's up, Chris?" I ask. "How're you doing today? Did your mom leave the keys in the van, or are they in the house?" I always have to fight the impulse to make my voice go higher when I'm talking to him, the way people do when they're talking to little kids.

"On the driver's seat," he says in his wobbly, raspy voice.

"Cool. Sorry I'm late."

It takes me a couple of minutes to get him secured in the back of the van, but he's patient. Chris is nice to everybody, always smiling, always polite. He was the stats manager for the baseball team, so he came to all our games, which is where I really got to know him.

I get into the driver's seat, pull out of the driveway, and creep down the street at about ten miles an hour.

"This thing can go faster," he says.

"Sorry, just getting used to it." I speed up a little. Driving him is going to take some getting used to. I hit the button for the radio, but nothing happens.

"It's broken," he says. "Gotta get it fixed."

46

"Sure." I wonder whether they don't have the money. Chris's dad works at my dad's company, but I think he's way, way down from him.

"What do you think of the Mets?" Chris asks.

I could probably list their starting lineups for the last ten seasons from memory, but I can't think of anything going on this year. It's a total blank, and it hits me just how distracted I've been. Whatever's been happening these last few months, my head's always been someplace else.

"Not sure about the bullpen," I say. Always a safe bet.

"You're telling me." Chris launches into an analysis of middle relief, and I try to follow along, but it's happening again. It's like a magnet is pulling my thoughts away from what's actually going on around me. I'm focused, just not on what Chris is saying. I had an idea this morning, as soon as Cole told me that his refrigerator isn't as full as I thought it was.

"Hey, Chris," I interrupt, "can I ask you something?"

"What's up?"

I'm not quite sure how to start.

"You get prescribed a lot of meds, right?" I ask.

"Oh, man, you have no idea."

"Like, what? Pain meds?"

"Sure, all kinds of stuff."

"You ever have any extra?"

He's quiet for a moment. "What do you mean, 'extra'?"

This is insane. Chris's parents will be on the phone to my

parents by dinner, and I'll spend the rest of the summer in mandatory rehab.

"Just, you know, some extra pills," I say. "The doc prescribed me stuff for my elbow, but I hardly use it. I've got a bottle that's mostly full in my bathroom."

"Yeah," he says cautiously. "Sure. Lots, actually. It builds up."

I'm holding the steering wheel hard with both hands. I look in the mirror. Chris is looking back at me.

"Think you might be interested in getting rid of some of it?" I ask.

There's a pause, and then he nods. "I might be."

I slowly let out the breath I didn't know I was holding and relax my grip on the wheel. "Nice. Here's the thing, though, Chris. I can't really get at any money right now. It's a long story, but . . . I mean, you trust me, right? We're buds. I could get you cash this fall, winter latest." At some point my parents have to get tired of watching my account. I could take money out in lots of small withdrawals, maybe.

"I was thinking of a trade," Chris says.

"Oh, okay." I look in the mirror again and am startled to see that his face has turned bright red. "What do you want to trade?"

When he answers, his voice is even smaller than usual. "Stories."

"Stories?"

"Yeah."

"About what?"

"Can I tell you later?" he asks after another moment.

"Uh — sure." I have no idea what kind of a story I could tell him. I'm not any sort of a storyteller.

The PT clinic is coming up on our right, and I slow down way too early and creep into the lot. I jump out, open Chris's door, and get him out of the van.

"I'll wait here," I say when he's finally on the sidewalk.

"What about your session?"

I stretch my arm. The elbow pulls and aches, the pain shooting down toward my hand. "I feel good today. I think my mom canceled."

I watch as he drives his chair along the sidewalk toward the automatic door, and then I get back into the driver's seat. It's hot, I'm tired, and the air isn't moving. I want to roll the window down, but somehow turning the van back on seems like too much work. I rest my head on the window glass and close my eyes. I must have fallen asleep, because the next thing I know, Chris is calling my name from the curb and the clock on the dashboard shows that forty-five minutes have gone by. I struggle upright, wipe the sweat off my face, and open the door to get him in.

I don't know what I was dreaming about, but all I can think of is Sarah Jessup, and of taking that white ribbon out of her black hair.

Three

— *Cole* —

Grief is natural. That's what a counselor once told me. She said that it's the body's response to loss, just like a fever is the body's response to an infection. The pain is what healing feels like; suppress it, and your soul can't do its work. You can't ignore it. You can't hunker down and wait for it to pass. You can't drug it out of existence. You can't talk yourself out of it. You have to go through it, let it cleanse you of all the anger and fear that went with what happened to you, before you can move on.

Utter bullshit.

Grief is natural. You know what else is natural? Smallpox. Would you find that cleansing?

I'm back from Project Graduation, but Mom's the one who looks like she's been up all night. We're sitting at the dining room table, trying to have breakfast, but she can barely keep her eyes open. Her hair is pinned back but it's a mess, and it looks like she still has her makeup on from the ceremony yesterday. I made us toast and eggs, but she's hardly eating.

"You feeling all right, Ma?"

"I'm good, honey. Just not really hungry. I'll get a little nap and then I'll be fine."

Her little naps have been known to last for fourteen hours, but I nod and don't say anything.

"It was a lovely ceremony," she says. "They did a wonderful job."

"Yeah."

"And you had a good time last night?"

"Yeah." I feel her eyes studying me. In her pop-psych world of natural grief and making yourself do just one little thing every day, a day like yesterday is probably supposed to be some sort of a trigger for me. Maybe it awakens some old memories or trauma. I shrug. "It was fun. I played tennis."

"With who?"

"Matt." *Who else?*

"It's nice that he's working at Finn's this summer."

"I won't see him there much. Mr. Finn doesn't need two people at once. It's actually going to cut into my hours."

"Well, still. You'll get to see him sometimes. You'll pick up more hours when he leaves in the fall."

I stare at a pile of *National Geographic*s. There's a thin layer of dust on them, visible in the morning light. I reach out and doodle a pattern with my finger.

"Cole?"

"Yeah, Mom."

"Are you sure you're all right?"

"I'm just tired."

"I know, baby. You should get some sleep. We both should."

Sleep is the least of it. You should get some sleep, sure. You should also take the goddamned antidepressants the doctor prescribed you. The real doctor, not the quack who does "bodywork" with you three times a week and isn't covered by insurance. Not the "doctors" who write the books that tell you to "experience your grief."

"I will, Ma. I might just write for a little while. And then I will."

She smiles at me (a sad, worried smile) and clears her uneaten plate. I wait until she's gone upstairs and I hear her bedroom door close, and then I get up from the table and go into the living room. I take a pencil and pad of paper from the shelf and sit.

Dad had cancer of the pancreas, and then, after he died, Mom got a diagnosis too: Complex Bereavement. It basically means she can't get over what happened, not just the fact that he died, but how fast he went and how much pain there was at the end. Part of the problem, in my opinion, is that no one knew just what to say to her. That's why she keeps reading those ridiculous self-help books. Mom and Dad are both biologists—he *was* a biologist, I should say—and atheists, and all their friends were atheists too. Which is fine, but it's not very good for dying. Dad was buried under a tombstone without a cross but with a quotation by Charles Darwin. It was a good one. I can't remember exactly how it goes, though, and I haven't been able to bring myself to go back and check.

The room is too quiet, just the sound of cicadas in the too-tall grass outside and the hum of the mini-fridge in the corner of the room, still doing its job. I put the pad down and go over and open it, thinking of Matt and his crazy deal with Eddie. I wish we didn't have to work with the guy, but here's the thing: there are very few ways to get hold of a hot-air balloon in central New Jersey. Almost none, if you have limited funds and no flying experience. And Eddie is Eddie Deangelo, as in Deangelo Outdoor Adventures. As in crazy rides at carnivals that you generally couldn't pay me to go on. As in hot-air balloons. As in the central feature of my plan to win Viola's heart.

There's not much inside the refrigerator. I don't know anything about drugs, so I'm not even sure what Eddie would be interested in. There are some bottles, but they're mostly empty, and some pills that someone stuck in here, but not that many of them. There's also some weed in a plastic bag, about the size of a softball. Altogether, I don't think it's enough. I doubt that Eddie will think it's worth what we're asking him to do for us.

I close the fridge, pissed at Matt. He's the one who pushed for me to come up with a plan. Insisted, really. He's the one who offered to finance it, who said that money wasn't an issue, who told me that for once he was going to use his parents' cash for something that he actually wanted to use it for. And now we're making drug deals with Eddie Deangelo, and we can't even hold up our end of the bargain.

I grab my boots and very quietly let myself out of the house, through the back door and into the overgrown yard. There's a pond back here, tucked away at the edge of the trees. Dad and I used to sit and watch it when I was a little kid. He'd explain how it was a world in itself, how all the organisms — plants, animals, little things we couldn't even see — had adapted to live there, and how if conditions changed, if the water changed or the amount of sunlight it was getting, then they would adapt all over again, around and around forever, changing and adapting. That's what I'm waiting for now, for Mom to adapt to these new conditions, to Dad not being here, and if he still were, I'd ask him how long it usually takes for something to adapt and what happens if it can't, though I'm pretty sure I know the answer to that last one.

I haven't been to the pond all spring. It's all grown over with algae, cloudy where it used to be clear. I can't see anything moving. When I was a kid, I used to imagine that the frogs and little fish thought it was the whole universe, that they thought their pond was all there was and they couldn't even imagine anything else. They had no idea that it was just one little spot in the corner of a little yard on the edge of a little town.

I shouldn't be angry at Matt. If it weren't for him, I'd be doing nothing; I would have said goodbye to Viola this morning and I'd have no plan to ever see her again, and I can't even imagine what kind of state I'd be in. He'll come up with something. I'll get some sleep, wait for him to get off from Finn's, and then we'll see.

And then it hits me, all at once. The waiting. Waiting for

Matt. Waiting for Mom. Waiting for Viola. Waiting for inspiration. Waiting for things to change. That's what Matt was telling me when he told me I had to make a plan. He was telling me that everyone is leaving; he's going to Bucknell to play ball and Viola's going out to California, and I have to stop waiting.

I'm sick of waiting.

I kick a rock into the pond and watch the ripples part the algae. Then I turn and go back into the house.

The first thing I get is the book. I have no idea where wrapping paper is, don't even know if we have any, and I'm not sure how you wrap a present anyway. I cut up an old grocery bag and wrap it sort of like I used to do with my school books, except instead of wrapping the covers, I go all the way around, and after I've tried three times, it looks basically like a gift. I take the graduation card I bought and, after thinking for a few minutes, decide on simplicity: *For Viola, from Cole. Happy graduation.*

It's dead quiet upstairs. I go looking for the prescriptions. They're easy to find, in an envelope held to the refrigerator door by a magnet, tucked under a Chinese food menu. I take them out, study them, do five minutes of online research, and find a black ballpoint pen. A series of 5's need to be gently nudged into 6's or else they'll be out of date. Even then, it'll be at the pharmacist's discretion whether or not to fill them. I work as carefully as I can, study the results, and then stuff them in my pocket. I leave Mom a note on the off chance that she gets up before this evening, and I head to Dad's car, his green station wagon with the nearly bald tires. I get in, pop it into neutral so the engine doesn't wake Mom, let it roll down the driveway almost to the street, and then fire it up (to the degree that you can fire up an old Volvo).

Fifteen minutes later, I'm parked on Main Street in Wynnewood, two towns over. Wynnewood is a lot like East Ridge but busier and more crowded, and they have direct bus lines into New York. People don't know everyone else the way they do in my town. I get out of the car and go into the pharmacy, wandering through the smell of medicine and cheap plastic, looking at bottles of sunblock and disposable razors, finally arriving at the back of the store. The pharmacist is standing at the counter and talking with a very old woman with a walker. I linger at the end of an aisle where I can see them, and I try to look busy.

The woman seems to be hard of hearing, because the pharmacist is speaking slowly and loudly, trying to get her to understand that two medicines can't be taken together. He goes over it three times, until I have a complete understanding of the way in which the first drug can lower her blood pressure too much for her to take the second drug. I'm not sure that she gets it, but she finally nods, and he stops talking. He drops the bottles into a white paper bag, swipes her card, and she very, very slowly moves away from the counter. No one else is there. I realize that I've been standing in front of an adult diaper display for the last couple of minutes, and I make my way over to the counter.

I'm making certain assumptions about this guy, all of which I'm hoping to be correct. He wears the sleeves on his white coat rolled up almost to his elbows, and you can see tattoos on both forearms. He's got thick plastic hipster glasses. I step up and pull the folded prescriptions from my pocket.

"I'd like to fill these, please."

He takes them and leans low over the counter, pushing his glasses up on his nose with his left hand, rapidly twirling a pen from one finger to another with the right. He shuffles through them, flipping each one over as he scans it, and then looks up at me.

"These are for you?"

"For my father. He can't come in."

"Have you been here before?"

"Yeah, I think he's filled things here."

He scans me up and down. "I need to see an ID." I fumble with my wallet and produce my license. He takes it. "We generally won't fill prescriptions like these unless the patient is present. Or if it's for a child."

"He can't come in; he's too sick."

"They won't fill these at the prescribing doctor's hospital?"

"I don't know—my mom just gave me these and asked me to fill them. I don't know what the story is with the doctor." It occurs to me for the first time that he might call the doctor to clarify the story, which would obviously lead to him learning that the patient in question doesn't need pain management because he's been dead for months. "I mean, my mom called the doctor and all. He told her just to fill it at, you know, a regular pharmacy."

"What doctor is it again?"

It's a test. This is an easy one, though. I went to a lot of appointments with my dad, and my parents talked about the oncologist all the time. He was a short, Jewish man, old enough to be my father's father, and he shuffled when he walked like he was making his way over a sheet of ice. "Dr. Myers. Robert Myers."

The pharmacist nods. "I can fill most of these today. One of them is out of date, and I can't give you two of them on the same day, so you'll have to come back for one. Can you wait for the rest?"

I tell him I can, and instead of waiting in the sad little sitting area by the counter, I buy a Coke at the front of the store and go stand on the sidewalk. I carry a notebook for moments like this so I can write down observations and stray lines that come to me. Some of my best poems have started this way, when something just hits me out of the blue. Nothing's happening now, though, because I'm starting to get nervous. The guy seemed more uptight than I thought he would be. I guess he should be, right? These are heavy-duty meds. I watch the cars go by on Main Street and wonder what will happen if he figures it out. Is there something in the computer system that should flag it if a patient is deceased? Some sort of a public record? Something with the government or the insurance company?

The insurance. I feel like a complete moron. Who did I expect was going to pay for the pills? The pharmacist will try to use his account, and it will come up as closed.

I'm starting to sweat, and I look up and down the street as though I already expect police officers to be closing in on me.

Should I just leave? But the guy has the prescriptions, he could call the house, and with my luck, it would be one of the few times my mom picks up the phone. He could call the cops. I need to go inside and make up some sort of excuse. What am I going to say? "I'm sorry, sir, but I forgot that my father actually passed away several months ago and so I won't need those medications after all."

I throw the mostly full bottle of soda into a trashcan and go back into the store. This time I don't make any pretense of browsing, I just go straight back to the pharmacy counter. The only thing my brain is coming up with is the truth: I can tell the guy the truth and hope he feels sorry for me and just throws the prescriptions away and tells me to go home. How old can he be, anyway? Maybe in his midtwenties? He has to understand. I'll tell him that I'm not planning to use the pills or sell them (barter, yes, but that's not strictly selling). I'll tell him that I'm in love and I'm short on cash and trying to set something up, and that I wasn't thinking clearly and that I'm sorry.

The pharmacist has a white paper bag like the one he gave the old woman, and he's tapping on his computer and looking annoyed. I stand by the register and wait for him to say something.

"There's something up with your dad's insurance."

"Really?"

"I see he's filled these meds here before and they've been covered, but I'm getting an error message here."

"Oh."

He gives the top of his monitor a final tap and turns to me. "These insurance companies are sons of bitches, you know? They shut down their systems just to slow the outflow on their payables. Know what I mean?"

"I think so . . ."

"And I'll tell you something else." He glances around to make sure no one else is nearby. "This place is no better. Let me tell you something, okay? They want us to tell people that we can't completely fill their prescriptions and that they have to come back to get the rest another day, regardless of whether or not that's true. Know why?"

I shake my head.

"They want you to come into the store an extra time. If you come in twice to get your meds, you're twice as likely to pick up gum or a magazine or some crap by the register. See?"

I nod and furrow my brow in a look of what I hope is knowing disapproval of corporate depravity. The pharmacist's name tag says Kiernan. He leans back and looks at me in satisfaction, maybe feeling that he's shocked me or that he's done his part to spread the word about his employer. I don't know what to say. I just want to get out of here in a way that minimizes the chances of a felony charge.

"Here's what I can do," he says. "I can let you take the generics, and I can run them through the system later. Your dad still has his insurance, right?"

I nod, feeling terrible.

"So, I can't let you take the brand names, but three of these are generics and you can take 'em and I'll run them later. Chances are the payment system will miraculously be fixed and come back up in an hour or so. These three should get him through, you know? They're potent. Then you just have to come back for the rest."

"Yeah," I say, "all right. Thank you."

He takes a few bottles out of the bag and sets them aside, then hands the rest to me. I give him the twenty-dollar copay.

"Do one thing for me," he says. "When you come back in, don't buy a goddamned thing, all right?"

I smile and nod, thank him again, and get out of the store as quickly as I can. I'm never going back, and I'm going to have to think about what to do if Kiernan calls the house when the insurance doesn't work. Hopefully he'll just decide that we're being permanently screwed by the company and he'll forget about it, though I have a feeling that he's going to be in trouble for letting me walk off with these pills. I can't think about that right now, though. I need these, and even with them, I'm going to need more, given how empty most of the bottles in the fridge are. I'm going to need a lot more.

I leave Wynnewood behind and drive back to East Ridge. I'm almost home, lost in my thoughts, when I realize I'm going in the wrong direction. I make a U-turn and drive over to one of the newer developments on the west side of town. The houses are huge here, and the trees are puny little saplings they put in after they bulldozed everything down. Totally weird and out of proportion, but everyone wants to live here anyway. It's hard to figure out the streets, since everything looks sort of alike. They're named for presidents: Grant Avenue, Reagan Circle, and I turn onto Wilson Street and approach Viola's house.

I've been here once before. It was in April. AP English, and I'd managed to get myself into her group for our spring project. I don't know if she ever noticed that, but I did it a lot. We were in the same lab group in chemistry, the same study group in history. Anyway, this particular project was on *The Waste Land* by T. S. Eliot, and the other three kids in our group were complete-and-total morons. We didn't get anything done until the weekend before it was due, and I could tell that it drove Viola crazy. She got A's in everything. She always did the extra credit. She retook a chemistry test to try for a higher grade after she got a ninety-seven on it the first time. She would have done the Eliot project alone if we weren't partly being graded on teamwork.

So the five of us met at her house to get it done at the last minute. It was a rainy spring day, and it was slow going; the other people in the group hadn't even read the text—or if they did, they hadn't understood it—so Viola and I did most of the work. I mean, basically she did the project and I helped out, while the others screwed around and did just enough that we could honestly say it was a group effort. She was pissed the whole time, snapping at people and blowing her hair out of her eyes in a way that meant she was annoyed but that I absolutely loved.

By the end of the afternoon, I figured she hated us all,

including me, but when I was packing up to leave, she leaned over and squeezed my arm and whispered, a secret just between the two of us, "Holy fucking Christ, Cole, do I love Eliot."

The combination of that smiling whisper and her English accent would have been enough for me to fall in love with her right then and there, if I hadn't been in love with her already.

I've replayed it a million times in my mind. I'm replaying it now as I glance over at the package sitting on the passenger seat beside me. Which is a mistake, because when I look up, there's a dog directly in front of my car. Not just any dog. Viola's dog. A bulldog named Winston. Viola calls him Winnie, and she clearly adores him.

I pull the wheel hard to the right and try to accelerate past Winston and into their driveway, except that instead of getting out of my way, the idiot darts toward me, and I have to pull the wheel harder and drive straight, and I mean straight, into the Grey family's nicely painted mailbox.

It's no match for a Volvo. The post breaks like a toothpick, and the whole thing goes down. I get out of the car to survey the damage, and I see that in addition to the ruined mailbox, I've torn up the grass around it.

Winnie darts around, yapping and growling. We immediately hated each other the first time we met. He growled at me and nipped at my legs, and I laughed and told Viola and her mom that it was no big deal while fantasizing about punting him out the window.

"Fuck you," I growl at him. "Fuck you, you stupid little bastard. Fuuuuuck you."

"Cole?"

I turn from the dog, and there's Viola, standing in the middle of the lawn, staring at me and the dog and the car and the mailbox.

"Are you talking to my dog?"

I look down at the little shit baring his teeth and staring up at me. "No, I was talking to myself."

She walks over and looks at the mailbox, her eyes wide. Then she throws her head back and bursts into laughter, eyes still on me. "What in God's name are you doing?" she asks.

"I seem to be trashing your lawn," I say. As at the pharmacy, I can't come up with any excuse but the awful truth.

"Are you all right?"

"Oh, yeah . . ."

"Is your car okay?"

"Yeah. But I'm not sure the mailbox is going to make it."

"No, I don't think it is. I'm so sorry; this is my fault, letting Winnie get out of the house like this."

"No, it was my fault—"

"You just wanted your walk, didn't you, you little beastie?" she says to the snarling bulldog.

"I was just driving by, and I didn't want to hit him—"

"You were driving by?"

"Well, I was driving here."

"Why?"

Why, indeed. Well, I got her this present, and I was going to drop it in her mailbox while she was at work and then I was going to call her later and say that it was just something I randomly came across that made me think of her and maybe does she want to get coffee and talk about it? Except that I've crushed her mailbox and almost killed her obnoxious little dog, and she's obviously not working today. So things are clearly not going according to plan.

I wish I could disappear into the ground. I feel my face burning and my stomach seizing up, and for an awful moment I think that I could actually vomit.

I don't. "Just a minute," I say. I take a deep breath and get into my car and back it off the lawn and over to the curb while Viola clips a leash to Winnie's collar. The dumb animal is totally cooperative for her. I get out with the present in my hand.

"I thought you were going to be working today," I say.

"I took the day off, since I knew we'd be up all night. What's that?"

"It's for you."

"You got me a graduation present?"

"Sort of—it's just something I found, and it made me think of something you said, so . . ."

It's just a little something that's one of my prize possessions. Just a little something I'm staking my dreams to.

I hand it to her.

"Thank you!" She opens the card, scans it and smiles, and then pulls off the brown paper.

She does it just the way I imagined she would, carefully pulling it apart at the seams rather than tearing it off like a little kid.

"We were out of gift-wrap," I tell her. I hate the moment when someone opens a present.

"Oh, Cole, this is lovely," she says. She's holding my copy of *The Collected Works of T. S. Eliot.* She turns the book over in her hands and opens the front cover, studying the name on the inside. "This was your father's!"

"Yes . . . but it made me think of you. I mean, I thought, I thought you would like it because, you know, you like Eliot and all."

She closes the book and runs her hand across the cover. "It's beautiful. I love it. Thank you."

My stomach relaxes a little bit, though I can still feel my face burning. I want to freeze this moment in time, standing here on Viola's lawn, hearing her say that she loves it. It's quite possibly the best moment of my life.

And then Winnie bites me on the ankle.

"Fuck!" I shout, louder than I should.

"Winnie! Bad dog!" Viola tugs on his leash and pulls him away from me. "Cole, I'm so sorry! I don't know what's gotten into him; he never behaves this way!"

"It's okay . . . It's fine . . ."

"Is the skin broken?"

66

He got me on the sock, right on the Achilles tendon. "No, no . . ."

"Do you need some ice?"

"No, I'm fine, really." I want to kill this dog. Literally kill it.

"I think he needs to go for a walk and get some energy out."

"Okay."

She looks at me. "Do you want to come?"

"Oh . . . uh, I've got to . . . I think I'm supposed to work this afternoon."

"Well, all right. Can you just hold Winnie for a moment while I put the book inside? It's so lovely."

"Sure."

I take Winnie's leash and watch Viola retreat across the lawn and hate myself with a whole new level of intensity. How many chances like this is the summer going to give me?

Winnie and I spend an uncomfortable thirty seconds glaring at each other until Viola comes back outside.

I'm doing it again. I'm waiting.

"I'll go with you."

"Oh, fantastic." She takes the leash back, and we set off toward Jimmy Carter Avenue, me trying not to limp because my ankle actually does hurt. I can't think of a thing to say.

"You get some sleep?" I finally ask.

"A little bit, yeah. How about you?"

"Not really. I was writing." There is truth in this. I sat with a pen and paper for about fifteen minutes.

"What were you working on?"

"Just . . . stuff," I say.

"You're writing 'stuff'?"

"Yeah, well . . . poems. I'm working on a poem. I'm actually a little bit stuck with it." I want to tell her that I've published three of my poems, but I can't think of a way to do it that doesn't sound like bragging. "Do you ever write?"

She laughs. "No, not unless you count practice SAT and college admission essays."

"Well, it seemed to work."

"I suppose it did."

"What do you think you're going to study at Berkeley?" I ask.

"Major in econ, minor in Asian studies."

"That's pretty specific."

"That's how I tend to be."

"Specific?"

"Yeah. Well, precise. Planned out."

"So, you've planned what your major and minor are going to be?"

"Oh, Cole, I've planned lots of things. I could tell you where I'm going to be and what I'm going to be doing an hour from now, and a week from now, and a year from now, and probably ten years from now too. It makes life very . . . predictable."

I want to ask her more about those plans and how negotiable they are, but instead I nod and say, "That's not really how I think of Berkeley, you know? I think about hippies protesting and people walking out of class and stuff like that. I don't think of people majoring in econ."

"Well, I think I may wind up being the only strait-laced conservative in Berkeley. I'll be the one-woman College Republicans. It should be interesting."

We're walking along Rutherford B. Hayes Drive now. I'd have a tough time finding my way back to the car by myself; we've taken a couple of turns, and everything looks the same. The dog stops and starts to circle around by the side of the road, and we both stop with him. I look at the huge houses to our right, big green lawns swooping up to their front doors, chandeliers visible through arching windows. "It's nice here. The houses are nice."

She shrugs. "It's okay." We watch as Winnie elaborately prepares to take a dump. "Where do you live?" she asks.

"Other side of town." I tell her the street name, but she doesn't seem to know it. Most people don't. It's a small street, not many houses, by the woods. I'm sure that's why Mom and Dad chose it. The dog apparently decides to find another spot, and we walk on.

Rutherford B. Hayes Drive is long, straight, and empty. There isn't a sidewalk, and since there are no cars around, we walk right down the middle of the street. The heat is starting to come up out of the smooth, fresh asphalt. Off to our left, the grass slopes down to a line of trees, and I can see the sun glinting off some water.

"What's down there?"

"Down where?"

I nod toward the tree line.

"I actually have no idea."

"Really?"

"Yes, really."

"It looks like a stream."

"Do you know, I walk Winnie down this street every day, and I've never really looked. There *is* a stream, I think. You can sort of see it in the wintertime, when there are no leaves."

"Let's go see."

"Should we? Whose property is it?"

"Just the town's, probably. It's fine." I veer off, stepping up onto the curb and setting off across the grass. This is the sort of thing Dad always did with me when I was young. We'd be driving somewhere and he'd spot something, some clearing or rock formation, and he'd pull over and we'd explore it. It might seem weird to other people, but it's totally natural for me. He saw things that no one else could see.

I glance back. Viola is hesitating, standing in the street, holding Winnie's leash. He's sitting next to her, staring at me. "Come on!"

Viola smiles and catches up with me, tugging Winnie behind her. He looks like he'd rather be heading home. We walk down the slope and into the trees. It's cooler in the shade, and the ground is soft. I smell the leaves from last autumn, decomposing underneath our feet. Even here, in the middle of this development, there's a little bit of nature, and it's a relief to step into it.

We pick our way around rocks, down to the stream. It's small and slow moving, going nowhere fast. Still, it's pretty. Water always is. It ripples over a bed of pebbles, and there's even a tiny waterfall where the rock bed drops off by about six inches. Winnie wanders over and sniffs the water.

"I can't believe I didn't know this was here," Viola says, looking around.

I nod, looking at the sun filtering down through the trees. "There was a spot like this behind the old school," I say. "You could get to it from the playground. We weren't supposed to go back there at recess, but we did. Andy, Matt, and I."

"Andy was Paul Gerber's brother?"

"Right. His twin."

Viola nods. She doesn't say anything, and I can't tell whether the silence is awkward. "Where did you go to school back then?" I ask.

"Outside of London. A little all-girls school."

"Was it nice?"

She thinks for a moment. "I liked it, yes. It was quiet. Very sheltered, very strict. It was a good place for someone like me, at that age. I like it better here, though. There's more going on, you know? More to do." We watch as Winnie laps at the water. "You're an only child, aren't you?" she asks.

"Yes. Are you?"

"I am."

It's a lot of house for three people, I think. It's the type of thing

71

my dad would have said to my mom. They didn't approve of developments like this one.

"Look at those," Viola says. "Aren't they lovely?"

I look across the water and see a cluster of small blue flowers along the bank on the other side.

"Are those forget-me-nots?"

"They are," I say. *"Myosotis scorpioides."* I say it without thinking, and then worry that it sounds like I'm showing off. "Hold on a moment." I step down to the water, pause, and then hop out to a flat rock in the middle of the stream, and from there to the other bank. I glance back. Viola is watching me, and Winnie is looking up at her, probably wondering who this person is that she found to walk with them. I walk along the stream to the flowers, pick one, and make my way back, managing not to fall in. I hand it to her. "Here you are."

She smiles. "Very nice. Thank you."

"Do you know the story of the forget-me-not?"

She shakes her head as she smells the flower.

"Well, there was a knight, and a maiden . . ."

"All the good stories begin that way."

"They do. And this particular knight was in love with the maiden and took her for a walk along a river, much larger than this one. He declared his love for her, and he went down to the water to pick her a flower. But he lost his balance, and he fell in, and he was wearing his armor—"

"He was out for a stroll in a full suit of armor?"

72

"Well, he was a knight . . ."

"I suppose. But still."

"These were medieval times. A dragon could have popped up out of nowhere, right? Plus, he probably looked good in it. Anyway, he fell in, and because he was in all that armor, he couldn't swim, right? And as he drowned, he threw the flower to the maiden and called out, 'Forget me not!'"

She nods. "Or . . . what did you call them?"

"*Myosotis scorpioides.* My parents were both biologists. Dad told me what all the plants and flowers are called." I look around. "He would have liked this."

"Well, I'm glad to know it's here."

We look for another moment, and then Winnie begins to tug on his leash, pulling back toward the road, so we make our way out of the little woods. We reach the street and continue on. "So, what are you doing this summer?" Viola asks.

"Working at Finn's, mostly. Not much else. I'm guessing you have yours pretty much mapped out?"

"To the minute."

"Anything fun?"

She wrinkles her nose. "Fun usually doesn't enter into the equation. I'm working a bit. Edward Riley?"

I shake my head.

"The CPA downtown. Not far from Finn's."

"Oh, yeah." I think a CPA is an accountant, but I don't want to ask.

"Yeah. So, I'm doing that, and then I'm also going to be away for three weeks in Haiti."

"That sounds cool."

"It'll be fine. It's a service trip; my dad set it up. It's for, you know—it goes on my résumé. Does that sound awful?"

"No."

"It doesn't? Do you do things like that? You know, to look good for future employers and grad-school applications and whatnot?"

Now it's my turn to laugh. "I think my best shot for graduate school is going to be putting some gum on my résumé and hoping that it winds up underneath yours."

It seems to take her a moment to realize that I'm joking. "Really? It's really not something you think about?"

"No. Maybe I should."

"No, you shouldn't! I mean, maybe you should; I'm not sorry I do, not really . . . but it must be nice. It must be nice to do things without worrying about how they're going to look to the world. Like write a poem. I've never written a poem."

The clouds from earlier in the day are moving on, and the sun is coming out. Viola takes a pair of sunglasses that had been hooked over the collar of her shirt and puts them on. I left mine in the car. It's a rarity; I'm hardly ever caught in public without them.

"I think I know what you mean," I say. "About worrying how you're seen. For me, it was different. You know, I was famous—

74

my *face* was famous, at least—from when I was really young. People look at me, even now. They look at me for an extra second, or they look at me twice, or they look away. I mean, you're sort of making a face for yourself, right? With your résumé. With the job and the trip and stuff. It's the face you put out to the world. You want to get yourself out there. I just think about things differently. The only thing I've ever cared about is trying to take my face away."

Viola looks at me thoughtfully but doesn't say anything, and I immediately feel like I've spilled way too much. Jesus, why can't I find a middle ground? Still, she looks like she's considering what I said and like she's about to say something back, but it's in that moment that Winston finally decides to crouch down and take a crap on the side of the road.

I really do hate dogs.

Viola has a plastic bag tied around the leash, and I watch as she unties it and puts her hand inside. I realize that she's going to scoop the shit up, and I stop her and tell her I'll do it, taking the bag off her hand and putting it on my own. I really don't want to, but it seems like the right thing to do, and anyway I don't want the image of Viola picking dog shit up in her hand to be stuck in my head. I bend over, grab it, and pick it up. I can feel the warmth through the plastic and I think I might gag, but I don't. Then I realize I'm not totally sure what to do next.

"Turn it inside out and tie it," Viola says.

I do, and now I have a neatly packaged dog turd in a bag. I look around for somewhere to put it, but of course there's nothing.

"I'll take it," she says.

"No, it's fine," I say. We start to walk again, Viola holding the leash and me holding the bag dangling from one hand, trying not to think about its weight.

"You know," she says, "I've never really talked to anyone about this stuff before. It's interesting, what you're saying. It's sad, but it's interesting."

As usual, I'm not sure what to say. A small plane flies overhead, dropping down toward the county airfield. She watches it as it passes.

"Even our vacations are supposed to accomplish something," she continues. "Later this summer, after Haiti, my parents want me to go with them and some friends of theirs up to Nantucket."

"What's that supposed to accomplish?"

"Oh, you know, they're not really friends. They're some sort of business associates. They're somewhere in the web that connects my dad to all the other lords of the universe. I don't want to go. I really don't. Do you know, the son in the family, Conrad, is an ex of mine?"

"An ex?"

"We dated for a summer. He went to Northfield Academy. He's a year ahead of us. He's at Yale now."

"Huh."

"And Conrad, of course he had to be the valedictorian of his class, so I'm really not sure I can stand to be around him right now."

"Right, right." My final class rank was eighty-six or eighty-seven. Maybe eighty-nine, now that I think about it. I was just happy to be in the top half.

"Anyway, they have their own plane. He flies it. He's supposed to fly everyone up to Nantucket for a long weekend in August. Doesn't that sound awkward?"

"Yeah . . ."

"But that's the point: I don't think my parents have even thought of that! They're not inconsiderate people, but it's just not the way they think about things. For them, going away with this family serves a purpose, and me being there serves a purpose, and the idea that I might not want to spend a long weekend flying around and sitting on the beach and whatnot with my ex-boyfriend doesn't even occur to them."

And whatnot. I feel a sudden hatred for Conrad. And for everyone else who goes to Yale and summers on Nantucket. And especially, particularly, deeply, and truly for each and every asshole in the world who flies his own airplane.

"Parents try," I say. "They do their best."

"I suppose."

"You could refuse to go."

"Oh, that would be quite the rebellion, wouldn't it? Very unlike me."

"It would be. Have you ever rebelled against anything?"

"Well, I'm going to Berkeley instead of Stanford. My parents very much preferred Stanford."

"That's . . . it?"

"That's not good?"

"No, it's fine. It's, um, a good one. Yeah."

We've arrived back at her house, following the names of presidents I mostly half remember from history class. I guess you can have only so many Washington and Lincoln and Roosevelt streets before you have to dig a little deeper. Martin Van Buren would probably be tickled to know that a cul-de-sac with million-dollar houses is named for him in central New Jersey.

"Well, here we are," Viola says, turning to me and trying to unwind the leash from her legs as Winnie darts around, probably angling for another taste of my ankle. I keep my distance.

"I'm sorry about your mailbox."

"Don't worry about it."

"There's probably some sort of insurance or something."

"I'm sure there is. This has been nice, Cole. Thank you so much for the book. It's very thoughtful."

It's actually an expression of unbridled, unexpressed passion, but sure, we can go with "thoughtful."

"It was nothing," I tell her. "I'm glad you like it." I start toward my car. I'll wait a few days and then maybe call her. Wait until Matt comes up with a plan B for Eddie. Wait until there's some good reason to go by the accounting agency. When are taxes due? Not until April, I think.

I reach my car.

I can see the end of the summer, way out in front of me, months away, but I'm rushing toward it like a plane racing down a runway.

I'm fucking sick of waiting.

"Hey," I call to Viola. She's halfway across her lawn, Winnie jogging by her side, acting like he's not a complete psychopath. She turns. "You want to get lunch with me sometime? We could meet up at the diner."

She pulls her sunglasses off and squints at me. The sun is to my back.

"I've never been to the diner," she says.

"Never? In four years? You're not telling me you've lived in Jersey for four years and never been to your town diner?"

"I haven't. Is it good?"

"'Good' isn't quite the right word for it. But if you want to get away from the predictable, try ordering their seafood special and see what happens."

She laughs and nods. "Sure. Let's do it."

"Yeah?"

"Yeah."

"We can talk about Eliot," I say. "There are a few in that book that I haven't even read."

"You're funny, Cole. You make me laugh. You still have my number?"

"I think so. Somewhere." *Etched into my soul.* "I'll text you."

She gives me a smile, a beautiful smile, the best I've gotten out of her, and then she turns and walks away. I turn the engine on and drive Dad's Volvo out of the neighborhood, feeling happy.

Here's the pathetic truth: I've never really had a girlfriend before, and I'm not entirely sure how to get one. I don't know how to make it happen. Matt's had a few girlfriends, but it seems like he doesn't really do anything, like they just show up for him. Probably because he's an athlete, I suppose.

It's the kind of thing that makes me wish I had a big brother. Or my father back, of course.

I'm halfway home when I realize I have a cooling bag of dog shit on the passenger seat beside me. I pull over and throw it deep into the woods.

Four

— Matt —

It's the morning of the second-to-last day of June, and I can't sleep. There are thoughts bouncing around my brain every time I close my eyes. All kinds of stuff, like different parts of a movie that are out of order. Kids I haven't thought about in years, the lake, the old school. Principal Schultz; the time in kindergarten when I got called down to his office. I don't even remember what it was for. I remember that I was scared, though, and that he was pretty nice and let me off easy for whatever it was. I remember that he smelled like after-shave, like my grandfather used to smell, and I remember looking at a picture on his desk, of him and his kids at Disney World. He was grinning in it, his arm around Mickey Mouse's shoulder, and I remember staring at it and thinking how weird it was for the principal to have a family and to go to Disney.

I wonder what happened to the picture. I wonder what happened to all the stuff in the school when they tore it down.

I finally get out of bed and go downstairs. The lawn guys

are mowing outside, and someone's cleaning the pool. There's a cellophane-covered plate in the fridge with a note from Mom, the carb content laid out in her perfect handwriting. I warm it up, check my glucose level, and give myself some insulin. I eat the meal she prepared, then make myself some more toast and eat that, too, not bothering with an extra dose. I find some clothes in the laundry room, throw them on, and come back upstairs to find Dad in the middle of the living room. He's waving a golf club with one hand and holding a cellphone to his ear with the other.

"Sure," he barks into the phone. "Sure! Just make sure it gets done by Friday." He glances at me and winks. "Ken . . . Ken, you're doing a great job. You just need to get this done." He looks back at me and rolls his eyes, then swings one-handed at an imaginary ball on the carpet.

I used to love to listen to Dad talk on the phone. He has a study on the second floor, and I'd wander in and sit in one of the chairs and listen to him go at it. He sounded so sure of himself and of everything else. He sounded like the boss.

"All right, my friend. I'll talk to you soon." He puts the phone in his pocket and turns to me. "Finally awake!"

"I didn't know you were home," I say.

"Just heading out. Up for some golf?"

"No."

"Elbow too tender?"

"Yeah. Uh, yeah."

He frowns, leans the club against a section of the couch, and walks over to where I'm standing. "Let's see you extend it."

"It's fine, Dad. I'm doing the PT."

"I know. Just let me see."

"Christ, it's fine. Look." I flex and extend my right arm three times, feeling like a piece of meat. "I just don't really feel like golf today. I'm going to see someone."

"Anyone I know?"

"An old friend." He shoots me a knowing look, and I turn away so that I don't have to return it. Let him imagine that I'm going over to a girl's house. Let him think that we're some sort of buds. "I'll see you later."

I go outside. As I get into my truck, I realize that I left the plate on the counter, something Mom absolutely hates, but I'm pretty sure this is one of the days when people come in to clean.

It's already hot when I pull up outside the Gerbers' house. It's nice, though not even close to being as nice as ours. You'd expect a broker like Mr. Gerber to have a much bigger place. It's the same one they had when Andy and Paul were little and Cole and I would come over to play.

Mrs. Gerber is surprised to see me, but she invites me right in and apologizes for the mess. "Frank," she calls, "Matt Simpson is here!"

"Matt?" a voice comes back from deeper inside, and right away I'm feeling weird about coming. When was the last time I was in this house? There must have been something, some sort of get-together, something for Paul? No. There were two Gerber boys the last time I was over, years and years ago.

It's very quiet, and they don't seem to have AC, and I'm feeling like I shouldn't be here. It's like I'm showing up too soon after something bad happened, and I'm intruding. It's awkward. Still, Mrs. Gerber seems genuinely happy to see me, just like she was happy at the store when I said I'd come by, and she's already bringing me in and offering me something to drink. We enter the living room and find Mr. Gerber sitting in a recliner in his pajamas and bathrobe, newspaper spread on his lap, fumbling around with the lever to lower his feet. He manages to still look well-put-together.

"Matt, my boy, what brings you here?"

"Good morning, Mr. Gerber. I'm sorry to drop in on you."

"Not at all. Have a seat."

I sit on a hard green sofa. I'm facing the fireplace; I seem to remember the mantel being covered with photos when we were young, but there aren't any there now, just a weird modern sculpture that's not of anything in particular. Mr. Gerber is pouring himself some coffee and offers me some, and I take it because I can't seem to wake all the way up.

"How is work, Matt?"

"Fine; it's good. I like working at the store."

"Good practical business experience working there, though I don't think it's where you're headed, is it? The grocery industry?"

"Probably not, Mr. Gerber. I'm not sure where I'm headed yet."

"I'd definitely have you at the firm this summer; internship position, but I'm sure we could find some money to throw at you."

"Thank you, that's . . . kind. But I'm happy at the store." It's close to being true. "Is Paul home? I was—I've been thinking about him. Just wondering if, you know, he'd like to go out. I'd take him out. Like, get some ice cream and go for a drive, whatever he—whatever he likes to do these days."

Both of their faces go soft. "Oh, that's lovely, Matt," Mrs. Gerber says, and she really seems to mean it.

"He'd love that," Mr. Gerber says. "He doesn't get very many visitors. Do you want to go upstairs and see him, ask if he wants to come out?"

Mrs. Gerber glances at him like she isn't sure it's such a good idea, but then she turns back to me and nods. "Go ahead, Matt. You remember. It's just at the top of the stairs. I'll grab him a clean T-shirt from the dryer."

I take my mug of coffee and go up the stairs, the back of my neck tingling. There are still pictures here, framed photos on the wall, family vacations with two kids and then with one. I stop by the last one with Andy in it, the summer before first grade, and I look closely. They're at the Grand Canyon, the four of them at the top, their backs to it, smiling into a camera that must have been held by some friendly tourist. Oblivious. No idea what was coming in less than a year. I look into Andy's squinting face. I told Cole that I had forgotten what Andy looked like, and that was basically true. I stopped being able to imagine him, to see him in my memories, but standing here and looking at this photo, I know that I never forgot at all. Every feature is familiar. It was always there, inside me; it just got lost for a while.

I continue on to the top of the stairs. There is a hallway, closed doors on either side, and the open door to a bathroom ahead. I pause. I imagine what it must have been like here that day, while I was home in bed and Cole was being carried out of the school. Who called them? Was Mr. Gerber at work? Who told Paul about Andy? How did they make him understand? I wonder about that day, and about the day after, and then all the days after that. And then I go left when I know I should go right. I open the door and step inside.

Andy's room is just as I remember it. I don't know what I expected to find; a sewing room, maybe, or just boxes of stuff, or some sort of bizarre shrine to the shooting, but I'm happy to discover that it's just Andy's room.

Nothing's changed from when me and Cole and Andy were crouched on the floor playing with Matchbox cars—and there it is in the corner, at the foot of the bed, the official plastic car-carrying case that I'd been so jealous of and wanted so badly for myself. There is the *Star Wars* poster above the bed. There is the crappy painted ceramic dinosaur on the dresser from Cole's fifth birthday party (mine broke a long time ago). I look around, and I can see it: the three of us, rushing in after playing outside. Maybe coming back from the lake, smelling of sunscreen. Hot and sweaty, pushing past one another for the best, fastest

Matchbox car as though that were the most important thing in the world, which is exactly what it was.

The air is so still in here. There's a little bit of a funny smell, though I can't quite place it. I can't imagine that they ever open the window.

"We haven't changed a thing." Mrs. Gerber is standing in the doorway behind me.

"I'm sorry—I, uh, it's been a while; I forgot which one—"

"That's fine, Matt." She steps inside the room and looks around. "Paul has a very hard time with change. 'Wedded to sameness' is what his psychologist calls it. Isn't that sort of a poetic phrase? So we felt that we couldn't just take the room away, change it to something else."

She trails off and looks around. *Not able to change anything.* *"Wedded to sameness."* It makes me think of Cole's house.

"I made the bed that morning," she says. "After he left for school."

I look at the bed. A *Transformers* sheet and matching quilt are neatly tucked up over a single pillow.

"I wish I hadn't."

We stand together in the silent room, looking at the empty bed, which seems smaller than it should be, and then Mrs. Gerber lays a hand on my shoulder and brings us out into the hall. She knocks on the door that I should have gone through at the start, after first carefully and firmly closing Andy's door behind her.

Paul's room is a disaster. Unwashed clothes and dirty dishes, old toys like in Andy's room but in much worse shape, and Paul sitting on the floor in the middle of it, cradling a laptop. He doesn't look up as I step in behind his mother and stare at him.

There's something I've been wanting to ask Paul ever since I saw him at the grocery store, but I'm not sure how. I don't even know if he really has actual conversations.

"Paul," Mrs. Gerber says, "guess who's here?" Paul looks at her first, then at me. It's like he's looking through a telescope; he focuses on one thing and then on another, not able to take everything in all at once. "Matt came by to see you," she continues. "It's such a hot day, and he thought that you might go out for an ice cream."

Paul seems to register this without any expression, but he sets the computer down and gets to his feet. Ten minutes later he is getting into the passenger side of the Explorer, and I'm wondering if this is such a good idea after all, but it's too late to back out now. The Gerbers are standing on the front porch, and they look too happy to disappoint. Still, it seemed like an ordeal for Paul's mom to get him dressed and ready to go, and I wonder what will happen if Paul gets upset while we're out, or if he decides to run away or something. He did a lot of that when we were starting high school, before they put him on all the meds. I start the car, and we head down the road and into town.

There are a few places nearby where we could stop for ice cream: the diner; or Finn's to buy a pint and a box of cones. Instead, I turn the radio on and roll down the windows and step on the gas, heading out toward the lake. I glance over at Paul, who is looking straight ahead, out the windshield, his hair blowing in the wind.

"This okay, Paul? Not too much wind? I can turn on the AC instead."

Paul nods, though I'm not sure which part he is nodding to, being okay with the windows down or wanting the air conditioning on. He doesn't seem unhappy and I want the windows open, so I don't change anything and we continue on.

When we were little kids, Cole and I always wanted the Gerber boys to be even more alike than they were. We wanted to play games where we had to figure out who was who, but it was always too easy, because no matter how alike they looked, even if they were dressed in the same clothes, it was no mystery. For one thing, Andy was just a little bit taller than Paul, plus it was clear as soon as one of them opened his mouth. Even before that, though, the look in their eyes gave it away. Andy was sharp; he didn't miss anything, ever, while Paul looked at you like he was studying everything from a distance, the details of a situation slowly coming into focus.

The lot at the beach is crowded. It's mostly young kids; when we got older, we wanted to go to the pool instead, and then we wanted to go to the shore. I park in the shade and climb out, stretching my legs. We cross the lot to the beach, and I'm wondering what Paul would want to do. He's not in swim trunks. How do you make a plan with someone who barely communicates? He keeps going, though, down to the water's edge, where he sits in the wet sand, grabs a stray plastic shovel, and starts to dig. His shorts are going to get wet, and a couple of families playing nearby give him long looks, but I just watch as he digs a hole, packing the sand into a wall facing the lake. There's a plastic bucket nearby, and I take it and set it down by the sand wall. Paul looks at it, then looks up, making eye contact with me for the first time.

"Thank you," he says. It sounds as though he's reading from a script.

"No problem. What are you building?"

He doesn't respond. He's busy using the edge of the shovel to etch around the edges of the wall. I'm watching him as he continues to dig and pile and shape, with his hands and with the shovel, his focus completely on the work in front of him, and I'm startled by a voice from behind me. I turn to find a girl who had been in my senior math class. I can't remember her name.

She seems to know who I am, and we start talking, me pretending to be more familiar with her and her friends than I am, keeping the conversation going because I like her white two-piece swimsuit. I figure out that her name is Danielle. She's here with her baby sister, and as we're talking, she keeps irritably turning to glance at a young girl splashing in the shallow water along with a little boy.

I have to make an effort to keep the conversation going. Talking to girls has always come easily for me, but I'm not feeling it now. I've never been in love, I'll tell you that, though I've had a couple of girlfriends. I've never felt the way Cole obviously feels about Viola, and to tell the truth, I'm not sure I ever will. I don't think I could feel anything real for this girl, but I wonder whether she would make the rest of the summer go by a little bit faster.

Then she asks me about Paul.

"He's just a friend of mine. The brother of a friend. I'm just taking him out."

"Who's his brother?"

"Andy Gerber. This is Paul; his brother was Andy Gerber."

Her eyes widen and flicker from my face to Paul, sitting in the middle of a growing sand castle, and back again. "Oh . . ." She sounds impressed, interested. What's the word? *Titillated.*

I try to place Danielle. Which year did she move to town? I can't remember.

Her interest in Paul has ruined the moment, ruined the conversation, ruined whatever might have happened for the rest of the summer. It feels totally wrong. It feels like she's butting in on something she shouldn't be. This must be what it's like for Cole all the time; walking around, hoping no one recognizes him, hoping they won't connect the dots. No wonder he doesn't want to talk to people.

I want this girl to leave me alone, but before I can think of a way out of the conversation, her sister pulls a shovel out of the boy's hand, sending him tumbling. He begins to wail, and

Danielle turns and runs over to her, screeching about what a problem she always is, and drags her away with an embarrassed wave, which I don't return.

The boy's mother wades into the water, helping him to his feet and brushing wet sand off him. She seems old to have a kid this age, and she's not Asian like he is, and I wonder whether she might actually be the grandmother. The kid stops crying and goes back to digging. The woman turns to me, and I recognize her right away.

"Hello, Matthew Simpson!"

"Hello, Mrs. Maiden."

"I didn't expect to see you here at the beach!"

"No, I don't come much. I'm just here with Paul." I nod toward him. I wait for her to say how lovely it is that I'm paying attention to Paul and taking him out, but Mrs. Maiden just nods as though it were the most natural thing in the world.

"Well, it's a good day for the beach."

"Is he, um, with you?" I ask, nodding toward the little boy.

"Oh, of course he is! I don't think you've ever met my son, Stephen. Stephen, come over here and say hello to my friend Matthew."

The boy wades out of the lake and stands before me, dripping, shovel in his hand. He looks me directly in the eye and says, "Hello, Matthew."

"Hello," I say, and, not knowing what else to do, I put my hand out, and the boy shakes it. He has a good handshake. We stand, looking at each other, and then Stephen nods, turns, and goes back to digging.

Mrs. Maiden laughs. "He's such a pistol."

"How old is he?"

"He's eight. He's small for his age. He was in an orphanage for the first few years of his life. He came to me when he was three years old. He'd gone to a foster home by then, but he was still malnourished. I don't know if he'll ever make it back up, no matter how much I pour into him."

"Does he go to school?"

"Well, naturally he goes to school! He's going to be in the third grade at Harrison in the fall."

Harrison Elementary is what they built to replace the old East Ridge Elementary School after they tore it down.

"He's one of the smartest ones in his class," Mrs. Maiden continues. She turns back and looks at me. "Speaking of smart, I understand you're going off to a very good school in the fall, Matthew."

"I'm going to Bucknell. But it's for baseball."

"You're just joining the baseball team? You won't be taking classes?"

"No, I will; it's just . . . I meant that I got in because of baseball."

"I know what you meant. But you think too little of yourself."

The comment makes me happier than I'd expect. It means something, coming from her. Unlike all the other parents who lost kids that day, Mrs. Maiden continued on with our class. She knows all of us. She came to our events: concerts, awards ceremonies, games, the elementary-to-middle-school step-up party. I saw her there at the high school graduation, too, handing out programs.

Stephen gives up on digging and finds a handheld fishing net. He's standing knee-deep in the lake, spinning in a circle, one arm dragging the net through the water and the other extended toward the sky. "Mommy," he shouts, "I'm going to catch us a fish for dinner!"

"Of course you are!" she calls back. She watches him and laughs out loud.

I watch him spin. I know that Mrs. Maiden's husband has been gone for many years; they were one of the first couples to break up after the shooting. Even as kids, we heard things. I know that Kendra had been their only child, so she must have been alone. But here she is now, with a child of her own. Another child. Starting over again. I don't know what to think of it. She looks at me for a long moment as Stephen continues to fish.

"You look sad, Matthew."

"I . . . no, I'm fine. I'm fine." I study the structure Paul is making in the sand.

She nods, eyes not leaving my face.

"I'm just tired," I say. It's true. The sun is beating on my head. I don't think I ever woke all the way up.

She turns back to her son. "Stephen," she calls, "we have to be going. We have Dr. O'Hara." Stephen wades out of the water and stands at attention, the net over his shoulder, like a little soldier with spindly arms and a sunken chest. "Most children hate going to the dentist," Mrs. Maiden says, "but not Stephen. He likes to show off what a good job he's doing with his teeth." The boy grins at me, displaying flashing white, and I can't help but smile back at him.

Stephen and his mother gather up a few things, and she turns to me once more and lays a hand on my arm. "Be gentle with yourself, Matthew," she says. Then they are gone.

I sit down in the sand and stare out at the water. I wish I could sleep. Paul is directly in front of me and doesn't seem to be going anywhere, so I lie back in the sand and fold my hands in front of my eyes and try to rest. Maybe I do. My mind drifts, not really dreaming but not awake. It feels like a long while, but when I finally sit back up, only a little bit of time has gone by. The sun is really bothering me. I look at Paul and the sand castle, which is actually surprisingly good.

"Hey, Paul." No response. "Paul!"

Paul looks over.

"Feel like an ice cream?"

Paul nods, and I lead him up the beach to the Snack Shack. We stand in line, and when we get up to the counter, I wait for him to place his order. When he doesn't, I ask him what flavor he likes, and then I have to relay the answer to the guy working the soft-serve machine. I get a chocolate cone for Paul, pay for it, and then on second thought, I get another cone for myself. Vanilla, covered in rainbow sprinkles. My parents hardly ever let me get ice cream at the beach when I was young; it was a treat for special occasions, always carefully measured, never any sprinkles to throw things off. But now, standing on the hot sand with this cone, I'm remembering when the other kids all had treats like this, melting over their hands, and I was the only one left out. I check my phone: blood glucose of 224. Too high. The extra toast at breakfast.

I shouldn't have this. I should take some insulin. Instead, I take a bite.

The sprinkles mix with the soft vanilla cream in my mouth. It's incredibly good. I turn to Paul, who is attacking his chocolate cone and getting a fair amount of it on his chin.

"Paul, do you remember Andy?"

His eyes flicker; then he goes back to his cone.

"Andy. Your brother. Your twin brother, Andy. Do you remember him?"

"Andy."

"Do you remember when I used to come over to your house? Me and Cole? We used to play in the backyard."

He doesn't respond. I go back to the counter to take a handful of napkins and then return to his side. I eat more of the ice cream. I'm going to finish it, even though I'd sort of told myself that I'd eat only half. I stare out at the lake, thinking that I almost made it across.

I spot someone off to my right, slipping through the crowd. A woman in a bikini, long black hair tied back, ponytail shimmering in the sun. She's gone in a moment, and I turn and follow her. There are more families on the beach now, and for a moment I lose sight of her behind a big umbrella, but then there she is again, and I walk faster, not taking my eyes off her. I step around sand castles and moms rubbing sunscreen onto their kids, closing the distance, and I tap the woman on the shoulder just as she pauses by a beach chair. She turns and immediately looks alarmed. I've never seen her before.

"Yes?"

"I'm sorry. I thought you were someone else."

She looks at the now-soggy cone I'm gripping in one hand, ice cream running over my wrist. My phone blares suddenly, alarmed at the sudden spike in my blood sugar, and we both jump. I take it from my pocket and swipe the screen. It reads 256, with an arrow pointing straight up.

"Are you all right?"

"Yes, I'm sorry." I turn and walk away. My body feels dry and brittle. Sugar coats my mouth and the inside of my throat, and I know that inside me, large globs of it are circulating in my blood, clogging things up, taking their toll on my kidneys and my eyes. I need to take insulin, now. More than 250 is dangerous. More than 300, and the app automatically sends a message to my mom.

I retrace my steps and find that Paul is nowhere to be seen.

I look up and down the beach. Kids are running everywhere.

97

I keep on walking, back toward the spot where we'd been sitting when Mrs. Maiden found us, scanning the sand and the water's edge for him. The sun is too bright, and black spots are popping up in my vision. There's a throbbing pain behind my eyes. Paul should be easy to find; he was wearing orange-and-black checkered shorts and a Rolling Stones T-shirt. I pass his half-finished sand castle—I'd been thinking that he might have come back to finish it—and I reach the edge of the beach area. There's a path here that runs along the side of the lake to a smaller beach, mostly gravel, directly across from the Monument. A mom is sitting on a blanket with two toddlers.

"Excuse me," I say. "Did a young guy come through here a few moments ago?" I describe Paul, and she shakes her head. One of her kids offers me an animal cracker. I take it and turn back to the beach. Does Paul know how to swim? Where's the lifeguard? I can see the chair, but no one's in it. I'm still holding the cone, which is a sticky mess now, and I throw it into a trash bin as I head back, my eyes on the water. I'm coming up to the empty lifeguard chair when I hear a noise and see a stir of activity up by the Snack Shack. I walk toward it.

Paul is there, behind the building, crouched on the ground, the remains of his ice cream cone lying between his feet. People are gathering around him and speaking to one another, and as I approach, Paul shudders and makes a sound like a gulping bark. The people probably think he's upset because he dropped his cone, and one mother is rummaging in her purse as if she's getting ready to buy him another. I crouch down and try to look into his face.

"Paul," I say, "Paul, settle down."

He isn't looking at me. His eyes are on the ground, and he's shaking his head.

"Hey, look, I'll buy you some more ice cream and we can, we can go home." Even as I'm saying it, I know that the ice cream isn't the problem.

Paul continues to shake his head, rhythmically, bouncing a little bit on his heels. I look up. Some of the people have moved away, but a number of them are still here. I feel like telling them to move along, but I don't, and I turn back to Paul just in time for the ice cream to hit me full in the face. He's scooped it up from the ground and flung it in one motion. Someone screams. I can't see for a minute, and I stand and use the wad of napkins to wipe it away. When I look up again, I see that Paul has also risen and is staring directly at me.

"I remember Andy."

We look at each other for a long moment. I don't know what to say. I'm not angry, and I'm not scared. To tell the truth, what I want to do is talk more about Andy, but there are people all around, so I just wipe my face some more. Then I turn and walk toward the parking lot, glancing back once to make sure he's following me. I get into the truck, and so does he. Paul fastens his own seat belt without being asked. My phone goes off again: 298. I have to pee, badly, my body struggling to purge the excess

99

sugar, but I don't want to leave Paul alone again, so I go and pee standing in front of the truck. I text my mom with my free hand, letting her know I'm going to take my medicine and to ignore the alert. Then I get back into the truck and we drive back to the Gerbers' house in silence.

Mr. and Mrs. Gerber are waiting for us in rocking chairs on the porch. Mr. Gerber has switched over from coffee to something in a cocktail glass. They both stand up.

"How did it go?" Mrs. Gerber asks.

"We went to the beach," I tell her. I look at Paul, who is looking at the ground. "We had some ice cream, too."

"Oh, that's great. Let me pay you back."

"No, no, that's all right."

The four of us stand silently for a moment, the two of them on the porch looking down at us. Some kids are running around on the lawn across the street, having a water-balloon fight. "I'd like to take him out again," I finally say.

"Would you like that, Paul?" Mrs. Gerber asks. "Matt could come by again sometime, and you could go out together. He's going to be gone in the fall, you know. Off to college."

Paul doesn't say anything, but he looks up at his mother and he nods, maybe to acknowledge the truth of my leaving; maybe in response to a thought of his own rather than to anything his mother said; maybe to say that he'd go out with me again. His mom clearly chooses to believe that last one, and she claps her hands and says, "Wonderful!"

100

Mr. Gerber comes down off the porch to shake my hand and clap me on the back, and I can smell the liquor on him now. He squeezes my shoulder hard and reminds me that an internship is mine for the asking, and I thank him again and get back in the truck.

I wonder for a moment, as I'm pulling away from the curb, how tired and desperate these people need to be to allow a passing eighteen-year-old, someone they barely know, to take a kid like Paul out with him on a moment's notice, without even knowing where they're going.

I come to the stop sign by Route 21 and realize that I never took any insulin.

I accelerate out onto the empty road, roll all the windows down, turn on the radio. I'm beyond tired. I should crash for ten or twelve hours. I can't do it, though. Every time I lie down, the thoughts close over my head, like I'm sinking into deep water.

I step on the accelerator. The road ahead of me is empty, and for just a moment, not very long, I close my eyes, letting the dice roll.

And then I open them again and continue on, looking for a reason not to go home.

Five

— *Cole* —

"Over here."

Matt's voice comes out of the darkness, and I stand for a moment at the edge of the parking lot, letting my eyes adjust. It's late, the Snack Shack is closed, with a big padlocked board across the window, and the beach is just a black strip with the blacker lake behind it.

"Where are you?" I ask.

I hear a rock hit the water once, twice, three times. Even when he was a little kid, Matt was able to get at least three skips out of the least aerodynamic stone.

"Fuck you," I call. "I have the beer."

"In that case . . ." Matt emerges from the darkness farther down the beach and grins. "Is it cold?"

"Ice-cold." I toss the lukewarm six-pack to him, and we walk down to the overturned lifeguard boat. Matt pulls himself up onto the hull and twists a can free, popping it open

102

and holding the foaming edge to his mouth. "Is this all we've got?"

"You're welcome." I pull myself up next to him and twist off one of my own. Dad left lots of beer in the garage. I doubt that Mom even remembers it's out there, and she definitely has no idea exactly what and how much he had, so I can bring some whenever I want. But it's not cold.

Matt grunts, drinks, and looks out at the water. "Did you know," he asks me, "that Mrs. Maiden adopted a kid? A Chinese kid? I saw them out here a few days ago."

"Sure. Everyone knows that."

"Where was I?" he asks.

I shrug. Where is Matt usually? Somewhere off in his own head. "I don't think they made an announcement or anything. I've just seen them around town. They go into the diner all the time."

"Isn't that kind of crazy, though? Adopting a little kid like that? I mean, what is she, sixty or something?"

"I don't know. How old she is, I mean. I don't think it's so crazy. What else is she supposed to do?" We sit for a few moments, drinking our beers and looking out at the dark lake. "How are things going with Finn?" I ask. We almost never see each other at the store.

He shrugs and drains most of the rest of the can. "It's fine," he says. "It's a job, right?"

I almost laugh. It's the first job Matt's ever had, and here he is, sounding like a working guy. He takes it way too seriously.

"Here's the thing," I tell him. "I was kind of counting on some extra hours this summer. Some overtime hours."

"For what?"

"For money, genius." It comes out harsher than I intended.

"All right, calm down."

I sigh and finish my own beer, reaching for a second. "It's just that I'm thinking about something in the fall. A plane ticket. Out to California."

"Yeah?"

"Yeah." It's been a little more than a week, but I haven't told Matt about giving Viola the book. I guess I've just wanted to tell him in person, and he was working, and then I was working. I talked to him on the phone once, but he seemed out of it. "So, I . . . went by her house."

"Yeah? And?"

"And I gave her the book."

"The J.R.R. Eliot thing?"

"No, it's . . . yeah. That one."

"And? Did she fucking love it?"

I grin in spite of myself. Matt can always make me grin like no one else can. "She loved it."

He throws back his head and laughs, slams his beer down so that it foams over the top, vaults off the hull, and does a standing backflip in the sand. I've only ever seen him do that after turning a double play. Now I'm laughing too, helplessly, like an idiot.

"And you're going out to the West Coast to see her this fall?"

"Well, if she wants me to . . . I mean, she's going to be busy starting college and everything, but . . . I might ask her, eventually. We're seeing each other. Day after tomorrow. We're, um, getting lunch at the diner."

Matt laughs again, cackling up at the moon. "You son of a bitch!"

"It's nothing definite—"

"Motherfucker, I will personally drive you to California if you can pull this off." He pulls himself back up on the boat, claps me hard on the shoulder, and drains the last of his beer.

Sometimes I wonder if Matt and I would be friends if we met for the first time today, and of course we wouldn't be. What do we have in common? He's a jock; he's a good baseball player. A great player. People like him; girls like him. When he walks down the hall or comes into a room, he's not really paying attention, in the sense that he doesn't need to, in the sense that he's fine on his own and doesn't need anybody else's approval. Even when we were little, it seemed like he and Andy were closer, and I was always chasing along behind.

Matt burps, wipes his mouth with the back of his hand, and asks me how my mom is. I tell him that someone called the house about an overdue bill the other day, looking for "Mr. Hewitt," and I pretended to be him and told the person that they'd get the check ASAP.

"I saw her the other day," he says.

"Where?"

"At the store. She came in. She looked pretty good. She was joking around with Finn. And she asked me about college and stuff. I think she feels bad that you're not going, maybe."

I shrug. That doesn't sound right. She does have her better days, but not that good.

We let it go quiet. I like that we don't have to talk when we're around each other. And even when we do, we don't totally have to listen. I'll talk about my poetry sometimes and know for a fact that he's not listening, and he'll go on and on about baseball and I'll process maybe twenty percent of it.

I want to ask him about graduation. About sitting in that chair. Everyone saw it, but no one's talked about it. "How are you doing?" I ask him.

He lets out a slow, loud belch. "Good. I'm all good."

"Yeah. But, I mean, you're doing all right?"

"Yeah. I'm good, dude."

"Because, I was just wondering. About graduation and all. The chair."

He's quiet for a moment. "I don't know," he finally replies.

"You don't know why you did it?"

"I didn't even know I was going to do it until it happened."

106

"Are you thinking about it? The shooting?"

He shakes his head. "No. I'm not. What's there to think about? I wasn't there."

It's true, but it never used to stop him. He'd ask me questions endlessly, never seeming to really understand that it was all a blank. It's like a missing chapter from a book, I told him once. I can read right up to it, and then it picks up after.

We sit and finish our second beers. There are only two left now, and he hands one to me. I weigh saying something more, decide not to, and we both pop our cans open at once, the sound preceding by two heartbeats the blast of gunshots from the right side of the lake. Then there's a silence when neither one of us moves or speaks, and then another shot.

We both slide down off the boat and stand frozen on the sand. "What do you think that was?" I ask, which is stupid. There's no mistaking gunshots.

He shakes his head.

"It's probably just some kids screwing around," I say. "We can get out of here. I guess we should probably call the police, maybe?"

Matt shakes his head again. "Let's go see." He throws the beer can hard into the sand and starts walking in the direction the shots came from. Usually, the best way to get Matt to do something is to imply that he shouldn't. I follow him. We're leaving the beach and heading toward the Monument.

We enter the woods and follow the path alongside the water. It's quiet. Matt's leading the way, and I can feel my heart beating

107

and realize that I have to pee. I'm still holding the can in one hand. I tell myself it's just some stupid kids screwing around in the woods.

In the dark, tripping over tree roots and dead branches, it takes us about five minutes to get to the spot where the white birch tree breaks the path in two. We pause there, and I think about taking a leak, but then we hear laughter and someone shouting. Matt looks at me and then sets off down the path to our right, and I follow him.

It takes us another few moments to come out into the clearing. There are three people there, and a garden gnome who's about to be executed. They have a blindfold on it and everything. There's another one, alongside it, and the shattered pieces of a third on the ground. Matt and I stand in the shadows at the foot of the path, watching. I take a sip of my beer, and that's when they spot us.

The first guy is named Tom something. Higgins, maybe. I can't remember. He was in our class but didn't graduate with us. I think he went off to a different school freshman or sophomore year. The second is Mike Antonucci, who played football and never seemed too smart, but I never had a hard time with him either. The only class we had together was math, because I'm not very good at math. I don't know the third guy at all, and he's the one with the gun. He's tall and has black hair tied back in a ponytail, and when he looks at me, I have to do a double take because his eyes don't focus on the same spot. His right eye looks at me, but the left one looks off to the side. I think that's what *cockeyed* means, though I'm not sure if that's something people say anymore.

We all say hi to each other, and Mike comes over and shakes Matt's and my hands like we're friends and like it's been a long time since we've seen each other, neither of which is true. Tom asks if we have any more beer, and I tell him we finished it off back at the beach and that we came out because we heard the shots, and they all start laughing, and Matt and I laugh too, even though I'm not sure what's funny.

There's more moonlight making its way down through the branches now, or maybe my eyes are just continuing to get better in the dark, or maybe I can't really see it that well at all but I remember it and my memory is filling in the blanks on the side of the rock: FUCK SAM KEELEY. Matt's talking to the other three, but I'm not really paying attention. The one with the ponytail and the gun has a bottle of something in his other hand, and he takes a drink and turns from the group, raising the gun and sighting along it.

"I'm gonna do it this time, faggots," he calls out, and everyone turns to look at him, and he does. He pulls the trigger, and there's that unmistakable, unapologetic bark of a gunshot, and we all flinch a little bit while the garden gnome, having apparently been previously spared by this guy's poor aim, explodes into shards. Mike and Tom cheer. The guy slowly lowers the gun, admiring his handiwork, and Tom, laughing, is hanging off his shoulder and slapping him on the back and trying to grab the bottle from him all at once. The acrid smell of gunpowder reaches me, and I wince, immediately nauseated.

My bladder is going to burst, so I say something about taking a leak, turn, and walk off into the woods until I'm a respectful distance away from the Monument and behind some trees, and I set the now-empty can down among the roots. Those guys are idiots. I know exactly where the gnomes came from and just how stupid it was to steal them. Sam Keeley hasn't lived in that house for twenty years; it isn't his, and it isn't his family's. People still talk about the place over on Pine Street as "Sam Keeley's house" even though it's just where he lived for one year, two decades ago, when his family was passing through town and he was a little kid.

No one actually remembers him from back then. He went to school for a year, and then they moved on, went out West, moved a bunch more times, and no one ever knew why this was the place he came back to. Different families have lived there over the years. They probably don't even know the history when they buy it. The current owner has a bunch of stupid ceramic gnomes in the yard, and apparently these losers decided to steal a few and bring them out here and shoot them as though that were fun but also meant something. And I don't think the guy with the gun is even from East Ridge.

It takes me a while to relax enough to start peeing. I'm still sick to my stomach from the gunpowder. I just want to get out of here. Out of these woods, away from these guys. Even away from Matt. I zip back up and take a few more steps farther into the trees. It's quiet out ahead of me, and dark. I shiver. I wish I was the kind of guy who would go off hiking and camping by himself at night. Climb up a mountain somewhere and build a fire, dance around and jump over it and find a way to get out of this skin. Maybe everyone wants to be someone they're not.

I'm standing here just thinking about this stuff when I realize that the voices behind me have changed. One of them — it sounds like the kid with the ponytail — sounds angry, and then I hear Matt shout something. I turn back toward the rock and start walking. I've come a little bit farther than I thought. The voices are all in a tangle now, arguing about something, with someone — not Matt — saying to calm down and chill out. I start to jog, stepping around trees and over roots, hands balled up into fists, and I want to be back there with my friend, but I'm scared because there are three of those guys and one of them has a gun. I'm thinking that it will work itself out if I give it a minute; they'll just settle down, and I'll walk out into the clearing by the Monument and we'll all stand there for a few minutes and talk about some bullshit or other and then Matt and I will head back to the beach.

I get there. I step into the clearing, and everyone is standing really still. Matt is face-to-face, nose-to-nose with the guy with the ponytail. The other two are off to one side. The guy still has the gun in his hand. I want to say something, at least step up to

Matt's side, but I freeze for a moment. One thought takes over my mind: *Matt is going to get shot here.*

I see everything in front of me. The little names in red paint on the side of the rock, rising up into the darkness, dominated by the massive block letters of their killer. That's not the way it should be, though. I've seen it a hundred times, but this is the first time I've realized it. His name shouldn't be there. It should just be them, the ones we lost, their names, and the rock should be beautiful; it should be painted and decorated by new first-graders every single year; they should be brought out here on the last day of school, on the last day of first grade, a day the kids in my class never got to see; and they should paint all the things they love on this rock so that by now there would be eleven years' worth of flowers and baseballs and dogs and cats and who-knows-what-else sloppily painted here by little kids instead of what we have: a monument put up by our class, announcing its hate, announcing that it will never forgive or forget or understand and that, no matter how much we try to remember the ones who were killed, we will always remember their killer more.

In that moment, before I can speak or move or find out if I have the courage to do either, Matt brings his left hand around in a wide, perfect swing. His fist arcs through the air, and in the moment before it strikes Ponytail's face, I see the kid's expression: surprise, and fear, like a little boy's. He's a guy I've never met before, acting like an ass out in the woods by a monument that isn't even his, and he's holding a gun and I'm scared to death of

112

him, but in this moment I feel sorry for him too, because he's about to get hurt and there's nothing he can do about it.

And then there's a smack; I should be able to come up with a better way to describe the sound, but that's exactly what it is, a loud *smack* of flesh-on-flesh, of Matt's fist driving into the side of the guy's face, and the gun goes flying and the kid goes down and for another moment everyone's quiet, and then everyone's yelling, and I run a few steps toward them and then stop again. Matt is still standing there, not saying anything, and the other two guys, Tom and Mike, have shut up too, and everyone is looking at the kid on the ground who has rolled over onto his knees and is halfway up. Everyone is waiting to see what he's going to do.

He doesn't do anything. After another one second, two seconds, three seconds, the spell is broken and I can move again, and I find that I don't turn and run out of the clearing; instead I walk over to Matt and grab him by the arm and start to pull on him. The kid on the ground is muttering something, cursing, pissed off, but he's not getting back onto his feet, and neither one of the other two guys is doing anything either.

I pull on Matt's arm some more and he finally takes a step backwards, watching the others, and then another, and then turns, and we walk to the edge of the clearing, and then I stop, because I'm leaving something behind. I walk back, the three guys staring at me, Ponytail still down, his gun lying only a bit out of his reach, and I pick up the third, surviving gnome from where he's standing in the ceramic shards of the first two. I look at Ponytail, then at his friends, one at a time, and then I walk back over to Matt, holding the gnome on my shoulder like it was a baby, and we leave the clearing together.

We walk silently through the woods, Matt leading the way, me holding the gnome, back to the birch tree and down the path toward the beach. I'm trying not to think about the fact that there's a kid back there with a gun who's probably on his feet by now. I glance over my shoulder.

Matt reads my mind and laughs. "Relax, Cole. That asshole isn't coming after us."

God, I hate him sometimes. I wish that just once he would be scared and lost and wrong.

"What were you doing?" I ask. "That was crazy. What the fuck were you doing?"

We're walking along by the lake now, the water glimmering in the moonlight off to our right, and we'll be back at the beach soon. I'm trying not to listen, but I am, and I don't hear any footsteps or voices behind us. There's another spot to park, off the road about two hundred yards through the woods back behind the Monument, and that's probably where the other three left their cars. Hopefully they're walking in that direction right now.

Matt doesn't answer my question right away. "He was just being a dick," he says. "He was talking shit and then he wouldn't back down. I can't even remember what he said."

We arrive at the end of the path and look out at the beach. I can see the inverted hull of the lifeguard boat silhouetted against the sand, and beyond that, the dark shape of the Snack Shack, and beyond that, the lit parking lot and our cars. There's still no one here. Matt turns to me. "Cole," he says, "just what are you doing with that thing?"

I look at the gnome. It's about two feet tall. It's a little grinning guy with a stocking cap and a beard. It's hideous.

"I don't know," I say. "It just wasn't his. It wasn't his gnome."

Matt starts to laugh. "It wasn't his gnome?"

I look at it, then look at him, and then I burst out laughing myself. "It wasn't his fucking gnome."

"It wasn't his fucking gnome!" We're both laughing now, me so hard that I have to bend over and put my hands on my knees, tucking the figure under my arm like a football. We're laughing at the gnome, and laughing at what just happened, but also laughing at each other laughing. It's been this way since we were little kids. I remember this from sleepovers in his basement, or in a tent in my backyard.

After we catch our breath and I sneak one last look down the dark, empty path, Matt puts his arm around my shoulder and we make our way to our cars, two friends for whatever reason, friends even though it doesn't make any sense, the brother I never had, my co-defender of lawn gnomes. Just because, for as long as either one of us can remember, that is the way it always has been.

Pine Street is on the far edge of town, a fifteen-minute drive from the lake. We didn't talk about coming here, but we both knew where we were going. I pull up behind Matt's truck and turn off my engine, sitting in the dark for a moment before getting out and joining him on the sidewalk.

"So, we're just going to put it back?" I ask.

"I guess so."

I go around to the other side of my car and open the door. I have the gnome belted into the passenger seat. I get him out and carry him back around.

"I don't know where he was," I say. In the glow of the street-light, we can see that there are gnomes all across the lawn, some as big as the one I'm holding, some smaller, a few bigger. They're arranged in all sorts of scenes. Some are in groups; some are on their own. There's a little gnome family playing on a miniature swing set. I can just see, in the shade of a bush, a gnome squatting with his pants down, a plastic bird perched on his ass.

Matt opens the chain-link gate, and I follow him up three concrete steps and onto the grass. I'm looking around, trying to decide which scene I want my little guy to join, when I'm blinded by a light coming from the direction of the house. I freeze.

"Hold it right there!" The light drops just a little bit so that it's not directly in my eyes, and I can see that there's a figure on the front porch.

"Where are my other two?"

Matt and I look at each other. He speaks up first. "We're not the ones who took them!"

There's no response. It occurs to me that this is going to be hard to explain. It also occurs to me that this person might have a gun, and that it might be legal to shoot people creeping around a lawn in the middle of the night. I imagine us lying here dead among the gnomes.

"We found it," I call in the direction of the house. "We recognized it, that it goes here. We were just bringing it back." It sounds unlikely, though probably less unlikely than our stealing three and returning one. The spotlight switches off, and a moment later a porch light turns on, and I can see a woman, maybe in her sixties, in a bathrobe and slippers. No gun in sight. She steps down off the porch and approaches us.

"That's so kind of you," she says. "Thank you so much." She holds out her arms, and I hand her the gnome. I look over at Matt. He's standing beside me, but he's not looking at the woman or at the bizarre gnome garden. He's studying the house.

"Would you like to come in for some tea?" she asks us, and before I can tell her no, Matt enthusiastically replies that we would.

Five minutes later, we're sitting at her kitchen table, a teapot heating on the stove, a plate of cookies in front of us. Matt is next to me; the woman, who it turns out is named Mrs. Marjorie Ryan (she introduces herself with the "Mrs."), is sitting across from us. There's a fourth chair, occupied by the gnome, who is apparently named Jorge.

Mrs. Ryan has put three teacups on the table. It would have been time to leave if she'd put out a fourth.

"So," she asks as the water in the teapot begins to bubble, "where did you find my little friend?"

I start in on a slightly stripped-down version of the story, omitting the beers and also the fact that we knew who the kids in the woods were. She listens, getting up to pour the tea and then sitting back down. I usually don't eat sweets in front of Matt, but while I'm talking, he eats one of the cookies in two bites and then helps himself to another. I finish with our exit from the clearing, and Mrs. Ryan shakes her head sadly.

"Poor little fellows."

"Did they have names too?" Matt asks through a mouthful of cookie. I want to kick him under the table, but Mrs. Ryan laughs.

"No, goodness, no. If I named them all, I'd never keep track of them. Jorge here is special. Mr. Ryan and I purchased him on a trip to Spain for our thirtieth anniversary."

"Ah," I say.

"He was a bit too big for the airline to let me carry him on my lap, so Mr. Ryan bought a third ticket. I didn't want him in with the luggage. I so appreciate your bringing him back to me."

"Of course."

"Mr. Ryan would have appreciated it too."

She gets up again to pour herself more tea. Matt reaches for a third cookie. "Take some insulin," I whisper.

"Thanks, Grandma." He takes a giant bite, his eyes scanning the kitchen, leaning over a bit in his chair to peer into the next room.

Mrs. Ryan sits back down. "Are you diabetic?"

"Uh-huh."

"So was Mr. Ryan. He got it toward the end of his life. What a headache, hmm?"

"He probably had type 2," Matt says.

"Yes, I believe that's right."

"I have type 1. It's a totally different disease." He finishes the third cookie. Matt hates it when people mix up the types and think that their uncle or sister or someone has the same thing he does. Mrs. Ryan blinks in confusion, and I clear my throat.

"Well, I'm really sorry about what happened to your other, uh, figures, but I'm glad we could bring Jorge back to you, and now I don't—"

"I've always wanted to come in here," Matt says.

"In my house?"

He nods.

"Matt . . ." I say.

"Did you know," he asks, "that it was the Keeley place when you bought it?"

Mrs. Ryan sighs and takes a sip of her tea. "Well, yes, we did. The realtor was quite honorable and told us. But we didn't think it would matter. It's just a place, you know? People move on, and it's just a place. And, to be honest, I'm not sure we could have managed to move to East Ridge otherwise. This house probably cost fifty percent less than it would have."

"Are you sorry you bought it?" Matt asks.

She shrugs and sighs again. "I suppose that's why they took the gnomes, isn't it? Sometimes people pull up outside and take pictures. Once or twice, people have knocked on the door and I've had to tell them to go away. And they filmed the outside once, for that documentary. People are interested. It's natural, I suppose. You're interested, aren't you?"

"We were in the class," Matt says. "Both of us."

She breathes in sharply. "Oh! Oh, I'm so sorry."

I really would like to kick Matt now. Either that or disappear into the floor. My skin crawls as Mrs. Ryan turns her wide eyes to me and then back to Matt. If she recognizes me as the kid from the photo, I'm going to get up and walk out.

Matt shrugs. "It's all right."

Easy for him to say; he wasn't there. He'd blow a gasket if I said that out loud, and I'd never do it anyway. It would be cruel. I know how it eats at him.

"But I was wondering," he goes on, "I was wondering if we could have, you know, a look around."

"Uh, Matt—" I begin, but Mrs. Ryan interrupts me.

"Of course." She stands up. Being a survivor gives you a certain level of privilege. We leave Jorge with the cookies and tea, and she leads Matt out of the kitchen. I follow them.

Mrs. Ryan is right. It's just a place. It's a house: walls, floors, ceilings, stairs. Too big for an old woman on her own, but neat and tidy. It looks like she hasn't changed things much since her husband died; she points out his chair and his guitar in a corner. Sort of like Mom with my dad's stuff, though not as messy. More like a museum than a house.

Matt's phone squawks in his pocket. "Take your medicine," I hiss at him. He responds with a raised middle finger, discreetly placed behind his back so that only I can see it. We come to an upstairs hallway.

"My sewing room," Mrs. Ryan says, directing our attention to a doorway on the left. "And the powder room. And the master bedroom, down there at the end." There's one more door, on our right, closed.

"What's in there?" Matt asks.

She lays a hand on the knob but doesn't open it. "Storage. I don't need that many rooms, really."

"Was it his room?"

She grimaces. "Yes, I understand that it was. That's what I was told."

"Can I see it?"

She looks at him for a moment, then opens the door but doesn't go in. Matt steps past her. I follow him with an apologetic raise of my eyebrows.

Matt has stepped to the middle of a mostly empty room. I grope along the wall for a switch, find it, flick it on, but get only a pale, sickly light in response. There's a fixture in the ceiling, but it looks like two of the three bulbs are burnt out. The room is hot and airless, the windows closed, the shades down. For a storage room, there's not much here. Some cardboard boxes, an old ironing board, a bed frame without a mattress.

Matt is circling the periphery, looking closely at everything. He opens a closet door and pulls a string hanging from the ceiling. A bare bulb turns on. I walk up and look over his shoulder. Just a few board games on the floor in ratty old boxes: Battleship, Connect Four. He flips a chessboard open with the toe of his shoe. There are a few pieces inside, a knight and some pawns, but most of them are missing. I wander over to the window, pull the shade aside, and look down at our cars.

This is just a place. It's just a room.

A phone rings somewhere in the house, making me jump. "Excuse me for just a moment," Mrs. Ryan calls from the doorway, and she leaves us alone. Neither one of us says anything as I wander around the room and Matt studies the contents of the closet.

"Do you smell that?" Matt finally asks.

I inhale deeply through my nose. "It's musty, that's all."

"No, there's something else."

"I don't smell it."

"Come over here."

I go over and stand next to him in the closet door. Nothing.

"It's like in the woods," Matt says. "I think it might be gunpowder."

"I still don't smell it."

"Do you think he kept stuff in here? Like, ammo and stuff?"

"What, when he was a little kid?"

"They said he must have been born like that. He was probably always fucked up."

"Where would a little kid get ammo? And how would a closet still smell of it all these years later? A bunch of families have lived here since then."

He shrugs and continues to study the empty interior. "It smells like piss, too."

"I don't smell that, either, but it makes more sense. There might be mice."

His phone rings and he takes it out of his pocket, looks at it, and hands it to me. "It's my mom. Would you answer it?"

I roll my eyes and swipe the screen. "Hi, Mrs. Simpson . . . Yeah, Matt's right here. Well, not right here; he's in the bathroom. He left his phone . . . We're, uh, just hanging out at a friend's . . . You got an alert? No, he's fine . . . He probably just ate something and forgot to dose . . ." I glare at Matt. "I'll tell him to take some as soon as he comes out." I hang up and hand the phone back to Matt. "What's the matter with you? Take your goddamn medicine."

"I will. Soon as I get back to my car."

Mrs. Ryan returns and clears her throat from the hallway.

"We should go," I say.

Matt turns off the closet light and closes the door. He looks around the room one more time, breathing deeply as though he's trying to take it in. "He was here," he says. "For, like, a year. This is where he slept every night."

"Yeah. But he's gone. It's just a room. It's just a room full of junk."

He shakes his head. "No," he says, "it's not." Then he walks out without saying anything else.

We thank Mrs. Ryan for showing us around, and for the tea and cookies, and she thanks us once more for bringing Jorge back to her as she shows us to the door. We cross the yard, passing through the assorted gnomish scenes, and let ourselves out through the front gate.

"You working tomorrow?" Matt asks as I open my car door.

"Yeah."

"So, listen—good luck the day after, okay?"

"I'll need it."

He grins and cuffs me on the shoulder. "Just be your usual self. Only better."

"Right." I smile back. "I'll let you know how it goes."

"You better. And don't worry, I'm working on our problem. Eddie's going to be fine."

"Thanks," I say.

Matt winks at me and gets into his truck. I start to get into my car, and then I remember something. I walk up to his driver's-side window and knock on the glass. He rolls it down.

I pause and stare at him for a moment, suddenly struck by something. "You look just like your father."

"What?"

"I've never seen it before, but you do."

"You came over here to tell me that I look like my father?"

"No, I came over to tell you to take your insulin. Then I noticed that you look like your father."

"Cole, brother, two things. First, I am absolutely nothing like my fucking father, and second, you worry too much." He winks once more, puts the truck into drive, and pulls out, leaving me standing alone on the curb.

I turn and contemplate the house and the yard for another moment. I don't know when Matt started hating his dad. Mr. Simpson has always seemed like an all-right guy. He does stuff with insurance, and I know that he helped my parents with paperwork when Dad was sick. He and Matt were close when we were little, or at least I think they were. They played ball together all the time. And then, at some point, Matt seemed to lose faith in him. He decided his dad was some sort of a fake. Basically, I think he figured out that his dad wasn't the person Matt thought he was when he was a little kid, and he couldn't stop being disappointed in him. I wonder if that's part of growing up for everyone. I wonder if I would have eventually looked at my own father that way.

I turn away from the gnomes, get into my car, and drive away.

Six

— Matt —

Chris Thayer is waiting for me in his driveway. "Can you come inside?" he asks.

I raise my eyebrows. "Do you—"

"I know where it is, but I need your help getting it. And we have to be quiet; my mom's asleep. She was working last night."

I seem to remember that Mrs. Thayer is a nurse. I nod and follow him up the driveway and onto the metal ramp. From up close, I can see tons of rust spots, and it feels a little bit rickety. I've never walked on it before, never been up to his house.

The place is a mess inside. Piles of stuff, clothes and medical gear, with a path through the living room just wide enough for his wheelchair. I try not to stare, but it's hard not to. My mom would go nuts if our house was one-tenth this bad.

"Sorry about the clutter," Chris whispers. "My parents would have cleaned up—"

"Don't worry about it." We've reached the kitchen. A table is pushed up against the wall. It's covered with papers. Three places are cleared on it, and there are two chairs.

"Up there," Chris whispers, nodding toward a cabinet above the microwave.

I step forward and open it. There are little plastic baskets inside, all of them filled with pill bottles. I take them down and put them on the kitchen table, at the open spot that doesn't have a chair. Chris starts to sort through them with his one mobile hand and tells me to get a gallon-size plastic bag from on top of the fridge.

I stand next to him and watch as he looks at the bottles one at a time. He replaces some in the baskets and drops others into the plastic bag as I hold it open. He cautiously shakes one bottle by his ear and then hands it to me. "Open this one up."

I do, and he peers inside.

"Okay, you can take about a third of these."

I pour the pills into the bag, probably closer to a quarter than a third. I don't want to leave him without meds he probably needs.

"What are these, Chris?"

"Muscle relaxants. Really strong stuff."

I nod, and glance at the nearest pile of paper as he continues his sorting. It's some kind of medical bill. I absently scan the lines of mysterious charges until my eyes arrive at the bottom, at a number that I literally cannot believe. I whistle softly. Chris looks up and follows my gaze.

"And that's just one of them."

"Jesus. They actually want you to pay that?"

"That's what a bill means. My folks would have been better off if Keeley's aim had been just a little bit sharper."

"Dude!"

"Joking. You've got to be able to joke, right?"

"Chris?" The voice comes from the back of the house. We both freeze.

"Just heading out, Mom," Chris calls softly.

We both wait, but there's no response. After a moment, he nods toward the table. "Put it back."

I quickly put the baskets back in the cabinet and take the plastic bag from the table. Chris turns his chair and leads me back to the front door and down the ramp. I breathe a sigh of relief as I tuck the stash under the driver's seat in my truck and return to Chris, who's waiting beside his van.

"Boys!"

Mrs. Thayer is coming out of the house. She's hurrying down the ramp, wearing slippers and a puffy pink bathrobe. Her hair is all over the place. Thoughts of a call to my parents and summer-long rehab flash through my mind.

"Hi, Mrs. Thayer."

"Hello, Matt." Mrs. Thayer gives me a warm smile as she approaches. "Chris, honey, you need to bring in a check today." She reaches down and tucks the folded paper into his chest pocket. "Just remember to tell her it's there."

"Okay, Mom."

She studies him. "Your dad get you ready before he left?"

"Yeah, of course."

"Hmm." She reaches out to smooth his hair. "I got in around three. What time did he leave?"

"Um, I don't know. Around six?"

She rolls her eyes. "Which actually means five. Which means that he got you up at four."

"It's fine, Mom. I got a lot of reading done."

I shuffle my feet and study the ground. You'd think that my dad, or one of his fellow assholes at the top of the company, would tell Mr. Thayer that he can come in late.

"How's your arm, Matt? Working hard in PT?"

"It's getting better, Mrs. Thayer."

"You'll be ready to play in the fall?"

"I'm sure I will be."

"That's good. Thank you again for driving Chris."

"I don't mind at all," I say.

"He gets tired of his mom driving him everywhere he has to go, don't you, baby?"

"Never, Mom. You're the Tonto to my Lone Ranger. You're the Robin to my Batman. You're—um, who was the sidekick, Laurel or Hardy?"

She laughs. "You're very funny." Mrs. Thayer reaches out and squeezes my hand. "Take good care of him." She bends, adjusts Chris's glasses, and kisses him on the forehead.

"Mom . . ."

"I'm sorry. I know. Not in front of the guys."

She smiles and winks at me, then turns and walks back to the house. I get him into the van and start it up.

"Thanks, Chris, this is awesome. I'm just wondering, uh . . ."

"There's more. That was just one stash. You should see what's behind the mirror in the bathroom."

"Right. Great. Awesome." I back us out of the driveway. I'm getting more confident with the van. "So — you wanted a story?" I still have no idea what to expect. He's quiet as we drive down the street, but when I check the mirror, he doesn't look red and embarrassed the way he did last time. He looks determined.

"I want to hear about something." He takes a breath, and then another. I look back again, worried he's having some sort of an attack.

"Okay . . ." I say.

"I want to hear about you and . . . and Rosie."

"Rosie?"

"Rosie Horowitz."

"I know who Rosie is. I just don't . . . What about her?"

"I want to hear about sex." I have no idea what to say, but Chris plows on. "You need something, Matt, and I'm giving it to you. I need something too."

"You want me to tell you . . . like, about . . ."

"I want you to tell me what happened. Where you were, what

130

you did, what it was like. All of it. And it has to be true; that's the thing. I can look stuff up online, but I want this to be real."

This is not what I was expecting.

"Yeah. I mean, yeah, I can do that . . ." I say.

"You probably have a bunch of stories."

"Sure."

"So, that's the trade, okay? Stories for more pills."

"Okay. Okay. I can do that."

This is going to be one of the weirdest things I've ever done.

"So, yeah, here we go . . ." We're maybe eight, maybe ten minutes from the PT clinic. I have no idea where to begin.

"Where were you?" Chris prompts. "The first time."

"The first time, we were at her house. In her, uh, well, in her parents' bedroom."

We drive on, me describing, trying to imagine that I'm telling him about someone else, like about a movie I saw, Chris sometimes stopping me to ask for more details. By the time we get to the PT center, I'm about halfway through. I wait in the van again while Chris goes in. I stretch my elbow, bending my arm behind my head, and it throbs. I stare at the low, brick building in front of me, the big sign announcing PHYSICAL THERAPY.

Sarah Jessup hasn't come back into the store. I keep an eye out, but I never see her. I don't know why I can't stop thinking about her. She's pretty, but she's not someone you'd stop on the street to stare at. Still, she's stuck in my head. Her face, her voice. I keep on replaying that last moment, when she walked away.

What did she say? I'm not as cute as I think I am? I don't think of myself as cute. I know she was sort of insulting me, but there was something else. It's like a knot that I can't quite untie.

I should be working on my arm. I know I should. They're expecting me to start at second base in the fall, and I don't know what I'm going to do the first time they ask me to throw the ball. Somehow, though, it doesn't feel like a problem. It doesn't feel real. It doesn't feel like the fall is ever going to come.

I get out of the van and walk around the mostly empty parking lot, watching my shoes tracing the edges of cracked asphalt, weeds pushing their way through, slowly stretching my arm one way and then the other.

I think about the night before. I'm still happy about Cole. I can't believe he actually did it; he actually went over there and gave Viola that stupid book and asked her out. I can't imagine Cole on a date. When I think about his future, it's easy to see him married but impossible to imagine him dating.

And then there was that crazy shit in the woods. I was more curious than anything else when we went back there, and then I was mainly disappointed that it was just some losers shooting at a statue. I laughed when that dude shot it, but it wasn't really funny. Still, I wasn't pissed or anything. Not until they started talking about Cole.

Mike Antonucci was all about the gun, which was his, giving us stats on it that I didn't really understand. I don't like guns. I looked around, at the Monument and the gnomes, and wished that Cole would come back so we could leave. He had gone off to take a leak.

"That's Cole Hewitt, isn't it?" Mike asked. "What's up with the little motherfucker? I had math with him. He usually looked like he was about to cry."

"He had a tough year," I said. I didn't like him badmouthing Cole.

"He was always having a tough year," Tom said, laughing. "He was always like that."

"What the fuck do you know about it, Higgins?" I asked, taking a step toward him.

"Whoa, whoa. I didn't mean to offend you, Simpson."

I shook my head and looked around. It was time to leave. Where was Cole?

"What happened to your boy?" the kid with the ponytail asked. "He have a problem? He have to sit down to pee?"

That's the kind of stupid, pointless comment I really hate. The kid was trying to sound tougher than he was. He probably lived in a two-million-dollar house in Alpine Falls. He probably drove his daddy's car over here to act like a badass while pretending to do something righteous by messing with Sam Keeley's old place. Before I knew it, I took two more steps toward him. I heard my own voice in my ears, louder than I meant to be, and the other two guys were yelling too, trying to calm me down by drowning me out. It wasn't working.

The kid with the ponytail didn't look scared, which only

made me angrier, and then he stepped right into my face and his eyes darted to the right, looking at something over my shoulder, and he smiled and whispered, "Your girlfriend's back."

I had a sudden image of the gun coming up in this kid's hand and going off. I imagined a bullet hurtling off into the night, past me. I imagined Cole lying in the grass in front of the Monument, bleeding his life away in front of the names of kids who died the same way eleven years before. In front of Andy's name. And then, before I could even realize what I was doing, my hand had come around and made solid contact with Ponytail's face, dropping him to the ground.

I would have kicked him, too. Standing over him, I was lining myself up. I was going to break his fucking ribs. Crack them all. I wanted to kick him in the balls so hard they'd burst. I don't know exactly what I would have done, but in the moment before I did it, Cole grabbed me and pulled me back. And we left.

I've circled the PT lot ten or eleven times when I see Chris come out the front door. The session went by quickly. I sigh and head back across the lot to open the van, getting ready to continue the story.

I get back to Finn's after dropping Chris off, and I punch in. I pause and hold my timecard alongside Cole's. I figured when I took this job that he'd think it was cool for both of us to work here. Then it turned out that things were slow and Mr. Finn didn't need us both at the same time, so we basically never saw each other, but that was all right. Our aprons hung side by side and we could swap stories about rotten produce and shitty customers. It wasn't until last night that I understood that Cole doesn't want me here. Every hour on my timecard is an hour off his.

I feel like such a rich kid. I feel like an idiot. I put the cards back in their slots and start sweeping the floor. I'll find a way to make it up to him. I'll make sure he gets to California, somehow, if he wants to go.

A few minutes pass by, and then I hear a voice from the other side of the stockroom door. "Hello?" I push the swinging doors open and find Cole's mom in the produce section.

"Matt, how are you?"

"I'm good, Mrs. H. How are you doing?"

"I'm well."

She looks well, just like she did the other day. I think she even has makeup on. I'm glad to see her like this. She looked like shit for a while there.

"Something I can get for you, Mrs. H?"

"More of those peaches from yesterday?"

"I don't think so. Maybe tomorrow? I can go ask Mr. Finn . . ."

"No, no, I'll ask him myself." She gives me a smile and heads for Finn's office. I go back to the stockroom, finish sweeping, and take my break. I hoist a box of candy up onto a table, my elbow screaming at me as I lift it, and open it up. I'll have a Milky Way. I'll keep an eye on my phone, and I won't let myself go over 300. I sit down on another box and take a bite.

It *is* good to see Mrs. H. I feel badly that I don't go over much anymore, but it's a weird place to be. She needs to get better so that she can move on, and so that Cole can move on. Maybe she's moving in the right direction. Cole seemed surprised when I told him about his mother last night, that she'd been in. It was almost like he didn't want to hear that she was doing well.

I finish the candy bar, throw the wrapper away, and get back to work using my left arm as much as possible. The afternoon goes by. Sarah Jessup doesn't come in. I get off at five and drive over to the Gerbers', thinking I can take Paul out again, but no one's home. I walk around to their backyard and stand there, memories flooding back to me. There used to be a jungle gym over there, and a swing set, there. That spot over by the patio is where they set up the wading pool, the three of us—me, Andy, and Cole—splashing in it while Paul did his own thing and our moms sat nearby in floppy hats and big sunglasses.

All of it is gone now. The yard is empty. It looks like someone tried to start a garden over to one side, but it's all grown over. It's quiet. I stop by the picnic table and look up at the house.

Mrs. Ryan said that her house was just a place, but she was wrong. Places aren't just places. Things stick to them, things remain, even when people move on, even when people die.

The alarm on my phone goes off. I curse under my breath, quickly text my mom, and turn the app off. I go back to my car, trying to think of somewhere I can go other than home. A kid is watching me from the yard across the street. He's a redhead. He's lying on his stomach, holding a plastic toy rifle. He aims it at me. I step up on my running board so that I'm looking at him over the top of the truck. I smile, make my fingers into a gun, aim at him, and drop my thumb.

"Bang."

He looks back at me, not impressed. "You missed," he calls.

I probably did. I shrug, blow imaginary gun smoke away from my index finger, get into the truck, and drive away.

Seven

— *Cole* —

What's worse: finding condoms while looking under your late
father's bed, or the fact that you were searching for stray pills
when you found them?

I'm willing to call it a tie.

It's the third of July. I've got my lunch date with Viola, and
then later on, Mr. Finn is finally going to give me a few hours
of overtime, but this morning I had an hour free and was nervous, really nervous, so to keep busy, I decided to do some quick
cleaning up. This place had one really good cleaning after Dad
died, by an aunt I had never met before, Mom's brother's second
wife, who lives in Ontario. They'd come for the funeral, and
although I don't remember much about those days, I do remember this harsh-looking woman who seemed to think that the best
thing she could do for us was to clean the entire house. It stayed
clean for a while, but now there's dust and mud that I've tracked
in; there's grease all down the side of the cabinet by the stove
where the pots and pans spatter; there's an ungodly amount of

newspaper and mail and even some flowers that someone must have sent that have dried up in the vase they came in. Mom keeps on saying she's going to hire someone to help, but it never happens.

I opened up some windows and the back door to let the air in. I found a bottle of cleaning spray and paper towels, and I went to work. It felt good. It felt like progress. I was thinking about Viola, and about Matt's and my plan, and that made me think about the pharmacy and wonder how we were ever going to come up with something for Eddie. And then I had this idea that maybe under the bed there was something. It was stupid, because if there had been, it might have been one pill, not some stockpile, but I got down to look anyway, and there wasn't even that.

There was something else, though. Three foil condoms under the couch nearby, attached to each other in perforated lines, two with their contents still inside and the third torn open and empty.

So now I'm sitting and looking at these things. *All right*, I think. *So the nurse, the hospice nurse, had these in her purse and she dropped them and they got kicked under the couch when she got up. Simple.*

Except that there had been only one nurse, and she was pretty open about liking other girls and telling us all about her girlfriend, so what use would she have for these things?

Well, what use would anyone who'd been in this room have for them?

Mom and Dad, I think. They'd tried to do it one last time in the hospital bed. It's a thought that's completely gross and also makes me really sad. And hopeful, in a way. Like, I hope that they did do it here.

Still, I can't quite believe it. I get up and stuff the rubbers in my pocket and keep cleaning, making my way into the kitchen. I want to put some music on, but I'm afraid it would wake Mom, so I work in silence and there's nothing to keep my mind from racing. People had been in the living room. Matt came to visit, didn't he? They could have fallen out of his pocket. But he hasn't been here in months, and there was lots of dust under the couch, and the condoms were on top of the dust, not covered up by it.

It's eating at me now, partly because it's a weird mystery and partly because it makes me feel like I'm outside of something. Like there's a club that I'm not a member of, and everything would be clear to me if I was. All the satisfaction has gone out of cleaning. I have the stove half done, and I leave it that way and retreat upstairs. I'll admit that my room's a mess, but it's comforting. It's *my* mess. I plow through piles of laundry to get to my bed and throw myself down.

It's hot in here, stuffy, and I should open the window, but I like it this way. I wrap a blanket around myself despite the heat. It feels like a cocoon. I make myself breathe slowly and deeply. Slowly and deeply, one breath at a time.

He who was living is now dead / We who were living are now dying / With a little patience.

I've been reading Eliot.

I roll over and wrap the blanket more tightly.

I should get changed. I'm meeting Viola in just over an hour.

The awful daring of a moment's surrender / Which an age of prudence can never retract / By this, and this only, we have existed.

I want to show her one of my poems. One of the ones I published. But thinking about it now, it seems pretentious.

I turn my face into my pillow.

The doorbell rings. I struggle free from the blanket and stumble out of my room and down the stairs, but Mom's gotten there first. I thought she was out cold, but she looks awake and freshly showered, and she's dressed for the day. It makes me think of what Matt said about her coming into the store and looking normal.

Mrs. Maiden is standing on the doorstep with her little boy. Mom invites them in. It's not the best house for a kid to play in, and for a moment I imagine him getting up and bouncing on the hospital bed, but Mom somehow produces a box of my old toys, and the boy—Stephen—settles right down in the middle of the dining room floor with some Transformers that I haven't seen in years. I'd kind of like to get down there and play with him, see if I can still convert Optimus Prime into a tractor trailer, but Mom asks me to make tea, and five minutes later, I'm sitting at the table. They chat for a few minutes about nothing in particular, and then Mrs. Maiden leans over to glance at Stephen, sips from her cup, and turns to look at me.

"Cole," she says, "I didn't have a chance to speak with you at graduation, and I've been meaning to come by. I've been making the rounds, you see."

Mom nods as if she knows what Mrs. Maiden is talking about, but I don't, and my confusion must show. She takes another sip, blowing into the cup first, and continues.

"Cole, I want to tell you something, and I want to give you something. So, first things first: I want to tell you how proud I am of you."

Now I'm looking at her in complete confusion, not even trying to look like I know what's going on.

"I'm proud of all of you, although I have a special place in my heart for you, Cole. You've carried yourself so well, when almost no one else could have.

"After it happened, I remember you. That first holiday concert, the winter after. All of you onstage, all of us out in the audience. We were all so afraid, so overwhelmed. Could it be normal? Could we allow it to be normal? Such a mix of emotions. I can't even . . . well, but you, Cole. I remember you so clearly. You stood there onstage with the other children, in your little khakis and your button-down shirt, and you were just so — *earnest;* isn't that the right word, Samantha? He was earnest."

My mother nods again. She sets down her teacup, reaches across the table, and squeezes Mrs. Maiden's hand.

"You stood there and held your head up," Mrs. Maiden continues, "and you sang every song in the holiday repertoire with complete and utter conviction, as if it were the most important thing in the world. You were wonderful."

Mrs. Maiden came to all our class's events; she was such a regular that sometimes I had to remind myself that Kendra wasn't there anymore.

"I remember that concert," I say. "I was terrified." At that point, my parents still hadn't let me see any of the newspapers or magazine covers. I didn't yet know that I was the Boy in the Picture. I didn't know that everyone in the world had seen my face. Still, the weight of every pair of eyes in that auditorium was enough to petrify me.

"I don't know how you did it," Mom says.

I actually had no intention of doing it. I wasn't going to go on, and the music teacher was going to let me stay behind in the band room. And then Matt came over to me and took my hand. "You're shaking," he said. "I get shaky when my sugar's bad. Do you want some candy?"

I told him I did, and he gave me a few pieces of butterscotch that I'm pretty sure he was supposed to be saving for a hypoglycemic episode.

"When this happens to me," Matt said, "my mom says that I don't have to handle it all at once. She says that I only have to get through one breath at a time."

I tried that for the walk down the hall to the stage, taking one breath after another, Matt still holding my hand. Then I peeked out, saw the audience, and froze. "There are so many people," I whispered to him.

"Yeah," Matt whispered back. "But, you know something, Cole? Screw all of 'em." He laughed. Matt had an impressive mouth, even back then. I laughed too, took another breath, and then we both walked out there together.

I haven't thought about that concert in years. "Now, Cole," Mrs. Maiden says, "I want to say this as well. My heart broke for you when we lost your father. He was a wonderful, wonderful man, and he was a great loss, but my heart broke especially for you, because you've had to bear so much and it was just so, so unfair."

I nod and take a sip of my tea (even though I hate green tea, which is all we have), just to have something to do with my hands. Mom dabs at her eyes, and I hope she doesn't start crying.

"Cole," Mrs. Maiden continues, "I would like for you to have something. This is something that belonged to Kendra." She reaches into her purse and brings out a small, plain box, sliding it across the table. I open it. Inside, there is a brass pen, the decorative kind you can get at a kiosk at the mall. *Kendra* is engraved in script on the side. I take it out.

"I know you're a writer, Cole. Kendra was a writer too." She laughs. "Well, she was trying to be. My mother gave her this pen when she started first grade so that she could be a 'serious student,' and Kendra loved it. She kept it at home so that she wouldn't lose it, and she kept a little journal. She was precocious

144

with her spelling, although many of her entries still needed to be in picture form. She always used this pen, though. She sat at her desk right after school, before she had a snack even, and made her entries. Here; this is a photocopy of one she made about you."

Mrs. Maiden takes a folded piece of paper from her purse and smooths it on the table, sliding it over to me. Mom cranes her neck to look. It's a picture of two stick figures with big hands and happy faces, with a circle in between them that's probably supposed to be a ball, and a tree and a sun in the background. At the bottom it says, *me and Cole plaing bal.*

The three of us sit and look at it for a long moment, the only sound that of Stephen manipulating the Transformers on the other side of the room. When I finally look up, Mrs. Maiden is smiling at me.

"I'd like for you to keep it, Cole. And I'd like for you to have the pen, as well." Mom starts to say something, but Mrs. Maiden shakes her head. "Now, now, it's not such a big thing. I'm making the rounds, as I say, and I'm giving small tokens to many of Kendra's friends and classmates. It means something to me. I'd much rather see these things go on in the world, and be used and have life, rather than have them sit in a box under the basement stairs. Life goes on, Samantha. That has always been my solace. Seeing these children grow up, beautiful and strong. Seeing Cole become a man. It's the hope of the world, and I want a small part of Kendra to be in it."

I have no idea what to say to that. I look down at the pen

in my hand and feel its weight. Mom is crying now. We sit in silence for another long moment.

Different parents dealt with losing their kids in different ways. A lot left town; a few stayed but sank out of sight. Some got weird. Susie Edwards's mom, for example. For a few years after it happened, she still celebrated Susie's birthday and would have all of us over, and for some reason our parents would bring us. We'd play for a little bit—even though no one wanted to—and then we'd go out to a fountain she'd had installed in their yard, and she would have a cake and would have us all sing "Happy Birthday," and she'd be all happy, the sort of "happy" you are when you're trying too hard, when you're making yourself be, and she'd blow out the candles herself and lay the cake down by the fountain. Like she was making some sort of an offering. She'd say something about how Susie was watching from heaven and that Susie loved all of us and she was glad we were there celebrating her special day. And then we'd be expected to eat the cake and we'd all go home.

I don't know when that stopped; maybe someone finally said something to her. It was ridiculous. No one's watching anyone from heaven.

The silence is broken by Stephen yelling "Kaboom!" at the top of his lungs. We all jump as Transformers scatter, and Mrs. Maiden bursts out laughing. "There it is!" she cries, and although I don't what "it" is, I laugh too, and so does Mom, and then we sit and drink tea together. Mom and Mrs. Maiden talk about old times, and after a few minutes, I thank Mrs. Maiden again and tell them I'm meeting someone for lunch, and I excuse myself from the table.

I take the pen up to my room and put it in my desk drawer along with the photocopy of the journal entry. I change my shirt, change it again, and then go back to the plain blue T-shirt I'd been wearing to begin with. I look in the mirror and try to smooth my hair down, which is hopeless. I breathe against my hand, but I don't smell anything. I go into the bathroom and re-brush my teeth anyway, thinking about Matt's phantom odor and wondering if I just have a weak sense of smell. Finally, I take some of Dad's old after-shave from behind the mirror, dab a little bit of it onto my neck, and go back downstairs. I'm going to be early, but I can't sit around here. I say goodbye to Mom and Mrs. Maiden and Stephen, telling him that he's welcome to take any of the Transformers he wants and hoping that he doesn't take any of my old favorites. Then I head to my car, starting out on what is, horribly and ridiculously and depressingly, my first date.

Fifteen minutes later, I'm sitting at the counter in the diner, drinking a soda. I'm sure that Viola is the sort of person to be punctual, while I'm the sort of person to show up early. So I get to sit here, and sweat, and study the latest piece of wallpaper.

I've been coming here for as long as I can remember. Dad brought me when I was a kid lots of Saturday mornings. I don't know where Mom was; probably working. I think that was when she would have been finishing her dissertation. We always sat at the counter, and he let me order the pancakes from the adult menu rather than from the kids', even though I could never finish them. He'd pour the maple syrup for me from that glass container, the one with the metal button you have to push with your thumb to let the syrup out. I remember him leaning over me, his arm around my shoulder, pouring from the far side. His smell, soap and Old Spice, and the syrup pooling on an enormous stack of pancakes. When he finally stopped pouring, he'd plant a kiss on top of my head and put the syrup down, and then we'd eat.

The wallpaper wasn't there in my memories, though I suppose it must have started to appear when I was a kid. Piece by piece, over the years, the bills have covered the wall behind the counter, and then they've come out into the seating area. They're in the men's room, so you're staring at one while standing at the john and at another when you're at the sink, and they're even on the inside of the stall doors. I squint at the one directly across from where I'm sitting, taped to the tile just to the left of the little window where the cook puts the food. HR 2579, it reads, and just below that: A BILL TO REQUIRE BACKGROUND CHECKS FOR SOME INDIVIDUALS PURCHASING SEMIAUTOMATIC FIRE-ARMS. It's an old one, one of the first, I think. There's another one above it, a Senate resolution, and House bills on either side, both of them about background checks.

Some people really don't like it. I've heard them talking for years, around town, at Finn's. People who are pro-gun, of course, but other people too. They say it's gotten out of hand. They say it's been going on too long. That it makes it too hard to come in here. The woman who owns the place, Kathy, doesn't seem to care, though. She just keeps on putting them up, and I guess enough people keep coming in that she stays in business.

I finish the soda and crunch on the ice at the bottom of the cup.

"Hi, Cole."

I swivel around on my stool. She's right on time. She's wearing khaki shorts and sandals and a sleeveless T-shirt, and her hair is down. I literally cannot believe that she's here to see me. *Don't say anything stupid*, I think. *Please don't say anything stupid.*

"Cheers," I say.

She blinks, and then she laughs. "Cheers," she says, "though we usually say that when we're saying goodbye."

"Right," I say. "Of course."

"Of course." She smiles. "Do you want to get a seat, or shall we sit at the counter?"

Sitting at the counter, I can feel eyes on my back. It suddenly strikes me that the memories of sitting here with Dad must all be from before the shooting. When we started coming back here afterward, I wanted to sit only in the corner. "Let's get a table."

Kathy brings us two menus, and we settle into a booth by a window. I can see Finn's across the street. The façade looks especially worn down from this perspective. It looks like what it is: an old neighborhood grocery store that will probably be out of business in a few years. Viola takes the menu and looks at it, then looks at the Senate bill pasted to the wall beside the window. "Interesting décor."

I look at it too. It's newer, though I did see it the last time I was in. It has to do with banning silencers and certain kinds of ammunition. "That's right, you've never been here." I look around. "This is how it's decorated. Has been ever since. The first bill they introduced after it happened got voted down, and Kathy hung it up by the register to remind everyone. Then there were others, and she hung those up too. Everything having to do with anything about guns: background checks, automatic weapons, ammo, concealed carry, anything at all."

"She hangs up bills having to do with gun control?"

"Just the ones that get voted down."

"What about the ones that pass?"

"I don't think there are any of those."

Kathy comes back with our drinks and gives us a few more minutes to decide what we want to eat.

"Should I really get the seafood, do you think?" Viola asks.

"No. You should definitely not get the seafood."

"So what do you recommend?"

I study the menu. "The mozzarella sticks are good. So are the pancakes."

"Pancakes and mozzarella sticks?"

I shrug.

"Sounds delicious." She closes her menu and puts it on the table. "How's the store?"

"Finn's?" I shrug again. "Finn's is Finn's. It's a job. How's accounting-ing?"

"Accountancy."

"Accountancy."

"It's fine, I guess. Boring as hell. But it's not supposed to be interesting."

"Does it pay well?"

"No. Quite the opposite. It's a volunteer position."

"For the résumé?"

"That, and the connections. One of the men who owns the firm is friends with a business professor out at Berkeley. They went to high school together, or some such. It's going to get me a lunch when I'm out there in the fall."

"So you're working for free all summer for a lunch?"

"Well, it's the lunch, but then we stay in touch, you know? And I take some of his seminars, and then when I'm a junior, I might assist in one of his intro courses . . ."

"Also for free?"

She laughs. "Of course."

"And then?"

"And then I wind up with a grad-school recommendation from him, which is worth a lot, particularly at the University of Chicago, which is his alma mater and is where I'm supposed to go."

"Wow."

She raises her eyebrows and nods as she neatly pulls her straw out of its paper wrapper without tearing it anywhere but at the very end. She drops it into her soda and takes a long drink.

"It's like a long line of dominoes," I say. "One falls and hits another, and that hits another, and it goes on and on for years, and finally all your dreams have come true and you're in grad school in Chicago."

"Good metaphor. You must be a poet."

"That was a simile."

"Dammit!" She wrinkles her nose and bangs her fists on the table.

"Maybe that's why you were just the salutatorian," I say.

"Too soon, Cole. Too soon." She smiles. "You just can't leave it alone, can you?"

"It's a problem I have."

"Leaving things alone?"

"Yeah."

She looks out the window. "Damn salutatorian. Let me tell you something, Cole: That is the last time I am coming in second."

"You mean you've peaked? You're on your way down to the middle of the pack with the rest of us mortals?"

She laughs. "You know that's not what I mean."

"I know. You probably have your college valedictory address written already, telling all the Berkeley grads to grow up and stop playing Hacky Sack."

She squints at me. "It's half written."

"You have time."

"You're a writer; maybe you can help. Are your poems any good?"

"For the most part, no. But some have been decent. I've actually published a few of them."

"Really? Where?"

"Nowhere you would have heard of. A couple of little online journals."

"I'll google you!"

"I used a pseudonym."

"What was it?"

I look into my glass as I take a drink. Kathy comes back, and we order two plates of pancakes and an order of mozzarella sticks to share.

"So? Your name?" Viola asks after Kathy leaves.

"I'll tell you what. I'll tell you my pen name if you do something for me."

"What's that?" She looks wary.

"Do one pointless thing. One thing, just for fun, that doesn't have any future purpose. Have you ever done anything pointless?"

"Well, I am thinking about minoring in English."

"I thought you were going to minor in Asian studies."

"That too. Double minor."

"I'm not sure that counts. It should be something without a goal, that's just good in itself. Like writing a poem. What's the point of a poem?"

"You know, I love poetry but I don't think I've ever really met a poet before."

"There aren't many of us left. So?"

"Do it right now?"

"No, but before I see you again."

"Having lunch with a friend doesn't count?"

I look out at the new flowers Kathy has planted in the window boxes. *Aquilegia vulgaris.* "No."

She looks at me for a long moment. "All right. Something pointless." She holds out her hand, and I shake it.

"C. Maxwell Johnson," I say. "For Coleton Maxwell Johnson."

"Interesting." She draws the word out and widens her green eyes. "Is your first name really Coleton?"

"No, but I always wished it was. And Maxwell was the cat we had when I was a kid. And Mr. Johnson was my third-grade teacher, who told me I should be a writer."

"I like it. Who else knows about it?"

"Just Matt. He says that 'Max Johnson' sounds like the name for a porn star."

She bursts into laughter. "It does! It really does!"

I shake my head and close my eyes.

"Oh, Cole, but I still like it. And now I know what to google!"

"Now you know."

"Max Johnson."

"That's me."

Kathy arrives with our plates of food. Viola picks up one of the mozzarella sticks and studies it.

"Careful, it's probably . . ."

Too late. She takes a bite, and her face turns red. She starts bouncing in her chair and fanning her mouth, then spits into her napkin and takes a drink.

". . . hot. They're really hot when they come out."

"Oh, God," she finally manages to gasp.

"Sorry. I should have told you right away."

"I think the inside of my mouth is burned."

"Do you want more soda?" I look around for Kathy.

"I'm so sorry; that was so disgusting of me."

"Don't worry about it."

She shakes her head as Kathy puts a glass of ice water in front of her. "Take it easy, hon."

"Thank you." Viola takes a long drink while Kathy gives me a look before walking away. We both start in on our pancakes.

"Are you going to the fireworks tomorrow?" I ask her.

She shakes her head. "We've never really gotten into the habit of July the Fourth."

"I guess it would mean something different to you."

She frowns at me in mock ferocity. "We want you back," she growls, making my stomach do something that is very likely indescribable in prose.

"I have to be getting ready for Haiti, anyway," she says.

"Packing and all. And I'm trying to learn some French. Did you take French?"

"No. German."

"Too bad. You could have tutored me."

Jesus Christ, I would give anything to know French right now.

"So, can I ask you something?"

I nod, my mouth full of pancake and syrup.

"Do you think that would have made a difference?" She nods toward the wall.

"The bill?"

"Any of them." She swivels a finger to encompass the entire diner. "Any of these laws. Do you think they would keep another lunatic from doing something awful?"

The way she asks the question makes the idea seem silly.

"I suppose I do," I say. "I mean, something has to, right? We have to do something. Don't you think?"

She frowns into her glass as she drinks. "My father would say differently. He's an ardent conservative. He'd say that people will kill each other no matter what; you can't regulate it away. That Cain killed Abel with a rock. And he'd say that the shooters will have guns no matter what, so . . ." She looks at me and puts her fork down. "God, I'm sorry Cole. I'm such an ass. I shouldn't be saying this to you, should I?"

"No, you can say whatever you want."

"I mean, you were there . . ."

"I was there, but I don't remember."

"You don't remember it?" she asks.

I shake my head.

"Like you've repressed it or something?"

"Repressing something means you remember and then you make yourself forget. I've never remembered, even right after. The police had all sort of questions for me, and I couldn't answer any of them. It's like my brain just never made a recording." I shrug. "People get frustrated. They want to know things. Matt, for example. When we were little, he had all sorts of questions."

"He wasn't in your class?"

"He was, but he was home sick that day. His diabetes."

"Jesus."

"Yeah."

She shakes her head and cautiously returns to the mozzarella sticks, taking a small bite. "These are really good."

I nod. "They're classics." I take one too, bite into it, and study the bill hanging beside our table. "So you're saying that you're against gun control?"

She pauses for a moment, and when I turn back to her, she looks confused. "I suppose I don't know what I am."

We eat in silence for a few moments after that. It's not awkward or anything; we're just quiet and thinking. She finishes the mozzarella sticks and about half of her pancakes, then pushes her plate away and picks up the paper straw wrapper, twisting it around one finger. "Can I tell you something, Cole?"

"Sure."

"I'm not sure that *is* my dream come true. Chicago, that is. An MBA from the University of Chicago. Where all the dominoes lead."

"No? So why are you doing it?"

"It's like the dominoes are just falling. They started falling a long time ago, but I wasn't the one to line them up, and I wasn't the one to knock the first one over."

"See how useful a good simile can be?"

She smiles. "Very useful."

"Well, you don't have to do it, do you? I mean, no one's going to make you go."

"No. No one's going to make me. Honestly, if I said I wasn't, I think my parents wouldn't even be particularly angry. Concerned, but not angry. Disappointed. It's just—for some reason, I don't dare disturb the way things are ordered."

"'Do I dare disturb the universe?'"

Her face lights up. "Now, Eliot, he's *always* useful."

"He's like a Swiss Army knife."

"I love the book."

"I'm glad."

Kathy comes over to see if we need anything else. Viola tells her that the mozzarella sticks were "extraordinary," and Kathy laughs out loud and thanks her. I get coffee, just to make it all go on a little bit longer, and Viola gets tea.

"What about after Haiti?" I ask her. "Are you going to be around much?"

"I suppose I will. Working. Maybe going to Nantucket, if that winds up happening."

Yes, Nantucket. With Conrad. Yale-going, plane-flying Conrad. May his windshield ice over and a flock of geese fly into his engines.

"You look blue, Cole. Don't you want me to go to Nantucket?"

I feel myself flush. "Do *you* want to go to Nantucket?"

"Not particularly, but it's not like being sent to the tenth circle of hell."

"No. There are only nine circles, anyway."

"Oh, fuck you," she says sweetly. Kathy arrives with our drinks and with the check. Viola reaches for it. "We'll split it."

I reach into my pocket and find nothing but my notebook. My stomach drops about three feet. "I forgot my wallet," I say.

"It's no problem."

"I'm so sorry . . . I'll call . . ." Matt should be over at Finn's; I can run over and ask him for some cash.

"No, Cole, don't even worry about it. This isn't a date; you don't need to pay. You can get me next time."

I nod, not totally trusting myself to speak. I mean, we never officially established this as a date, but . . . and on the other hand, next time? All right; at least there'll be a next time.

We finish our drinks. I look out the window, over at Finn's. The front windows need to be washed. Maybe Finn will have me do it this afternoon.

"This has been nice, Cole. Thanks for introducing me to diner food. I almost lived in New Jersey for four years without experiencing it."

"That would be a record." She leaves money on the table, and we get up to go. There's an awkward moment when we reach the sidewalk.

"I'm going this way," she says.

"I have to get over to Finn's."

She looks across the street and nods. "Well, I'll see you soon."

"I'll swing by before you leave for Haiti."

"Sure." She smiles. Then she extends her hand. I shake it.

"Remember," I say, "one pointless thing. Before I see you."

"One pointless thing." She turns and walks away. I watch her go, and then I head over to work.

Eight

— Matt —

Cole jumps a foot in the air at the sound of the first blast and
looks like he half shit his pants. Another one goes off, and then
another. He pulls himself together, looks at me with a hurt,
pissed expression, and punches me in the arm. I feel bad for making him come here, even as I'm laughing at him.

They didn't do fireworks in East Ridge for years after the
shooting, and then when they started, it was a really small,
pathetic display. It's gotten bigger every year, though, and rumor
has it that this year they're going to outdo themselves. I believe it
as I watch the show start. The sky is filling up.

I'm not a complete asshole. I know why Cole doesn't want to
be here, and it's not just the crowds. But who knows? I might not
be around next summer. I have a feeling I won't be, and then who's
going to get him out of his house and down here to face his fears?
Is he going to avoid crowds and fireworks for the rest of his life?

"Hey, Cole?" I say to him, as the volley speeds up. "Cole!"

We're standing in the middle of a closed-off street, on the

161

edge of the crowd, the park in front of us. People have brought blankets and coolers, and there are carts and trucks with ice cream, cotton candy, funnel cake. A bunch of kids run by, shooting one another with squirt guns. One of them gets me in the leg, and I go down on one knee, pretending to be hit. He looks worried for a minute, then laughs and shoots me in the face. I get back on my feet and look at my friend, who is absolutely miserable. It's still hot, and he's wearing jeans and his work boots.

"Cole," I say for a third time, "did I ever tell you about the first time I flew?"

"No."

"So, I was maybe seven years old and we were going to Portugal or Peru or somewhere—"

"Those are on two different continents."

"Whatever. I just remember that we had to fly all the way down to Buenos Aires at night . . ."

"That's in Argentina."

"Dude, whatever, listen, this is what I'm trying to tell you. The point is, I was so scared to fly. Dad had to wrestle me into my seat and buckle me in. I was crying and kicking and screaming and everything. So what do you think happened?"

"You were the most popular passengers on the flight?"

"What happened was that the plane took off, and flew to Brazil or wherever, and it landed, and we got off. Get it? We were fine. I was fine. And then I've flown a gazillion times since then, and I don't even think about it anymore."

"Okay."

"That's my point. If something scares you, you just have to go through it, and then it's better the next time."

"I'm not scared. I just don't *like* fireworks." He glances up at the sky, then scans the faces around us. "Let's get something to eat."

Cole sets off down the street, hovering on the edge of the crowd, head down. I trail behind him, looking up. *Pop-pop-pop*, a series of little pink ones and then red, white, and blue screamers and a massive red spider arcing over everything. I love it. I'm not sorry to be skipping Luther Schmidt's party. People are sighing and cheering and I trip over someone's stroller and look down and apologize, and then when I look back up, there she is.

I've thought I saw her so many times over the last ten days that at first I don't believe my eyes. I'm always looking for her, waiting for her to come into the store, waiting to see if fate is going to bring her back, and just when I started to think that it wasn't, here she is.

She's leaning against one of the barricades that's closing down the street, talking to a young police officer with a crewcut. He's a big guy; I know I've seen him around. He's paying a lot of attention to her, and he says something, and she nods but also looks away from him, and when I see her face in the red light of a firework, she doesn't look happy.

She still has that white ribbon in her hair.

I hurry forward and grab Cole's elbow. "Do you know who that is over there?" I ask him.

"Where?"

"Don't stare. The woman over there in the tank top, talking to the cop."

Cole goes ahead and stares, then turns away. "Yeah."

"Sarah Jessup."

"I know, yeah. So?"

I shake my head. "She came into the store the morning after graduation."

Sarah is talking to the cop again. She reaches out, pats him on the arm, and walks away, into the crowd in the park. The officer watches her go. "Come on."

"Um, I'd rather—"

"There are better food trucks over there, on the other side." I hurry after her without waiting for Cole to respond.

The first barrage of fireworks is getting slower, but all the people are still looking up. I weave in and out, stepping around picnic blankets and lawn chairs. I see her up ahead of me, walking fast, and I take my eyes off her for just a moment, and when I look back, she's gone. Just like that. She had been making her way down a pretty straight row between people, and then a moment later, that row is empty. She must have cut off to one side. I stop and try to find her, but there are too many people. I curse and look over my shoulder to where Cole is trailing along.

"Did you see where she went?"

He shakes his head. "I'm going over there to get some food."

Now I follow behind him, dejected. It's stupid; I didn't have anything to say. I just haven't been able to stop thinking about her, and I wanted to talk to her again.

We arrive at the food trucks, parked on another closed, crowded street running along the far side of the park. Cole goes to work; he's always loved this kind of food. He buys a soft pretzel at one truck, then moves down the line and gets a hot dog, a funnel cake, and by the time he gets his cotton candy, the pretzel and half of the hot dog are gone. I get a can of lemonade with the only money I have in my pocket and then stand off to one side and dose myself with insulin while watching Cole go down the line. After all these years, I'm still amazed at how much the kid can eat. I don't notice her coming up behind me.

"Matt the fruit guy."

"Hi, Sarah."

She has a cone of cotton candy. A tuft of it is sticking to her cheek.

"How's the lemonade?" she asks.

"Good. How's the cotton candy?"

"Delicious."

I nod, as if I'd always kind of thought that about cotton candy but never really known. I don't have anything smart or funny to say. I take a drink.

"God, that looks good," she says.

"Want some?"

She considers for a moment. "I forgot my wallet and spent my last cash on this."

"I did the same with the lemonade. Trade?"

"How about you just give me a sip of the lemonade?"

"That works too." I hand the can over. She takes a sip, pauses, looks at me, and then takes another. She tips her head back and continues to drink, eyes still on me over the rim of the can. It's empty when she hands it back.

"Glad you liked it."

She picks the cotton candy off her cheek and pops it into her mouth.

"Do you like the fireworks?" I ask.

"Not especially."

Her shirt has two fading, overlapping socks on it. "Red Sox fan?" I ask.

She looks down. "I don't really care about baseball. I think this used to be my boyfriend's."

"Oh."

"You're a baseball player, aren't you? You're supposed to be the star of the team or something."

"I was the team captain."

"Does that mean you were the best?"

"I don't know. The other players vote, so . . ."

"So, how are my Red Sox doing this season?"

"They're in first place."

The fireworks are building to a crescendo over the park. "I should get going," she says.

"Why're you here if you don't like fireworks?"

She shrugs. "I don't live far away. Walking distance. And there's not a lot to do around here at night, is there?"

"No, I guess there's not." Out of the corner of my eye, I can see that Cole is hovering with the remains of his funnel cake. "Sarah, this is my friend Cole." Cole shuffles alongside of me, wiping the back of his hand against his mouth and muttering something that might be "Nice to see you." I put an arm around his shoulder. "Cole's been busy trying to clean the trucks all out of food," I say as I give him a squeeze. She doesn't take her eyes off him, and I can feel him squirming under my arm.

"You're certainly taller than I remember you, Cole," Sarah says. I wince, the image of my friend held in her father's arms flashing into my mind.

"Dude," I say, "I'm thirsty and I'm out of cash. Want to grab us both something?"

Cole blinks, nods, and quickly steps away toward one of the trucks. She watches him go, then turns her attention back to me.

"So that's Cole Hewitt, all grown up?"

"Yeah."

"I look at him and I see the picture."

"I think he hates that."

She shrugs. "We don't get to pick how people see us."

"I guess not. Though it doesn't seem fair that he's stuck with something he didn't have any choice in. And I'd appreciate it if you didn't talk about it with him when he comes back. It makes him really uncomfortable."

167

She looks up at me, startled, and for a moment I think she's going to turn and walk away, which is the last thing I want her to do. Second-to-last thing, actually. I won't let anyone screw with Cole.

Instead she asks, "So, what do you do when there aren't any fireworks?"

"Not too much, I guess. Hang out. I mean, maybe go into the city, but that's a trip. Or go to the shore."

"Do kids still go to the lake?"

"Sure."

"Still bring cheap wine?"

"I think that wine tastes like month-old rat pee."

Cole reappears and hands me a Diet Coke. "Your friend gave me his drink," Sarah says.

"That was nice of him," Cole replies. He probably wishes he could fade into the air.

"I'm a nice guy," I say. "Ask me for anything."

There's a burst in the sky above us; red, white, and blue. Everyone else looks up. I keep looking at Sarah. I haven't been able to stop thinking about her, and I don't know why. She's pretty, but that's not it. I know lots of pretty girls. It's something else. Something about the way she looked at me when she came into the store. She tugs at something deep inside me. I feel like she needs something, and I want something from her, but I don't know what.

She looks back down and catches me staring. "Go ahead," I say, "anything."

She shrugs. "Do a somersault."

Without saying a word, I hand her the can and do a backflip, landing in the street without needing to take a single step backwards. She stares at me. "I can't believe you did that."

"What else do you want?"

"Cartwheel."

I was probably eight years old the last time I tried to do a cartwheel, but how hard can it be? I go for it, spinning hard to my left, and more or less pull it off. My elbow screams as it takes my weight. This time she cracks a smile. Cole shakes his head.

"Um—walk on your hands," she calls out.

That I can do. I flip upside down and start to make my way along the street, blind because my shirt falls over my face, and then I collide with something hard and fall onto the pavement, landing on my knees. Looking up, I see the police officer Sarah was talking with by the barricade, and I quickly get to my feet.

"Officer." He looks at me without saying anything. I glance at the name tag on his shirt pocket. "Lucas. Officer Lucas," I say. Now he grimaces.

I'm not one of those people who has a problem with cops. I just don't like it when anyone thinks they're better than other people and like they automatically get to control a situation. That goes for my dad, it goes for teachers, and it goes for the police.

The officer turns his attention to Sarah and to Cole. "Everything all right, Sarah?" he asks.

She smiles and nods. "Of course, Jeff. Matt here is just horsing around."

Officer Jeff doesn't seem amused. "I'm just going on break," he says to her. "You want to get something to eat?"

"Oh, I'm not sure . . ." She looks like she did back by the barricade. Unhappy; not just that, a little rattled. *Scared* would be too strong a word, but it's in the right ballpark.

"We were just leaving," I say, dizzy from being upside down.

"We were?" Cole asks.

"Were you?" Lucas asks Sarah.

Sarah nods. "I'm tired, and these gents were going to give me a lift home. The fireworks are giving me a headache."

"We're parked over by Finn's," I say. She nods.

"I'll see you, Jeff," she says, and we walk away, Cole trailing along behind, Lucas watching us go.

Finn's is all the way back on the other side of the park, and I lead the way. I don't seem to be able to shake off the dizziness of the handstand and the cartwheel and the flip, though, and as I step up onto the sidewalk, one foot slips, and I stumble and almost go down. "You okay?" Cole asks, hurrying to catch up. I nod, though I can feel a light sweat breaking out on my face and the tingling that tells me my blood sugar is plunging. It was the lemonade; I dosed for the whole can, and then Sarah drank most of it. I have way too much insulin in my system, and then on top of that, I went and jumped around, burning glucose. My entire life is a fucking chemistry experiment.

I weave through the crowd, Sarah and Cole close behind me, the faces and the bursts of light and the sound of the final blasts blending, mushing together into a mix of color and sound that I can't really take in. I pat my pockets, but I don't have my sugar tablets; they must be at home with my wallet. I check my phone: sure enough, my sugar reading is fifty-two and falling. By the time we reach the other side of the park and step onto the street in front of the grocery store, my knees feel like rubber, and there's no way I can drive. I glance back, and only Sarah is there.

"Where's Cole?"

She looks around. "He was just here."

I curse under my breath. I don't have the energy to look for him. I don't have the energy for anything, actually. The fuel is being sucked out of my muscles and bones and brain, and all I want to do is lie down on the sidewalk. I spin in a circle, wondering what to do, and then he's beside me, holding out a bottle of orange juice.

"You need this."

I take the drink and gulp half the bottle at once.

"I'll drive," he says. I hand him the keys to the truck, and Sarah and I follow him across the street and down the driveway to where I parked beside the dumpster. I climb into the passenger seat, and Sarah gets into the back. I've drunk the rest of the juice without realizing I was doing it, but it will be a few more moments before it takes effect.

Low sugars have been part of my life since I was a little kid, but I still hate them. I rest my forehead against the window glass as Cole cautiously takes us down the driveway. I gaze out at the people looking up at the sky; parents holding on to their children, children holding on to their ice creams, and then I see Officer Lucas, standing at the foot of the driveway, watching us. Our eyes meet through the glass. Cole doesn't see him. I glance into the back seat, but Sarah is occupied with her phone for the moment. I look back. He's still watching me, and then Cole turns and we're weaving around a food cart and a police barricade, picking up speed, leaving the park behind.

"Where do you live?" Cole asks Sarah, breaking the silence.

"Um, not far . . . over on Elm Street."

"Do you want to go home yet?" I ask.

"Where else would we go?"

"I don't know."

"I need to get home," Cole says. He's probably worried about his mom.

"Why don't we drop you off first?" Sarah says.

We don't talk anymore as Cole drives us out to his house and parks at the end of his driveway. "You all right to drive now?" he asks me. I nod.

"Thanks."

We all get out. Cole says goodbye to Sarah as she comes around to the passenger seat, and I circle to the driver's side. She gets in and shuts the door.

"What are you doing?" Cole asks, taking my arm.

"Nothing. Just going for a drive."

"With her?"

"Yeah, with her. Why not?"

"You know who she is?"

"Sure."

"Who her father was?"

"Yeah, so what?" He stares at me. His hand is still on my fore-arm, and after a moment, I pull away. "What's your problem?"

He shakes his head, turns without another word, and makes his way up the driveway toward the dark house. I watch him go, and then I get in and start the car back up. Cole can be a moody bastard.

"Where to?" I ask. I'm thinking maybe back downtown, to the diner.

"How about the lake?"

I glance at her and then, without comment, pull away from the curb.

It takes about ten minutes to get out to the lake, and we don't talk much on the drive. I put the radio on and roll down my window, and we watch the night go by. When I pull into the lot, I hesitate for a moment, then drive over to the far side, under the trees. Where I parked when I came for the swim; where I parked when I came here with Rosie. I turn the car off. I'm not sure what we're going to do, but Sarah undoes her seat belt and gets out. I follow her.

We cross the lot and step onto the beach. She bends down and slides her sandals off.

"I love the feel of sand on my feet."

I kick my shoes off too. It's surprising how cool the sand is at night. We walk down to the overturned rowboat. I hop up onto the hull and reach down to help her up. We look out at the water.

"What are you doing in the fall?" she asks.

"I'm going to Bucknell."

"Where's that?"

"Pennsylvania."

There's a train whistle in the distance. We sit quietly for a moment.

"It's nice out here at night," she says. "Do you come out here a lot?"

"Sometimes. When it's warm. Sometimes in the winter, too."

"Who comes with you?"

"Cole, mostly."

"I bet you've brought girls out here."

"Sure. A few."

"A few," she repeats. We sit quietly. The silence stretches on, but it's not uncomfortable. It's not like with Rosie, when I felt like I always had to be talking or doing something.

"What do you and Cole talk about when you come out here?" she finally asks.

It's a good question. What the hell are we always talking

about? We've been talking to each other since we even learned how; it's kind of amazing that we still have anything to say.

"Nothing much, I guess. We talk about life. Work. Cole's dad died last year. He talks about that a little bit, and his mom. His mom's having a hard time with it."

"Did he graduate with you? Is he going off to college too?"

"He graduated, but he's not going to college yet. He got in, but he deferred. He's going to stay home and help with his mom." There's another pause. "What about you? Did you go to college?"

"No. Dad got me the job at the insurance agency right after high school."

"Oh."

"It started out as the most boring job in the world, and it's just gotten worse."

"Why do you stay?"

"At the job?"

"The job . . . the town . . . New Jersey."

"I've stayed because I've stayed," she says. "I've got Dad's house, and . . . I've stayed."

"Do you live there alone?"

"Yeah. Mom left years ago, years and years. It was just me and Dad. And then he died, and it was just me."

I look at her Red Sox shirt. "You still have that boyfriend?"

"No. That's not it. That's not why I stay, though it was for a while. I thought I was in love."

"Huh."

She looks at me. "Have you ever thought you were in love?" she asks.

"No." Rosie had said it, whispered it against my chest in the back of the truck, but I didn't say it back.

"Never? Not even once? Would you even know it if you were?"

"Cole's in love with someone, a girl we graduated with. He follows her all around and talks about her all the time. He writes about her. He writes about everything, though. He's a poet."

"A poet. Huh." We're quiet for another moment. "You'll see," she finally says. "It's not so easy. It's not so easy to make decisions."

"I guess not."

"Did you make the decision to go to Bucknell?"

"Yeah. I mean, I sort of did, though it was also my dad and my coach, I think."

"I don't think I've ever decided anything." She slides off the hull, into the sand. "Come on."

"Where are we going?"

"There's another beach, a smaller one around the side of the lake, right? It's been years . . ."

"There is." I slide off the boat and we walk, side by side, across the sand to where the woods begin, and we step into the shadows of the trees. It's very dark here at night. We go slowly, picking our way along. There are a few scattered firecrackers in the distance, kids setting off their own now that the big show is over. Sarah stumbles over a tree root, I reach out without thinking, and she casually wraps her arm around the back of mine and takes me by the bicep as though it were the most normal thing in the world, as though we do this all the time and she doesn't have to ask. We don't speak for a few minutes, and before I know it, we've reached the little beach. She lets go of me and walks ahead. There's a lot of gravel here, but there are also sandy patches. She walks down to the water, dips a toe in, and then steps in with both feet. She looks back.

"It's not too cold."

I walk down the beach behind her. She's waded in up to her calves and is looking out at the lake.

"It's sort of beautiful here," she says.

I'm watching her, looking at her look at the water. There's something that doesn't seem real about being here with her. And then, before I know it, I'm reaching out. It's not something I mean to do, but it's not something that I don't want to do, either. It's sort of like it's something I was meant to do, and I don't have any choice in it.

I take one end of the white ribbon that's tied in her hair. She doesn't turn around, but there's something about her that goes very, very still. I hold it for a second, and then I pull as gently as I can. The bow falls away as if it had never really been there, the ribbon falls from her hair, and she turns around. We look at each other for a couple of heartbeats, standing in the water. She's studying me.

"Are you scared?" she finally asks.

I didn't realize I was until right at this moment. My heart

is beating too fast. It makes me feel foolish, like I've never been with a girl before, but I nod.

She raises her eyebrows. "I like that you told me the truth."

"Are you scared?" I ask.

"I'm always scared." She steps toward me, and before I can say anything or move or even take a breath, her lips are on mine. She still tastes like lemonade.

When we stop, she leans back, her eyes searching my face. Then she takes me by the hand and leads me out of the water and up the beach. I let her pull me along. She stops at a patch of sand, up near the tree line, and she sits and pulls me down beside her, and before I can think of something to say, she kisses me again and pulls my shirt off and reaches for my belt, and by the time she's pulling the Red Sox shirt off over her head and wriggling out of her shorts, I'm self-conscious that I've never been naked with anyone before. Even with Rosie, I kept a surprising amount of my clothing on.

It's not like with Rosie. With her, neither one of us knew what we were doing; we were just determined to do it, and even when I was embarrassed by how quick it was, there was part of me that wanted it to be like that. With Sarah, though, I lose track of the time. I'm not watching myself, I'm not thinking about myself, I'm not worrying about the sound we're making and whether it carries across the water.

I'm not thinking or worrying, but I am noticing everything, like the way her hair feels exactly the way I thought it would, soft and fine, and how it smells when it falls over my face and how soft the skin on her neck just under her ear is. I never noticed things like that with Rosie. Then again, I never wanted Rosie the way I want Sarah right now. Like I want to devour her so that there's nothing left.

By the time I do start thinking again, I'm lying next to her in the sand, looking up at the sky, wondering where the stars that were out earlier have gone. Eventually I sit up. For a moment I wonder whether she might be asleep, but then she reaches out and runs one fingernail along my back, scraping off the sand, drawing curving, looping lines back and forth across my spine. She gently pokes the sensor on my side.

"What's that?"

"It's a blood-sugar monitor. I'm diabetic." I reach out for my shorts and take my phone from the pocket, tapping on the sensor app. A healthy 143, nice and level.

"Checking your email?"

"Checking my blood sugar."

"Feeling okay?"

"Feeling like I want to do that again," I say.

She laughs. She has a great laugh. "Well, you're honest." She pulls me back into the sand.

Afterward we lie there together, her head on my shoulder, and she goes to sleep.

I look up at the sky and wait for it to rain, but it never does.

Nine

— Cole —

I've barely slept in three days, and when I climb out my bedroom window into the very early morning light, I have to pause
for a moment to make sure I'm steady.

I stand straight and take a few deep breaths. It's still cool,
though I feel the heat of the day lurking, waiting to come on.
Looking down, I see the layer of green on the surface of the pond
and how badly the grass needs to be mowed. I glance back. No
light on in Mom's window, but still, I'm not taking any chances
this morning. Her sleep patterns are as unpredictable as her anxi-
ety, and this is not a morning when I can stay home with her. I
make my way to the edge of the roof, put on my backpack, and
very gingerly reach over the side, find the trellis, and lower my
weight onto it.

Why haven't I been sleeping? Fear of what I'm going to be
doing this morning, I'll admit. Fear of flying is a hard one to
shake, and I'm heading to a flight. My dad isn't here to strap me

into a seat the way Matt's was. If I do take a plane out to California in the fall, I'll probably have to be medicated for it.

That's not the only thing, though. It's not even the main thing. The main thing is that I'm furious with Matt, and my anger won't let me rest.

I'm just over halfway down when I feel the wood begin to bow under my weight and the trellis starts to pull away from the house. I let go with one hand, look down, and decide to go for it. I drop into the tall, wet grass below, landing feet first and stumbling, falling onto my side. My left ankle twists, and I have to bite my lip to keep from calling out. I pause for a moment, resting on one knee, feeling like I might start crying.

It's stupid, I know. My ankle doesn't hurt all that badly, not after the initial impact. I just have these moments, more of them lately, when I feel . . . I just feel lonely. I feel like I'm the only person in the world and like I always will be. I blink my eyes, don't let myself rub them, and stare hard at the grass in front of me. I can spot three types of clover and name two of them. I get to my feet, adjust my backpack, glance up at the damaged trellis, take one tentative step on the ankle and then another.

Matt's truck is parked behind my car in the driveway. I limp up to the driver's-side window, and he rolls it down.

"What are you doing here?" I ask him.

"Did you get my texts?"

"Yeah. I thought we were going to meet there."

"I told you I'd pick you up." He takes out his phone and swipes at the screen. "Oh, I forgot to send that one. Whatever. Get in."

I look at my car. I sort of want to drive by myself, but I go around to the passenger side of the truck and get in.

"Let's see what you've got." Matt takes my backpack and looks inside, then shakes his head. "Lucky I brought some too."

"How much did you promise Eddie, exactly?"

"Well, like I said, I thought you had more . . ."

"Are we giving him all of this today?"

"Yeah."

"But I thought today was just, like, a down payment."

"It is."

"I don't have much left in the house."

"Well, we'll just have to get more." Matt puts the truck into reverse and backs down the driveway. I wince as he drives over a branch, imagining the loud crack carrying through the morning air and waking Mom.

We drive in silence until we get out to Route 21. Matt looks like he woke up about five minutes ago; his hair is rumpled, and there's a coffee stain on his T-shirt. He hasn't shaved in a few days.

To hell with this; he doesn't get to just show up like nothing happened.

"What happened the other night?" I ask him as he accelerates out toward the edge of town, nothing but terrifying open sky in front of me.

"With what?"

"With that woman."

"Her name's Sarah." I don't say anything. "Look, Cole, why are you pissed off about her?"

I shake my head, the anger of the last three days kicking in again. "It's just . . . it's fucking insensitive is what it is."

"I don't get it, dude. You don't even know her."

"Matt . . . it's like I told you when you were sitting in that chair at graduation. There are some things you just don't do. It's disrespectful."

He seems to think about that for a moment. "Look, I know sitting in the chair was wrong, and to be honest, I have no idea what I was doing. I was out of my head. I think I took some allergy medicine or something, and I wasn't thinking clearly. But dude, the woman isn't a memorial, you know? It's not like I'm fucking with those chairs, or with the Monument. She's just a person. She wasn't even there, she—"

"She's connected to it. She's part of it. She was his daughter." I stare out the side window. He doesn't get it. He's never going to get it.

"Do you not want me to see her?"

"You're seeing her?"

"I mean, there was the other night . . . and I was going to go over to her place tonight."

"How old is she?"

"Who cares? I think she's maybe seven years older than we are. So, like, twenty-five, I guess."

183

I exhale, watching my breath condense on the air-conditioned passenger-side window. "Do whatever you want."

"Cole—"

"I don't want to talk about it anymore."

He looks at me, then turns back to the road and switches on the radio. "Fine. I'm used to you not talking."

Neither one of us says another word until we're pulling up to the Central Jersey Fairgrounds ten minutes later. I'm sweating, and my heart is beating too fast. Eddie's truck is actually there; part of me hadn't really expected it to be. Eddie Deangelo never seemed like the earliest riser.

The fairgrounds are huge. They have carnivals here, and horse shows and all kinds of things. Eddie's truck is parked in a big field, tucked off to the side, surrounded by trees, and we drive through the parking lot and up onto the grass until we're alongside it. The sun still isn't all the way up and it's not very hot yet, but I can feel that it will be, the ground underneath my feet bracing to absorb another day's onslaught of sunlight. We get out, and the truck door opens. Eddie slides out and comes around to where we're standing.

"Bro." He swings his hand around, and I manage to catch it cleanly for once, clasp it hard, and then let go without any weird flipping around that I don't understand. He pounds me on the shoulder with his free hand, then turns to Matt and executes the same maneuver. "So. Let's see it."

I hand Eddie my backpack. He unceremoniously opens it

and begins arranging the contents on the hood of Matt's truck. Brown plastic pill containers, plus two glass medicine bottles and a bag full of weed that I thought looked pretty substantial but that Eddie tosses down with a contemptuous snort. "This isn't everything, is it?"

"It isn't everything." Matt has come up alongside us with a duffel. He reaches inside and begins to arrange medicine containers and plastic bags of pills alongside the stuff I've brought. I peer at one of the bottles. It's a prescription for Percocet, made out to him. It must be for his arm. It looks full.

Eddie picks up one of the unmarked bags and squints at the contents. "This is good shit. Where did you get it?"

"Don't worry about it."

"This stuff is hard to get."

"Yeah."

"They prescribe it for, like, hardcore neurological shit. This one's a muscle relaxant."

"You should be a doctor."

"This pays better." Eddie produces a gym bag of his own and carefully places everything on the hood inside, even the pot that he seemed so disdainful of. "So, this is half?"

"This is half," Matt says.

"Good. Let's get to work."

I take a deep breath, partly out of relief and partly to steady myself as I realize that we're actually going to do this. Eddie goes around to the back and whistles between his teeth for us to

185

join him. It's an old U-Haul, and as I walk around, I notice that there's still a faded cowboy on a bucking horse painted on the side that says TEXAS WELCOMES YOU. Over that slogan, there's a sign saying DEANGELO OUTDOOR ADVENTURES. Eddie slides the big door open, and there it all is.

"Let's get this mother set up."

Eddie surprises me for the second time this morning. Not only is he an early riser; he also knows what he's doing. This is the family business, I suppose. He's probably been doing it all his life. Matt and I follow his instructions as we carry various bits of gear out into the field, shoulder big bags, and then spread out a massive balloon. I catch Matt wincing several times as he lifts something heavy. He probably should have been taking the Percocet.

"We usually have a bigger crew," Eddie says, wiping his face and drinking from a dirty plastic bottle with the label peeled off. "But that wasn't bad. It'll go faster next time. I'll bring a guy when we do it for real."

My heart is pounding, and it's not from the exertion of setting it up. It's that I can't believe I'm about to get into this thing. I'm also worried that we've taken too long, worried that there's too much daylight. "Do we need a permit for this?" I ask.

Eddie shrugs. "We've got all the permits. We come out here all the time to test balloons or train new staff. No one's gonna give us a hard time." He takes a thick rope that's attached to the

186

basket and ties it to the front fender of the truck. "This ain't necessarily proper, but we'll be okay."

"What's proper?" I ask.

He steps back and examines his knot. "Six of these lines and a four-man crew."

"Really?"

"Don't worry about it; there's not much wind, and we're pretty far from those trees."

"What if the conditions are different on the actual day?"

He shrugs and grins, glancing at me through a lock of hair hanging over his eyes. "Can't control the wind, brother. Let's do this."

And the next thing I know, we're all in the basket, and I think I might actually throw up. Eddie's talking, pointing to different features, and he sees that I'm barely paying attention.

"Hey, you want to write some of this down? Mattie and I aren't going to be here on the big day."

I pull my notebook out and start taking notes, and it helps to settle me down a little bit. Everything here is basic physics, hot air rising over cold, stuff we learned in the tenth grade, though it took humanity most of its history to figure it out. There's really not very much to it, and Eddie is a surprisingly good teacher, showing me each step and then checking in: "Got it?" and I nod and make a note and then he takes me to the next step. Simple sequence. "It's just a tethered flight," he says. "Just going up and down. You're not actually going anywhere. There's a lot more to that, you know?"

I frown and nod. I cannot imagine.

"Okay, so let's make it happen," Eddie says.

And with that, I cram the notebook and the pencil into my back pocket and take hold of the edge of the basket in both hands. I give very serious thought to vaulting out, getting firm green grass under my feet, heading to the car, and driving home. I can surrender the drugs and the weed and let Eddie and any of his friends he chooses to tell know that I'm a coward.

But this is for Viola. It's a crazy plan, and that makes it the best plan I've come up with. To be honest, it's the only one I've come up with.

So I hold on to the edge of the basket but let go just long enough to give Eddie a thumbs-up. I observe carefully as he squeezes what I've just learned is called a blast valve, firing the propane burner.

When I was a little kid, I remember lying on my back outside, looking up at the sky. It was terrifying. All that space and nothing to stop me once the ground let go and I went hurtling off. I felt like I would literally fall up forever, and that's when I first got my head around the concept of eternity. That was probably what scared me more than anything else; I didn't *really* think the earth would let go of just me and me alone, that it would hold on to everyone else, all the cars and rocks and trees and animals, but select me to send plunging into the atmosphere. Even at a very young age, I could see that didn't make any sense. It was the idea that a fall upward would never end: the concept of never; the idea of forever. That was what sent me running inside, where my mom would find me and be convinced that I had hay fever and that was why I didn't feel well after going out to play.

And now here I am, eighteen years old, and the ground really is letting go. There's this huge thing over my head and this inexorable pull lifting me up, and I squeeze my eyes closed for a moment. When I open them, I'm looking over the treetops as we pass them by, the periodic breath of the blast valve and nothing else in the quiet morning, my knuckles white on the edge of the basket.

"Dude," Eddie says, observing my expression, "she must be some hell of a girl."

That's all I've told him, that I want to take a girl for a ride. He doesn't know who it is, and he hasn't been particularly curious, but he's right: she is a hell of a girl. This summer would be unbearable without her. It would be me and Mom and the empty hospital bed and the baking heat. It would be everybody else getting ready to go, and me staying behind.

The line runs out, and the balloon jerks to a stop. There's a sickening moment when I can feel the rope straining against the pull of the balloon, and then the forces equilibrate, and Matt and Eddie Deangelo and I are hanging there in the sky all together, far above the treetops, the trucks looking like Matchbox cars in the field far below. I straighten my back and relax my grip on the basket. The sun is coming up now, and there's a hawk circling over the forest below us, and some mist is rising off toward the lake.

It's beautiful, and I'm not thinking about the earth letting go. I'm not thinking about falling forever. I'm thinking about Viola's face when she sees the balloon, the look in her eyes when we get into the basket and begin to rise, the way she'll listen when we reach this topmost point and can look out at a scene like this one and I read her the poem I've been preparing. Her whole life is predictable, she said. I've made her laugh, but I've never seen her really, truly surprised. I'm not sure she ever has been.

That's what this is: something she could never imagine, could never expect. It's a surprise.

"Christ," Matt says.

"Pretty fucking awesome, huh?" Eddie asks beside me.

It is. It is *very* fucking awesome. We stand and look at it for five full minutes, my terror burning off with the morning mist, and then Eddie brings us back down to earth.

Taking the balloon down and disassembling it, folding the fabric and getting the components back into the truck takes even longer than setting it up. I'm soaked with sweat and dew by the time we're done. I thank Eddie, and we finalize our plan. I kind of want to write the date and time down for him, but he smiles and taps his temple in a way that I don't totally find reassuring but that does make me think I'll offend him if I insist that he take a note. Matt and I get back in the Explorer, turn in a wide arc across the field, and pull back onto asphalt, heading toward town.

"That was great," Matt says after a moment. "That was so great. What an idea, Cole. What an insane idea. You are one creative motherfucker."

"Thanks," I say. "Glad you liked it, but . . . half? That was just half?"

"Huh?"

"Because I have maybe at most a third of that back at home. How many more pain meds do you have?"

"Well, that was all of it . . ."

"All of it?"

He slaps the steering wheel with both hands. "Jesus Christ, Cole. Jesus Christ, would you listen to yourself? We just did something amazing, and all you can do is worry. You have a great plan, and it's gonna work, and all you can see are the problems. We'll come up with what we need."

"And if we don't?"

"If we don't? If we don't?" he says in a high-pitched, whiny voice. "We will. Just . . . we will."

When I look over, he's rubbing his elbow. "You've been saving your Percocet?" I ask him.

"Don't really need it. I don't like how it makes me feel."

"Pain free?"

He snorts. "Nauseous."

"Nauseated."

"Whatever. And it makes me think slow."

"Definitely can't have that." I glance back over, but he's not looking at me. "Sorry. Hey, I'm sorry for being a dick. I'm just . . . I don't know. I'm nervous. This summer is fucking with me a little."

It's fucking with both of us. I'm thinking about Matt sitting in that black-draped chair, Matt punching Ponytail in the woods, Matt running around with Paul Gerber and Sarah Jessup.

When Matt breaks into my thoughts, his voice is far quieter than I'm used to from him. "Cole, can I ask you something?"

"What?"

"It's about the shooting." I don't say anything, and after a moment, he glances over at me. "Can I ask you?"

"I guess."

"Do you remember where Kendra was sitting?" There's silence for a moment, and then he continues. "Because I heard her mom was going around and talking to all the survivors, and it got me thinking, and I was just wondering. She always sat at the front of the room . . ."

"Then that's probably where she was."

"Yeah. I mean, it's no big deal. Just, for some reason I've been thinking about it a lot."

It's been years since Matt asked me about the shooting. Years and years. There was a time, when we were a lot younger, when he asked a lot. He'd kind of sidle up to it, ask a few questions, trying to get at exactly what happened. He always wanted to know about Andy: what happened to him, what my last memory of him was, stuff like that. Things I couldn't tell him, because I didn't know. And then, when we were ten years old, I told him that I didn't want to talk about it anymore. I forget what he asked me that time, some question about afterward, when the police came in and took us out, I think, and I just told him I didn't know and couldn't remember a thing and never wanted to talk about it again. And we haven't.

It was very unlike me to stand up to Matt. It's not like he was a bully or anything; it's just that he always tended to be in charge. He'd decide what we would play, and I would follow along. But I couldn't stand it, couldn't stand talking about it, and so that one time, I spoke up for myself.

The road is humming under the tires, and there are no other cars, even though the sun is fully up now. I take a deep breath, feeling like I took a big pill and it didn't go down all the way. I can't talk about this. There's a place inside me, deep inside, that is totally private. It's alone, and it is still. It's old, older than my father's death, older than my mother's grief, older than my love for Viola. Almost older than I can remember. *Lonely,* that's the best word for it. Not in a bad way. Just in a way that has to be. It's where my poetry comes from. And this is trespassing, this question. Matt seeing Officer Jessup's daughter, that's a trespass, and this question is another. It's like he's trying to find his way into my story.

But how do you explain something like that?

How do you explain something like that to someone like Matt, who barely knows what's going on inside his own head, let alone somebody else's?

"I don't remember, Matt. You know I don't remember anything about that day."

"Yeah, but I just thought there might be a scrap. Like, when the police interviewed you or the counselors or something, they might have mentioned it."

"I think they were careful not to feed me information. Okay?"

"Okay, dude. You don't have to talk about it. It's just—"

"Just what?"

"I know it's fucked up, Cole. I know it is. It's just, you don't know. You don't know what it was like to not be there. I know it was terrible to be there, but it was terrible not to be, too. I feel like I left school the day before, and I never got to go back. I feel like every day since then, I've been an outsider looking in. I feel like I'm a ghost."

"I'd tell you if I could, Matt. I'd tell you anything if I could. I've got nothing. I never have."

I know it's hard for him. I want to sympathize. I try. It's just that when I look at Matt, all I can see is gold. All I can see is a guy who has the whole world at his feet. Girls love him; coaches love him; his family is rich. He's got diabetes, but that never seems to hold him back. And the one day when the worst thing in the world happened, he was lucky enough to stay home.

We don't speak again until he stops at the bottom of my driveway. He leaves the engine running, and we both sit, drained.

"Thanks for driving."

"No problem," he says.

"And thanks for the meds."

"No problem."

I open the door.

"You coming tomorrow?" he asks.

"Maybe. I guess." Matt's having some people over to his pool.

"I messaged Viola. I think she's going to come."

"Okay. I'll try."

"You should come, Cole."

I know I should. She's leaving for her service trip soon.

"Okay. I will."

"Nice. Great."

I slide out of the truck onto the gravel on the side of the road.

"Yo, Cole . . ."

"Yeah?"

"I'm sorry to ask."

I nod. "I know." I close the door and walk up the driveway, hands in my pockets. After a moment, I hear his engine roar as he cuts a K-turn and drives back up my street, off toward the big houses and clean pools on the nice side of town. I kick at the overgrown grass alongside the driveway and tell myself that I'll mow today, even though I know it's a lie.

As soon I open the front door, I'm hit by the smell of egg and warm vanilla. I warily step inside and make my way to the kitchen. Mom's up, cooking, singing along to the radio. She's wearing a clean apron, and it looks like she's showered. Evidently, this is a good day.

"I knew you'd turn up eventually!" she says with a smile. "Where have you been, early bird?"

"Uh, I went for a walk." I thought she'd be panicked if she woke to find me gone.

"I thought I heard a car."

"Matt gave me a ride home."

"He should have come in! We have enough here to feed a small army." She piles three pieces of French toast on a plate, smothers them with powdered sugar and maple syrup just the way I like, and slides it across the counter. I'm starving. She watches me eat, stuffing the food into my mouth without bothering to take it to the table.

"You need a shower, baby."

"I know. I'll take one. It's hot out already."

"Where did you go?"

"Just around. I couldn't sleep." I finish the plate and take the glass of milk she hands me, draining it in one long gulp.

"Are you all right, Cole?"

"I'm fine, Ma."

She looks at me doubtfully. "How's Matt doing?"

"Great."

"How's his arm?"

"Fine, I guess."

"He excited about Bucknell?"

"I'm sure." She's worried about me staying behind while everyone else leaves home.

"Can we talk about something, Cole?"

Christ, why does everyone want to talk this morning?

"Sure."

"Baby, did you give any more thought to what we discussed? To maybe taking a class in the fall?"

Mom started pushing this community-college idea about a week ago, telling me I should sign up for one or two courses and that I could transfer the credits later. She'd looked online and picked out a few things she thought would be good for me. That was when it hit me that she's got to be feeling guilty that I'm staying here to take care of her.

"Not really. Um—no. I'm just, I'm not sure that's what I want to do."

She nods thoughtfully, like some kind of therapist.

"I'm going to try to pick up more hours at Finn's. You know, when Matt leaves. He'll need me."

"Mr. Finn would love to see you taking a course or two. He'd make it work with your schedule."

"I just haven't thought about it much, Ma." *How does she know what Mr. Finn wants?* "I don't know. It's not really on my radar screen." The truth is that I can't imagine going over to the community college while Matt heads to Bucknell and Viola flies out to Berkeley and everyone else goes to other places you've heard of.

"There's no pressure, baby. I just want you to think about it."

"I will."

"Do something for me?"

"Yeah?" I know what she's going to say.

"Do one little thing today?"

The French toast in my stomach turns to cold cottage cheese. "Yeah. I'll do one little thing."

"Just something."

"I will. I already took a walk, didn't I?"

"You did. All right."

"And I'm going to a pool party at Matt's tomorrow."

"Wonderful! I'm so glad to hear it. More French toast?"

I shake my head. She reaches over anyway and puts two more pieces on my plate, then squeezes my hand and turns to the dishes.

I'll have to find a bathing suit. I don't think I even have one that fits, come to think of it. I don't go to a lot of parties. It's one more difference between Matt and me: he goes to the parties; he *has* the parties, while I'm trying to figure out what to wear. Generally speaking, actually, I never even know that there's a party going on.

I poke the French toast and notice that there are fresh flowers in a vase on the table. *Rosa . . .* my father's voice tells me but can't come up with the species. I look at them and take a bite of food.

"Is there coffee?"

"I'll make some, baby."

"Thanks."

It would be so easy to retreat. To go up to my room, with the notebooks and the binders, with the countless pages of quotes copied from overdue library books that are still piled by my bed. Go to that place inside me, alone.

There's something beyond that, though. Beyond the wall of wherever it is. Something normal and good. I need to see it.

I'm going to take a shower, I'm going to find something to wear, and tomorrow I'm going to go to that party. It'll be my last chance to see Viola before she leaves for her trip, and I'm going to make it count for something.

I keep looking at the flowers, and before I know it, I've cleaned my plate. It makes Mom happy.

Ten

— Matt —

I wake up on the floor, a couch cushion under my head, some sort of shawl or something covering me. The glowing hands on my watch say it's 8:15. Sunlight is coming in around a window shade. It takes me a moment to realize where I am, and another to realize that the watch is the only thing I'm wearing.

Cole would be pissed.

I roll over and raise myself up on one arm. Sarah's sacked out on the couch, her back to me, wrapped in a sheet. I push myself the rest of the way up onto my knees and pull it off her. She wakes with a start and rolls over, eyes wide. Then she smiles.

"Good morning."

I bend over and kiss one perfect nipple.

She pushes me away and stares hard, the way she did last night, the way she has every time I've been here over the last few weeks. She looks at me like she's trying to make a decision. Then she kicks the rest of the sheet off, hops off the couch, and tousles my hair as she leaves the room. I get up, wrap myself in the sheet like a toga, and look around.

Four times. I've been here four times since July Fourth. And this is my second time spending the night. I still barely know what her house is like. I open a shade halfway to let in some light. Specks of dust float across the sunbeam. I lean over, cracking my back and my neck, gingerly flexing my arm, and then stroll around the room.

It looks like she just moved in. No pictures, no little . . . what do you call them? Knickknacks, right? My mom has a million of them. A souvenir from every place she's ever been. This place is clean, though. Everything has a shine. It's just undecorated in the extreme. I should give her something, maybe, but what would she want? I have no idea.

Her father came back here that day. He carried Cole out of the school and then, eventually, this is where he came. Took off his badge and his boots, washed off whatever was on him. He was right here, in this room.

"Showing yourself around?"

She's standing in the doorway, wrapped in a bathrobe, holding a coffee cup.

"Yeah." I shrug. "You don't have much stuff, do you?"

"Travel light."

"I guess. This is your house, though."

"This is my dad's house." She sips her coffee and looks around the room as though she's seeing it for the first time. "It wasn't always this way. We used to have lots of things in here. Well, Dad, mostly. It was all his things. His pictures. His Nets stuff; he loved the Nets. Signed balls and framed jerseys. It's all boxed up in the basement. You like basketball?"

I shake my head.

She shrugs. "Well, maybe I'll just donate it." She looks around again.

"You should put something on the wall. Hotel rooms are more decorated than this."

"Yeah. I should."

"I mean, a poster, something."

She smiles, shrugs again. "I know. I just — I don't know what I want."

"Just get a picture of something you like."

She takes another sip from her mug and then looks at me for a long moment. "Maybe I don't know what I like."

"Do you like me?"

She raises her eyebrows and sets her mug down on a table. "You're all right."

"You thought I was better than all right last night."

"I said, you're all right."

"Okay. I'll take it."

She looks at me for another moment. "Lose the sheet."

I lose the sheet.

Forty minutes later, I'm jogging down her street, late for work.

I've been parking a few blocks away from her house. She seems to want it that way; embarrassed that I'm so young, I guess. I climb into the truck and start the engine. I could really use a shower, but Finn's expecting me. Maybe I should have called Cole last night and asked him to cover for me at the store, though he'd have been pissed as hell if I'd told him why. Cole's been in a black mood for weeks while Viola's been away. I think she gets back soon. Hopefully, that'll cheer him up. Give him a chance to do better than he did at the party.

Christ, the party.

I mean, at least he came. And I'm glad he came. Cole's unpredictable that way. But . . . polka-dotted swim trunks? That's what he wore. Black, with pink polka dots. They were brand-new; I had to peel the sticker off the back of one leg.

It was a good night, nice and mellow. Not too many people came, but enough. We had music, no drinks because my parents were home, but still, people had a good time. Luther was there doing cannonballs all night long. I didn't think there'd be any water left in the pool. Chris came, which was cool. I'd even called the Gerbers to see if there was any way Paul would want to come, but his mom said he's still not ready for something like that. She seemed really happy I'd asked, though.

And Viola came, which was the important part. She was leaving the next day for this big trip somewhere—Honduras, I think—but she came anyway. I'd told her that Cole would be there.

203

I will say this: He did a better job than he did at Project Graduation. He actually talked. To her. While looking at her. For a while, I was really proud of him. He even took his shirt off and got his pale, skinny ass into the pool.

And then things were winding down. The girl she had come with had to go, but Viola decided to stay, and it was as clear as anything could be that she wanted Cole to give her a ride home. Could. Not. Be. More. Obvious. To me, I mean. And anyone else with eyes.

Not to my best friend, though. Not to Cole.

So finally, I took him aside and I was like, "Dude, you should give her a lift home and maybe something'll happen. You know? Like, ask her if she wants to go for a drive. Maybe go out to the lake." I swear, she was giving him an open invitation.

And what did he tell me? That he had to get home, he was expected at home and had to get up and work the next morning, and he got all flustered and red. To be honest, he looked scared. He looked like the kid who's getting sent in as a reliever in the ninth inning and knows he doesn't have his stuff. He left without even saying goodbye to her, so I wound up driving her home myself.

Hopeless case.

I pull into the driveway behind Finn's and find that Cole's Volvo is there too. I go in, and he's cutting a box of bread open.

"Cole, what are you doing here?"

He looks up, surprise and annoyance on his face. "Uh, working?"

"*I'm* working this morning."

Cole straightens his back and shakes his head. "Not according to the schedule." He points to the whiteboard on the wall. He's right.

"Damn. I could have stayed in bed."

"Morning, boys. Scheduling mix-up?" Mr. Finn is standing in the doorway behind us. We both nod. "Matt, why don't you help Cole get all this unpacked and onto the shelves, and then you can take off. And Cole, that way you can knock off an hour early this afternoon." He winks and exits through the swinging door to the front of the store, whistling off-key.

"I could have really used that hour, Matt."

"Oh, Christ, will you chill out? It's one hour. I'll give you eight bucks or whatever it is we're making here."

"Fuck you."

I'd been tying my apron on, but now I stop and look at him, because he actually sounds like he means it.

"Look, I'm sorry," I tell him. "That was a shit thing to say. I can go; you can have the hour—"

"It doesn't matter."

"No, I'm sorry. I am. I was honestly confused about the schedule. I wasn't home last night, and I didn't have my copy with me."

Cole shrugs and shakes his head. "Let's just get this done."

We bend over a crate, emptying it, working in silence for a full five minutes before Cole asks, "Where were you last night?"

"Sarah's."

"Do your parents know?"

"I don't think so. Not yet, but it's not a secret, so I guess they'll find out, right?"

I'm actually not sure about the secret thing. Like I said, she wants me to park on another block and we've only ever been to her house, never anywhere out in public. Still, I'm eighteen years old. I can do as I like; my parents have no right to object. They'll be worried about the age difference, sure, and Dad will probably want to have an awkward talk, but I can get through that.

Cole attacks another crate, cutting too deep and ruining a package of English muffins. "So, are the two of you, like, dating? Is she your girlfriend now?"

I laugh out loud, see him wince, and wish I could take it back. "Sorry. I'm just laughing because it's a funny idea. The girlfriend thing."

Well, what is she, anyway? I can't come up with a word that seems right. *Lover?* That seems like something out of a movie. I don't want to think that we're just screwing, though.

"I don't know, Cole. I don't get her."

"What don't you get?"

"I mean, I don't know what she's doing. With me, you know? She's a lot older than me, and I'm pretty sure there are other guys who are into her."

Cole shrugs. He's probably the last person in the world I can get advice on this sort of thing from. "Maybe she's just having a good time?"

That's the obvious answer, but it feels like she's more serious than that. Still, she's never said anything serious. She's never said anything about being in love, the way Rosie did. She's never mentioned anything beyond the end of this summer. We're not a *couple*. It would be weird to walk down the street holding hands.

"You like her?" Cole asks.

"Yeah." *I do.* I already want to see her again, and I'm seriously mad at myself for wasting the chance to stay at her house when I didn't have to come in here after all.

We go back to work on the boxes. Five minutes later, Cole manages to slice his own thumb with the box cutter. It's not a bad injury, but it bleeds, and Mr. Finn seems nervous about it. They wash it and wrap it in a paper towel and tape, but it soaks through quickly, and Finn sends Cole home for the day.

I start to carry the fresh produce out to the front of the store. Mr. Finn catches me by the apples.

"Matt, does Cole seem all right to you?"

"He's fine, Mr. Finn. It's not a deep cut."

"No, that's not what I mean. I mean, from an emotional standpoint. He's seemed a bit dour these last few weeks."

Yeah, I'd have to say that dour *is about right for Cole.*

"I think he's just, you know, he gets down sometimes."

"Hmm." Finn studies the fruit and strokes his Adam's apple.

He's a funny guy, sort of old-fashioned and quirky. He's wearing a tie-dyed vest over his T-shirt. He strikes me as an aging hippie who thought it would be groovy to open a little store in a little town, then got stuck here for a couple of decades too long. "It must be a difficult summer for him."

I shrug. "I think he's all right."

"The significance of it."

"Of summer?"

"Of *this* summer. Graduation. All of you growing up, leaving home. It's brought it back to me, you know. Things I haven't thought about in many years. And he's facing it without his father. I wish I could be more help to him. He just seems . . . stuck, I suppose. Bogged down."

"I think Cole's going to be fine, Mr. Finn. Cole is Cole. He does things at his own speed. He's going to get moving again. He's worried about his mom, mostly, but once she gets better, he's going to pull it together and leave. I bet he'll be gone this time next year."

He nods thoughtfully but doesn't look convinced as he studies the avocados. He picks one up, squeezes it gently, and then holds it to his nostrils and inhales. "I hope you're right. I think that he and his mother need some space from each other." He puts the avocado down and begins to turn away.

"Mr. Finn?"

"Yes?"

"Where were you that day? Were you here, in the store?"

208

"I was. Of course I was. I don't often talk about it. I suppose I don't like to."

No one likes to. That's why I have to dig it out of them.

"How did you find out?"

He leans against a bin. "The radio." He pauses. "And do you know," he continues, "that Stevie Abrams's mother was also here? She came in every week to do her shopping. And she was here that day, just like any other day. She spoke to me about their summer plans. They'd just rented a house on Martha's Vineyard. She was very excited."

"And then what happened?"

"And then Mark Orlinsky came in, out of breath. Do you remember Mark?"

"No."

"He was the mailman for many years. He's retired now. He came in and told me to put on the television. Well, I've never had a television, but I put on the radio, and we stood there at the front of the store together and listened to NPR. At first, I thought it must be a different East Ridge they were talking about. I'd heard sirens, of course, but just the week before, there had been that big fire over in Wynnewood. No one remembers that. It was a five-alarm fire, and so for whatever reason when we heard all the sirens again, we thought it was a fire."

I don't remember anything about a fire. I do remember the sirens, though. I was in bed, reading comics, and even in my room, I could hear sirens in the distance. I could hear my mom moving around the house, the TV go on and then off, and then she was on the phone and I could tell she was upset, and she came and shut my bedroom door.

"Mark and I stood and listened to the radio," Mr. Finn goes on, "and at some point I looked up and saw Mrs. Abrams standing there at the end of aisle three"—he nods toward the spot—"with a look on her face that I'll never forget. She was listening and holding on to the handle of her grocery cart so tightly that her hands were shaking. I said something to her then. I said: 'I'm sure that Stevie's all right,' something of that sort. But she didn't say anything; she just shook herself out of her trance and ran out. And I will tell you, son, that she never came back. I can't quite recall when she left town, but I never spoke to her again." Finn puts the avocado down and sighs, looking up at a flickering fluorescent light. "I've always regretted saying that. Always regretted telling her that he would be okay. I had no right to do that." He finally looks at me. "I'm sorry. I don't talk about this very much, but having you boys here brings it back."

You boys. Like we're in the same group.

"It's all right, Mr. Finn."

He sighs again and pats me on the shoulder. "We'll never understand, Matt, but we'll always be in awe of boys like you and Cole. You survivors. You'll always have a place here. Even when you leave, you'll never really be gone." He nods in agreement with himself, stands silently for another moment, and then nods again and makes his way back to the front of the store.

I bring out the rest of the fruit and then ask Mr. Finn if I can take my break early. I go outside and lean against the back door by the dumpster. I look down at my boots. I got them new for this job, and they're finally starting to look genuine, the leather stained and nicked. I study them, and then I hear footsteps. I look up.

Officer Lucas pauses to look at my truck and then walks toward me. When he stops, he takes his time in studying me from top to bottom.

"You all right?"

I've been leaning against the wall, but I straighten up and wipe a hand across my forehead. It comes away wet. "I'm fine."

"Simpson, right?"

"Yes."

"Matthew."

"Yes."

He nods. He has very, very blue eyes.

"I'd like to have a word with you."

"About what?"

"You don't look good."

"You want to tell me that I don't look good?"

"You look sick."

I feel sick. "I feel fine."

He shrugs and sighs, as if he'll never figure something out and doesn't particularly care. "I'd like to have a few words with you about Sarah Jessup."

"What about her?"

Lucas shifts his gaze and stares at a spot somewhere up on the wall over my head, searching for words. "Give me a moment. I wasn't sure I would find you here."

"Take your time."

He flashes me a look of annoyance. "Look . . . I would imagine that Greg Jessup was probably a hero to you."

"Her father? I didn't know him. He wasn't anything to me."

"No? Coming into that school, carrying children out, that didn't mean anything to you? I believe you were in that class."

"I wasn't . . . I wasn't there . . . that day."

He studies me. "That boy in the photo with Greg, that's your friend?"

"Cole."

"Right. Cole Hewitt." Lucas inhales and exhales slowly. "Well. In any event, Greg Jessup was a hero to many people, even if he wasn't to you. But let me tell you something. I didn't know him well—he was much older than me—but my dad was on the force with him for years. And I can tell you that carrying your friend out of that school was just about the only good thing that man ever did, and it was just his good luck that someone took a picture of it and put it in every newspaper in the world."

"Why are you telling me this?"

"Because I want you to understand something about Sarah."

"I barely know her."

"I think otherwise. I hear she's been spending time with some young guy, and my money is that it's you."

I shake my head and start to open my mouth, but he smiles and cuts me off. "Just listen to me," he says. "Don't say anything. This is what I'm here to tell you. I know you're a rich kid, Simpson. I know your daddy's got money. You're hanging out here, playing at being a working guy."

"You don't know anything about me."

"Shhh. You're just to listen. You don't know what that woman's been through. Not losing her father suddenly, that's not what I mean. I mean what came before that. The way he treated her, like she was a piece of his property. I was glad when he had his aneurysm. His luck running out was the only lucky thing that ever happened to *her*. You don't have any frame of reference for that sort of thing. You understand me?"

"I have to get back to work."

"You understand me. And you need to understand this: I am not going to see her get hurt again. Sarah Jessup needs the right kind of man to take care of her. You hear me? The right kind of *man*."

He pauses, thinking, but I guess he's said everything he has to say, because he looks me up and down once more and pats me on the shoulder, just the way Finn did, then turns and makes his way back down the driveway without looking back.

I lean back against the wall of the store, and all the air goes out of me. *Fuck that guy*, I think. *Fuck him fuck him fuck him.*

Fuck him and every single last person in this shit town. I think it again and again and again, but there's no juice in it, and I realize that, whatever I'm making myself think, my hands are shaking and my armpits are sweating and there's no way around it: I'm scared. I'm scared, and that makes me madder than anything the cop or Mr. Finn or anybody else could possibly say.

"Matt?" Mr. Finn has come out the back door without my noticing. "Are you all right?"

"I'm fine. Sorry. I know my break's over."

"You look—upset."

"No. I'm not."

He looks at me doubtfully. "It's a quiet day. Do you want to take off?"

"It's all right, Mr. Finn; thanks, though. I have to go somewhere later. I'm doing a Little League clinic, so I can't go home anyway."

He nods doubtfully. "All right."

I make it through the rest of the workday and then grab my duffel from the back of the truck, change in the store bathroom, and head out to the new ball fields. The Principal Steven Schultz Baseball Complex. You can't get away from it, I think, as I drive onto the freshly paved parking lot. You can't get away from what happened in this town.

I take another minute to sit in the truck and eat a granola bar because my blood sugar's only seventy-one. Kids are getting dropped off at the edge of the field, nine- and ten-year-olds running across the outfield, tripping in stiff cleats, struggling with duffel bags almost as big as they are. These fields are nicer than anything I played on when I was a kid. Five diamonds with perfect brown dirt, level fields with fresh chalk lines, bleachers and backstops with no graffiti or rust. There are real dugouts, too. Even nicer than the ones at the high school. They opened this place up four or five years ago, and people said it turned out to be way more expensive than they thought it was going to be, but no one made a big deal. There wasn't enough the town could do for its kids after the shooting. They probably would have built us a domed stadium if someone had thought of it.

I finish the granola bar, get out, and make my way across the field. I usually feel better as soon as my cleats sink into dirt. Whatever has been on my mind, whatever is going on in my life, just goes away; it takes a back seat, and only the stuff in between the lines is real. It's been that way for as long as I can remember.

Not today, though. Today, all the shit rolling through my head comes right out onto the field with me, and so I'm standing by the mound on field three and Coach is introducing me to these kids as the best player he ever had, and I'm thinking about Lucas. The look in his blue eyes when he told me that I was *just to listen.*

And I'm thinking about Finn and the gentle way he patted my arm, thinking of me as one of the survivors.

And I'm thinking about Sarah.

Coach gets to the end of his speech, and I realize that I've missed what he said, but still I look out at these players in their too-big uniforms and I take their questions about varsity baseball and swinging with power and the most amazing catch I've ever seen. Then Coach asks me to say a few words about what I've had to overcome, playing with diabetes, and I don't mind that at all. I have a thing, a little speech, about how diabetes is a problem with energy, about how it makes you realize that you have only so much energy to spend, and you have to think about exactly what you're going to spend it on, how if you spend it on practice and homework, that will pay off in a way it won't if you spend it on video games. I hit my points about getting only one body and having to live in it and take care of it no matter what happens, and how if you do that the right way, you can do anything you want, and how you never, ever abuse your body with drugs.

As I'm rattling this off, I realize something: These kids, most of them listening hard, a few distracted by the buckles on their uniforms or bits of sod at their feet, hadn't even been born when I was in the first grade, and now they are older than I was then. Some of them probably don't even know what the shooting was; it's something their parents whisper about and agree to explain when they're older.

And they are so small. Little spindly arms sticking out of uniform sleeves, pants sliding down over hips, even with bright red uniform belts pulled as tight as they will go. Eyes looking up at me full of excitement and admiration. And something else: innocence.

How many are there here? I scan the group. It's a decent-size team, looks to be fourteen or fifteen. Almost as many as had been in our classroom. Someone looked out over a group just a little bit larger and a little bit younger and decided to go ahead and do what he had come to the school to do.

I try to re-grasp the thread of my story, about the way I'd hit a home run in extra innings against Alpine the previous fall. I've forgotten where I was and what point I'd been trying to make. I smile, shrug, and suggest to Coach that we try some drills. The kids are out of attention anyway, and they want to get on the field.

I jog to the outfield and take up a position ten or so yards behind the center fielder, running down long-hit balls from the coach and calling out advice to the boys in front of me. There's such a difference in ability at this age; some kids can see where the ball is going and get there first, running gracefully, pulling it out of the air. Others stumble around, letting the ball fall and then scooping it up and standing still, trying to compute where it should be thrown. I told them about the importance of practice, but in reality I know that it's something you're born with. It's just a question of whether you use it or not.

The kids are looking at me, all the players in the infield twisting around, Coach staring from the sidelines. There, about ten feet off to my right, a baseball is lying still in the grass. I have no idea how it got there. I run over, pick it up, and toss it to the second baseman. My elbow feels like someone slid a hot pin into it. "Sorry!" I shout. "Always keep your head in the game, right?"

A few kids laugh, and I jog back to my position and bend over, resting my hands on my knees.

The bat cracks, and a long fly ball arcs out toward left field. I'm not going to miss this one. I'm going to give these kids a show. I'm running away from it, able to see exactly where it's going to land, able to line up perfectly when I'll get there and when it will get there, and then I take just enough off my speed and launch myself through the air at the last moment, stretching out horizontal to the ground, snatching the ball out of the sky and then easily tumbling across the turf and springing back to my feet, tossing the ball to the waiting second baseman, ignoring the pain. The kids cheer. So does someone behind me. I turn and see Sarah, sitting by the outfield fence.

She's wearing cutoff jeans and a white blouse and she has a green bandanna tied in her hair, sunglasses on. She looks gorgeous, sitting there in the empty bleachers. She looks like a picture that I never want to forget. She gives me a big smile and she waves, and I wave my glove back at her and trot toward the infield and wonder why, instead of feeling as happy to see her as I should, I'm feeling nothing but scared and pissed.

Practice goes on, and I focus hard on the field in front of me, calling out tips to all the players now, even the pitcher, not turning back to the fence. Coach finally calls all the boys in for batting drills, and I join them by the backstop, sneaking a glance out and seeing that she is still there, still alone.

I take a bat and demonstrate my swing for the boys. I toss

a ball into the air and smash it over the center-field fence. Then another, then one out to right, and even though it burns like hell in my arm every time I swing the bat, it feels so good to make that kind of contact with the ball that I'd do it a thousand more times. The kids cheer and Coach laughs and asks me not to lose any more balls and I toss the bat in the air, spinning it end over end and catching it by the barrel. I go and sit in the dugout and watch the boys work on their hitting for a bit, until practice is over. The kids line up, giving one another high-fives, and I join them, letting them jump to tag my raised right hand.

Parents are making their way over from the parking lot, and Sarah is walking toward me down the third base line. "Anyone want to run a few infield drills?" I ask, even though I hadn't been planning on doing any more, and I'm relieved when three of the boys do. She walks up to me as I'm directing them to their positions.

"So, you're pretty good."

"Thanks."

"I heard about you, but I never saw you play."

I make myself smile. "I didn't know you were going to be here."

"I got off work early and didn't have anything better to do."

We stand for a moment after that, suddenly awkward.

"Does it bother you that I came?"

"No—I just thought, you know, it's a little strange to see you here."

"I didn't think it would be such a big deal."

"It's not."

"I'm not grabbing you and giving you a kiss or anything."

"I know."

"I'm not suggesting we go screw in the dugout."

"I didn't say you were."

She looks at me silently for a moment, then smiles and leans in. "You want to meet up later in the dugout?"

"Stop it. There are kids all around." People are looking at us, and I'm squirming and hating myself for it. I feel like Cole.

"I'm not talking loud, Matt."

"I know, it's just . . . I don't know."

"You don't want to be seen with me?"

"It's fine." It comes out way harsher than I mean it to.

"Whatever. Fine." She spins and walks away, cutting across the field toward the parking lot. I watch her go, watch the sun catch her hair where it spills out of her bandanna and down her back, watch the way her thighs are perfectly round where they disappear into her cutoffs, and I think that I'm probably the biggest pussy the world has ever seen. One visit from Mr. Police Officer and I'm a quivering bowl of jelly. I kick the dirt hard, spit in the grass, and turn to the kids who are waiting for me.

Forty-five minutes later, I'm done directing double plays, I've said goodbye to the kids, I've shaken Coach's hand and promised to stay in touch, and I'm back in the Explorer and pulling out of the parking lot, heading toward town, thinking I'll find Sarah and apologize for being a dick. I pass a pair of strip malls facing each other in a standoff across the four-lane road, each with a nail salon and a Chinese restaurant and some office space I'm pretty sure no one ever goes to. Traffic is light, and I'm lost in my own thoughts as I drive through a patch of marshland with trees hemming the road in on either side, and a second later I'm startled by the whoop of a siren. I look in the rearview mirror and see a cruiser with lights flashing. I glance at the speedometer. I don't think I was speeding and I figure the cop must be trying to get by me, so I slow down and ease over onto the shoulder. The cruiser stays with me and gets closer, and a voice comes over the loudspeaker: "Stop your vehicle immediately."

I roll to a stop and put the truck into park. I know what this is now. I reach over my shoulder and fasten my seat belt, roll down my window, and watch as the officer's door opens and he climbs out, adjusting his belt, settling his gun on his hip and straightening his hat, staring into the trees across the road. Finally, he turns and slowly makes his way up the shoulder of the empty road, coming to a stop by my open window.

My heart is pounding in my chest. My palms, resting on top of the wheel, are slick with sweat.

"Evening."

"Hello again, Officer." I manage to keep my voice steady by dropping it low.

"Do you know why I pulled you over?"

"Do you need my license and registration?"

"Do you know why I pulled you over?"

My mouth is dry, and I feel a surge of anger. "Was I speeding? Was I going a whole thirty-seven miles an hour?"

Officer Lucas straightens from the window and peers down the road as though searching his memory. He turns back to me in pretend surprise. "This is a forty-mile-per-hour road."

We stare at each other for a long moment.

"Do you know why I pulled you over?"

White kids don't get shot by cops in New Jersey, I tell myself, and I hate myself for thinking it, and I hate myself even more for feeling comforted by it. *Charlie Simpson's son doesn't get shot by a cop.* I don't say anything. Lucas leans closer, his head in the window, eyes searching the passenger-side foot well and the back seat.

"Turn off your engine."

I reach down and turn off my engine.

"Wait here."

Lucas walks back to his cruiser. I sit and watch in the mirror as he gets in and starts tapping on the computer next to the dash. He turns his attention back to the road in front of him. *There's nothing this guy can really do,* I think. *He'll just give me a ticket.*

Minutes pass. It's hot without the air conditioning or any wind. An occasional car goes by, the driver slowing and looking before speeding on. More time. I'm hot and tired and hungry. I need a shower, and I need to go to sleep. I look in the mirror again, and now Lucas is just sitting there, watching me through his windshield, not even pretending to do anything. I want to get out and walk back to him, but I know that is a very bad idea. I realize that my hands are still on the wheel and that my knuckles are white.

Lucas finally comes out of his cruiser, again goes through his routine of adjusting his gear and his hat, and walks back to my window. He stoops, looks in, and pauses for a moment before speaking.

"Do you know why I stopped you?"

"I know why you stopped me."

"Good. I'm letting you off with a warning." Without another word, he returns to his car, climbs in, and has pulled off the shoulder and around me before I've had the chance to restart my engine. I watch the cruiser disappear around the bend at the end of the road before I continue on, driving exactly thirty-five. I round the bend myself and have driven about two hundred yards when I hear the siren again. I step on the brake and look in the mirror. The cruiser is cutting out from behind some brush on the side of the road, speeding onto the asphalt and closing the space between us quickly.

I pull over again, put the car into park, turn off the engine, and place my hands back on top of the wheel. Sweat is beading on my forehead, and I have to reach up and wipe the moisture away before it runs into my eyes.

The police car stops a bit farther back than it had before, and at an angle so that the sun reflects off the windshield and I can't see inside. I wait. Thirty seconds go by. Another thirty. Sweat is running from my armpits and down my side. He doesn't get out. Then the cruiser starts rolling again, pulls back onto the road and speeds past me, away and out of sight and back toward town, leaving me sitting here alone, engine turned off, even though no one told me to this time.

I sit for a long moment and then bring my hands down hard on the wheel, letting go with every curse word I can think of. I turn the engine on and slam the gas, pulling back onto the road in a shower of dust and gravel without checking over my shoulder, accelerating to forty, fifty, sixty. I round the next turn and see empty road, maybe another three-quarters of a mile on a straight shot through the wetland. After that, the road bends again and reenters development. I step harder on the gas, heart hammering in my chest, hands and fingers tingling. Faster. Seventy miles per hour. Hands off the wheel and onto my lap. I shut my eyes and count.

How far away was the bend in the road? Half a mile? One, two, three. Slower. Make it seconds. Let the dice roll. Four-potato, five-potato, six-potato. I feel the road humming beneath my wheels, feel the gas pedal touch the floor under my right foot. *I'll go to ten. I won't tamper. I won't speed up the count. Eight-potato.*

I can't do it. I open my eyes. The bend is right there, in front of me. I see the trees, can feel the impact in my body, in the bones in my face that will splinter if I hit at this speed.

The Explorer has wandered over to the left side of the road. The speedometer says ninety-five. I grab the wheel and slam on the brakes, and if another car had been coming around the curve going the other way, everyone involved would have been dead. But there is no other car, and the truck grips the road and makes it through the turn, and I slow it down to fifty-five as I move back over to the right side of the street. More traffic here, more strip malls, more nail salons. I pull into a parking lot and stop.

Eight. I made it only to eight. Ten and I would have been dead. I'd be dead right now. They could put me in the ground, right where I belong, right beside Stevie Abrams and Andy Gerber and Principal Schultz.

I sit in my car shaking, the sweat drying on my face in the cool of the air conditioning, and I make one decision. I may be a coward, I may be a fake, I may be a ghost, but I will not be intimidated by that goddamned cop. If he is meant to fuck with me, if he is meant to kill me, I don't care. I'm not going to stop seeing Sarah, and I'm not going to hide from him.

I pull back onto the road, and five minutes later I'm sitting in my driveway. The car is still running when I hear tires on gravel; I spin around in my seat, but it's not a police cruiser. It's a minivan, and I recognize the woman who climbs out.

Mrs. Maiden approaches the driver's-side window, and I roll it down to speak to her. She's holding a large paper bag.

"Hello, Matthew."

"Hello, Mrs. Maiden."

"Are you just getting home?"

"Yeah. I was at baseball practice." I turn the engine off and slowly get out, then lean against the side of the truck, staring down at my shoes. I couldn't feel emptier inside. "I think my parents are out, Mrs. Maiden."

"That's all right. I wanted to come by and see you."

"Okay." It is an effort to look up at her. The sun is setting, and it catches every wrinkle on the side of her face; they spider out around her eyes and mouth. Her gray hair is braided together with a string of beads. She's watching me closely, like the way she looked at me at the beach.

"Do I still look sad?" I ask.

"You look angry now."

I shake my head and look down again. "I don't feel it."

"How do you feel?"

"I don't feel anything."

She nods as though it makes sense. I wait for whatever advice she wants to offer. I'll listen quietly. I don't think I can make myself play along, but I'll try to be kind, and then as soon as I can, I'll go inside and shower off, or maybe go right to sleep.

"Matthew, I want to give you something." She reaches into the bag, takes out a book, and hands it to me. *A Children's Illustrated Atlas.* There's a picture of the world on the cover, and around it are photos of different places: the Eiffel Tower, Easter Island, the Great Wall of China. The edges are worn. I open it up. *Kendra Maiden* is neatly printed in green crayon on the first page.

"I've been visiting everyone, touching base before you all leave town. You're my last stop."

I'd heard. I page through the book. There are maps, of course, and pages about various destinations. Each one has a little box neatly drawn in pen next to it.

"She made boxes next to every place she wanted to go," Mrs. Maiden says.

"She wanted to go to all of them."

"Yes."

"There's a check in the box next to Niagara Falls."

"We made it to that one, the summer before."

It's the only one that's checked off. I stare at it for another moment, a photo of the waterfall, millions of gallons of water pouring over the edge, into the mist, and then I close the book and hand it back.

"I can't take this."

"I want you to have it, Matthew."

"I wasn't there."

She nods. "I know. I wasn't either. And I hate myself every day for not being there with her."

"You didn't have any reason to be there."

"That doesn't matter one bit."

I don't look at her.

"We weren't friends, Mrs. Maiden. I hardly even remember her." I feel awful saying it, but I can't stop myself from going on. "She wasn't . . . I mean, we didn't ever do anything together. I wasn't her friend. I'm sorry. She wouldn't want me to have this."

She draws a deep breath and looks down for a moment before

turning back to me. "I know that you and Kendra weren't friends, Matthew. Maybe you would have been if she had lived. Who knows? Who knows who she would have turned into? Who she would have been friends with? I'm not trying to write you into a character you're not. And I'm not telling you that she would have wanted you to have this. *I* want you to have it. It's for me. I'd like you to take it, and have it, for me."

I look at her and see that, although she hasn't looked away, she has begun to cry.

"Will you accept it from me?"

I shake my head.

Another moment goes by before she drops her hand. "That's all right. It's all right, Matthew. You don't have to take it."

"I'm sorry, Mrs. Maiden—"

"You don't have to be sorry. Neither of us do. None of us do. We're all just trying to figure this out."

"I know."

"I hope . . . Matthew, I just hope that you don't have to be alone."

I hear her retreat to her van and get inside, and then the wheels rolling back down the driveway, onto the street. I don't look up until the sound of her motor fades away, and then I go inside.

Eleven

— *Cole* —

In ancient China, Buddhist monks used to practice Hua Tou.
It means "the point beyond which speech exhausts itself." Basically—and I may be getting this slightly wrong—they would
say or think the same phrase over and over and over again, just
examining it and examining it forever. Really, *forever*. They'd get
one for their entire lives.

Still, even the most devout monk would have nothing on the
way I've studied Viola's messages over the last three weeks.

Here's the first one:

> *Hey Cole at the airport & not sure when I'll have*
> *svc on my phone but fun seeing you last night*

So far, so good. Casual, but encouraging. She took the time
to text.

Still . . . "fun." You have fun with a friend. You can have fun
with a puppy.

Then the next one, sent right after:

Too bad you had to leave early

Just that. Seven words. Seven words I've read over and over again until they're burning in my brain.

And then the third:

maya walker winter get back

"Maya walker winter get back." A phrase which very slowly gave up its meaning over hours and hours of contemplation. After determining that there's no one named "Maya Walker" in East Ridge or in any nearby town and that she is not a famous person (although it turns out that there is a dermatologist in the city named Dr. Maya Walker). After determining that "Winter Get Back" is not the name of a poem, or a book, or a song. After hours of analysis, I think I have it. I think that she shot off one more message while heading for her plane and that she garbled it. I think the message was supposed to be "Maybe we can walk Winnie when I get back."

At least, I hope that's what it was. Because right at this moment, I am sitting on the hood of my car, outside her house, holding a dog bone and beginning to doubt myself.

I probably should have just texted her back.

Her front door opens, and I straighten, shading my eyes against the light from the rising sun, and then I hear a cry of protest.

"Winnie!"

The foul, evil beast is streaking toward me across the lawn, teeth bared, ready to do battle. I've never wanted to hurt an animal before, but I could now. I really could. Instead, I slide off the hood, take two steps onto the grass, and throw the bone.

It occurs to me, in the moment before he gets to it, that maybe this dog won't be interested. Maybe all he wants to do is to sink his dirty little British teeth into the soft flesh of my calf. But he's on it, grappling with the bone, slobbering and licking and biting, and I'm wondering whose dumb idea it was to domesticate wolves, anyway.

And then I hear her voice.

"Cole Anthony Hewitt."

She's walking across the lawn, her hair wet from the shower. Short white skirt, pink blouse, and a smile on her face that makes me want to tell the universe that if this is the best moment it ever gives me, then I won't have any complaints at all.

"How have you been?" she asks.

"Good. I've been good," I manage. "How was Haiti?"

"Lovely. A bit hot. How's the grocery business?"

"Thriving."

She laughs and watches Winnie wrestling with the bone.

"Look at that happy dog." She retrieves a leash from the house, and a few minutes later, the three of us—me, Viola, and Winnie—are making our way along Chester Arthur Avenue, the sun at our backs. I tell her about deciphering the text, and she laughs again.

"You never texted me back!"

"I—uh—I thought you didn't have cell service."

"We did, sometimes. Some of the places we stayed."

"I'm sorry."

"That's all right. You just left me to Conrad's tender mercies; I wound up having to message with *him* the whole time."

"Oh—Conrad. Did you, um, work things out about Nantucket?"

"Blech. It doesn't really get worked out at our level. It's a parent thing, you know?"

"Sure."

"I think it will kill the last few days before I leave for school, I'm afraid."

"Oh."

She sighs. I look at her, and she is looking down, one lock of hair hanging over the side of her face. I want to reach out and hook it back over her ear. "There are probably worse things," I offer, though at the moment, I'm having a hard time thinking of anything worse than the way I'm going to feel when she leaves with Conrad at the end of the summer.

"There are," she says. "There are indeed. It's just that it's a bit hard to really be comfortable with somebody when they've seen you naked, isn't it?" She laughs, then glances over at me in time to witness my face turning a color that, while indescribable and dramatic, only distantly reflects the chemical event that just took place deep within my gut. "Oh, I'm sorry, Cole. Sometimes I forget which side of the pond I'm on, you know?"

My reaction has much less to do with being an American prude than it does with being an American virgin. I manage a laugh and a shrug, and we lapse into an awkward silence as we walk.

"What were you building in Haiti?" I finally ask, although I feel like all the air has been let out of me.

She brightens. "A new school. You wouldn't believe what it was like out there, Cole. The circumstances."

"What did they have you doing?"

"I was in charge of the spackle." She seems proud.

"Really? The spackle?"

"Yes, you know, smoothing over all the nail heads."

"That sounds exciting."

"Cole, those children will be going to school in perfectly spackled classrooms."

I laugh. "I'm sure they will."

"Are you teasing me?"

"No, I'm just saying—"

"They were God . . . damn . . . perfect."

"I am one hundred percent sure that every wall in that school will be pristine."

She pauses for a moment, and then she laughs too. "I suppose I don't ever stop, do I?"

I shake my head. "Have you done your one pointless thing yet?"

"It's on my to-do list."

"You might be missing the, um—"

"I probably am." Her hair has dried in the sun and is hanging limply down her back. She pushes her short sleeves up onto her shoulders. "God, it's getting hot. Let's get home. Come this way."

Viola leads me on a shortcut between two houses and across a series of back lawns. Three of them have pools, but no one is in any of them. In fact, there's no sign of life, human or otherwise. No squirrels in the scrawny, newly planted trees. No birds. We're halfway across a huge lawn—perfectly green, with every single blade of grass cut to the same length—when I hear a hissing sound, and a moment later I'm hit by a spray of water. Viola cries out, Winnie yelps and barks like crazy, and we all run back, away from the line of sprinklers that have just come on.

"Oh, Christ!" Viola says, looking at my wet shirt. "I'm sorry, Cole, this is a crappy shortcut, isn't it? We'll have to go all the way around."

I look up the slope of the lawn at the spray of water. There's a shimmer of a rainbow in it. It felt amazing on my face, and a thought comes to me. Something I haven't done since I was a little kid. The exact thing that Matt would do right now, if he were here. The thing that I won't do if I give myself another moment to think.

I grin. "No, we don't." And I am off, running across the wet grass and then leaping through the spray. I land on the other side and spin around to see Viola and Winnie both staring at me. "Come on!" I call.

Viola shakes her head. "You're insane!" she calls back.

I wipe the water from my face. "It feels great! Come on, Viola!"

She smiles, takes a step, and hesitates. Winnie is sitting behind her, and it doesn't look like he's going anywhere. I hop back through the wall of water and jog down to them. "You can do it," I tell her. "You'll be glad you did." I scoop Winnie up, holding him under one arm like a football. He twists his head around but can't quite find an angle from which to sink his teeth into me. Viola is still holding on to his leash. "Ready?" I say. "One, two . . ."

And we're off, running alongside each other, connected by Winnie's leash. We jump at the same time, sailing through the spray, and we land, laughing, on the lawn beyond. I set Winnie down.

"See? That wasn't so bad."

Viola is still laughing and shaking her head. "Not so bad at all." She looks at me for a moment. "Let's do it again!" She grabs my arm and pulls me with her as she leaps back into the mist.

We run back down the hill, leaving Winnie to shake himself off and to sit, watching, from just outside the reach of the sprinklers.

"Now look what you've done!" I say. "There's only one way back . . ."

Viola is laughing so hard, she's doubled over. She lets out a whoop and charges back into the spray. I'm right behind her. Back and forth, jumping and slipping on the wet grass, laughing so hard we can't talk, even though there's nothing particularly funny, other than the other person being soaked to the skin. I try not to stare at the way her bra is showing right through her shirt. Winnie waits patiently.

"Oh, my God, Cole," she finally gasps, "I am a mess!"

I laugh and wipe the water out of my face.

"Come on," she says. She picks Winnie's leash up from off the ground and looks back at me. "Thank you. That was fun."

We walk on, and a few turns later, we wind up in her side yard, though I don't recognize it until we come around to the front and I see my car parked by the curb. All these big houses look just the same. Her driveway is empty; when we left, there had been a silver Mercedes parked here. Viola tosses the plastic bag with Winnie's poop into a trashcan, looks around, and then focuses on me.

"Do you want to come in?"

"Oh — sure."

She opens the side door and leads me into a mudroom nearly as large as my kitchen. "Just kick off your shoes." I do, and she does the same as she pushes Winnie into a cage and hangs his leash on a hook. "Make yourself at home. I'll grab us some towels."

I remember the inside of her house from when I was here for the T. S. Eliot project, but it seems bigger now that it's just the two of us. I wander through the family room, trying not to drip on the furniture, looking at the countless framed photos arranged over the bookshelves and the long side table. Viola and her parents snowboarding, parasailing, water skiing. All things I've never tried. There's not a spot of dust on any of the surfaces.

She comes in through a side door while I'm studying a picture of her in what looks like a tropical rainforest. She looks like she's eleven or twelve in the photo.

"Here, Cole, take this." Viola hands me a thick terry-cloth towel. She's rubbing her own hair with another. "Do you want something to drink? I'm going to get a glass of lemonade."

"Sure. Thank you."

She disappears for another moment and then returns with two glasses, setting them down on the glass coffee table and sitting on the massive L-shaped couch that dominates the room. I sit near her, just around the bend of the L.

"I looked up some of your poetry. You know, googled your alter ego."

"Oh . . ."

"I liked it. I did. It was good, Cole."

"Thank you."

"Sad."

"Yes, I suppose."

"Much of it inspired by your father's illness, I imagine."

I nod. "I started writing a long time before he was sick, but the pieces of published—yes, they're about him."

"And are you still writing?"

"Yes."

"About him?"

"Other things." *You,* I think. *I'm writing about you.* I don't say it, though. I look around the room again. I wonder where her bedroom is. I wonder how I could see her naked. I wonder what Matt would say if he were here in my place. He would know the way to connect the dots, to get from here to there. He knows the magic words that someone forgot to tell me.

"Do you mind if I ask whether you ever write about the shooting?" she asks. It startles me out of my reverie.

"I haven't," I tell her. "I've tried to do it, but it never seems to work out. I don't know. Maybe some things are just too big to write about."

"Maybe you'll be able to write about it someday."

"Maybe, but I don't think so."

"People go through big things and eventually write about them. Wars."

"This is different. It's hard to explain. It's hard to understand if you weren't there. I think it's impossible to understand."

"It's a very closed club."

"It's a club no one wants to be part of," I say. And that makes me think of something, a question I've wondered about. "Do you mind if I ask *you* something?"

"Not at all."

"Your family, moving to East Ridge. Not many people did after what happened, you know. For a long time. Maybe still not now; who knows? But definitely not many people with kids our age."

"I can understand that."

"But your family did. Did you not know about it? I mean, living in England—"

"Oh, I think we were aware of it. I was, certainly."

"But it didn't bother you?"

She thinks for a moment. "I don't know. There wasn't an option for me; my parents announced that we were moving and when and where, and we never talked about that aspect of it. I knew what had happened, and I'm sure my parents did too, but we never talked about it. It's not something they would have considered. My parents are very, very *practical.* They would have regarded that as an emotional consideration, you know? It wouldn't have factored into their decision making. They moved here because of the location, I suppose, and the cost, and the schools. That's all."

That's all. To other people, it's something that happened in the past. It's a date on the calendar. It's a bunch of plaques on benches and engraved bricks on paths, parks, and ball fields named for our brave principal and a kid in a wheelchair with an amazing attitude. For them, it's over.

239

"Cole?"

I've been staring into my glass, watching the ice melt.

"We shouldn't be talking about this," she says. "I'm sorry."

"No, I asked. I should—"

"Wait here."

Viola jumps up and hurries from the room. She's back in another moment, a book in her hand. The book I gave her, my father's Eliot. She sits again, a bit closer to me this time, balancing on one leg folded beneath her.

"Listen to this, Cole," she says. "I've read them all through, but poetry is meant to be read aloud, don't you think? This piece is amazing; it's very short and strange, sort of an early take on *The Waste Land*." She flips through the pages and finds the one she wants. "This is called 'Preludes.'" She pauses for a moment, then begins reading.

I've read this one. I listen to her voice, watch her eyes scanning the page. Even though my clothes are still wet and the air conditioning is on, the room is too warm. There's no point. I don't know what to do or how to do it. I'm never going to learn the magic words.

Viola finishes reading. She's right: it is short and strange.

"Now you read one." She holds my father's book out to me. I shake my head.

"I have to go."

"You have to go?" She stares at me in disbelief and closes the book as I stand up.

"Thanks for the lemonade."

"You're . . . welcome."

I can feel her eyes on me, but I don't look back as I let myself out through the mudroom. Winnie yaps at me from his cage, but I ignore him, slip my sneakers on without tying them, and hurry to the car. My eyes are burning, and I'm worried that I won't be able to drive, but I also don't want her to see me wiping them if she looks out the front window of her house, so I start the engine and squint hard and manage to make it away from the curb and around the corner before pulling over again, pounding the wheel, and screaming something so inarticulate and angry that it tears at the inside of my throat.

I'm a helpless, useless, dickless schmuck, and I always will be. Always.

I sit for a few moments, making myself breathe deeply. Then I wipe my eyes and my nose with the back of my hand and start driving again, and I'm more or less composed by the time I pull into my driveway.

I'm getting out of the car when I hear a noise from the garage, something falling down. Some sort of animal knocking things around, I think, but when I walk over and look, the door is closed.

The garage is detached from the house and is set back a little bit. The blue paint is peeling off, and it's full of junk. We don't use it for anything anymore, I just go out there when I want to get some of Dad's old beer. I make my way to the side and try to look in a window, but the glass is too dirty to see. There's another noise from inside. Maybe there's a hole in the roof, and a bird flew in. I walk to the front, take a firm hold on the door handle, and quickly pull it up as I jump to one side, waiting for something—possibly rabid—to fly or run out past me.

Matt looks up from the garage floor, where he's lying among scattered paint cans, and he bursts out laughing. "What's happening, Cole?"

I stare at him wordlessly. I haven't seen Matt in a few days, but I figured he was just busy with Sarah Jessup, and the thought made me so angry, so unreasonably but violently angry, that I ignored him the two times he tried to call.

"Is that my dad's beer?"

"It is your dad's beer, Cole, and I apologize for drinking it." He pushes himself up onto his elbows, puts the bottle he's holding to his mouth, and tips it up, sucking the last remnants. Then he peers inside, burps, and tosses it into the nearest corner, where it joins a pile of others.

"How long have you been out here?"

"What time is it?"

"About nine fifteen."

"I don't know, then. Few hours, at least."

"Let me see your phone." He hands it to me without protest, and I swipe the screen and tap on his blood sugar app. It's 112. Normal.

"How am I doing?"

"You're fine."

"Great. Hand me another beer?"

"How many have you had?"

"I've lost count."

"Then you should probably stop."

Matt pulls himself to his feet, looks around, and finally seats himself on Dad's old workbench. It looks like he'd tried to sit on a pile of paint cans, and that was what caused the noise. "Did I wake you up?" he asks.

"No. I was out."

"Where?"

"Viola's," I say, and I immediately regret it. He lets out a low whistle.

"Spend the night?"

"No, I did not spend the fucking night."

He looks hurt. "What's the matter?"

I shake my head. It's the last thing he could possibly understand. "Nothing. I'm just not sure—I'm not sure things are going to work out."

"With her? Why not?"

"I just don't think—"

"Dude, you haven't even done the balloon ride yet! I've been working on that. I have something for you!"

"What?"

"The shit for Eddie, Cole, I'm working on the shit for Eddie. I'm gonna have it for you. I'm working on it."

"Where are you—"

He puts a finger to his lips, almost poking himself in the eye. "Just trust me. You cannot give up on this." I stand with my hands in my pockets, looking around the garage. He probably can't imagine how badly I want to give up. "You look sad, Cole."

"I guess I am."

"Someone told me I look sad too."

"Who?"

"You should try having a drink."

"It's a little early."

"Let's go for a drive, then." He tries to stand up, but his knees give out and he sits back down, hard. "Ooof. You do the driving."

"That's probably a good idea. I'm going to drive you home." I pick my way across the garage, put an arm under his, and pull him to his feet. He's heavy, and he leans on me hard.

"Not home," he says. I don't answer as we thread our way through the tipped paint cans, around a big toolbox that's covered in spiderwebs, and out into the morning light. "Not home," he says again as I support him across the lawn. I don't have a good grip on him, and he's not taking much of his own weight. I need to lower him onto the grass; I mean to adjust my hold on him and stand him back up, but he sits all the way down. "Yo, Cole," he says, "you need to mow the lawn."

"I will."

"You want me to do it?"

"Not right now."

"And listen, Cole, I know you don't want to talk anything

about it, but would you please please please just answer me one question please? The first time I saw you," he continues, without waiting for me to respond, "the first time afterward, you told me something. We were out here, see, out here in the yard." He gestures toward the overgrown backyard, toward the pond. "There used to be a little, I don't know what, a little place out there."

"Vine Cottage." My dad built it out of plywood for me; he painted it and planted vines all along one wall. It's long gone.

"Yeah. We sat in there and had snacks. My parents, I think they brought me over to help. It was like a week after. It was the first time I saw you after."

"All right." I don't remember it.

"Well, we had snacks in, in, Vine Cottage, and our parents were in the house and you told me something. You told me about something you remembered."

I've never remembered anything. "What was it?"

"I . . . don't . . . know. Isn't that crazy? You told me something. I know you told me something, but I can't remember what it was."

"Well, neither do I."

"I didn't even remember being over here with you at all until I came out to the garage last night or this morning or whenever it was."

"Maybe you're imagining it. Sometimes that happens. People imagine things and think they remember them."

He shakes his head and stares out toward the spot where Vine Cottage used to be. After a moment, I get him back up, braced on my shoulder, and we start moving again. "Where's your truck?" I ask him. He hiccups and waves a finger in my face with his free hand. "Streets away," he says. "I've learned . . . you don't park right where you're going, am I right?"

"All right. We'll get it later." I hope to God he was at least a bit sober when he drove here. I lower him into the passenger seat of my car and go around to the driver's side.

"Cole," he says as I start the engine, "let's go somewhere."

"I'm taking you home." I wish he would just pass out.

"No, no, no, no, no. Let's go to Mrs. Ryan's house."

"No."

"Over on Pine Street."

"I know where it is. We're not going." I back the car down the driveway, shift into drive, and take off. I can have him at his house in five minutes. Both his parents are probably working; I'll get him up to his room, drop him in bed, and be done.

"I've been, you know."

"Been where?"

"Mrs. Ryan's!"

"I know, Matt. I was with you."

"No, since. I drive over. She has so many goblins."

"Gnomes."

"So many little goblins. I've given them names."

"That's great."

"She goes out, sometimes."

"Okay."

"She goes out at night."

"Right. You probably shouldn't be there, you know."

"Can I tell you something?"

"Sure. What do you want to tell me?"

"She doesn't always lock her back door."

It takes a moment for the implications of that to sink in. "Wait a minute. Wait a damn minute. Are you telling me that you've gone *into* her house? Have you gone into her house when she wasn't there?"

Matt doesn't respond. His head has rolled off to the side, and his forehead is against the glass. I try one more time to ask him, but he must be out.

I can't imagine that he's doing that, driving over to the old Keeley place and sitting outside in his truck, parking up the street, letting himself in when Mrs. Ryan goes out. Except that I can. Ever since he sat down in that black-draped chair, I've been able to imagine him doing all sorts of things.

I get to his house, pull as far up his empty driveway as I can, and shut off the engine. His head comes up when I open his door, and he's able to give me a little bit of help standing up, but not much. I get him up onto my shoulder, almost over my back, and support him as we slowly make our way up onto the Simpsons' patio. There's a code to the sliding back door, and I punch it into the keypad, open it, and get us into the chill of their central air. For the second time this morning, I'm standing in a mostly empty house far bigger and nicer than my own.

Matt's room, unfortunately, is on the third floor, and by the time we make it up to the landing, I'm covered in sweat, air conditioning or not. I pause, breathing hard. He raises his head just a little bit and speaks for the first time since the car.

"You all right, Cole?"

"I'm great."

"You seem out of breath."

"Come on." I haul him down the hall, his feet tripping over each other, my arm around his waist, his arm over my shoulders and gripped tightly in my hand, the muscles in my legs and back and abdomen screaming at me. We finally make our way into his room, and I get him over to his queen-size waterbed and lower him down onto it. I even get his head squarely on the pillow and try to stand up, but he's still holding on to me.

"Cole," he says, squeezing my upper arm.

"You're down," I tell him. "You can let go of me now."

"Cole," he says again, "I gotta tell you something."

"Okay," I say, "but you can let me go."

"Cole." He squeezes my arm harder, feeling the muscle, the tendons. "Cole, you are much, much stronger than people think you are."

He lets his arm drop to the bed. I straighten up with a groan and stretch my back and shoulders, looking around his room. It's been a long time since I've been in here, not since we used to have sleepovers when I was younger. The *Star Wars* posters have come down and been replaced by lighthouse prints, probably chosen by his mother. It's been repainted, a color that would probably be called cosmic blue or something like that. It doesn't feel like it's Matt's room.

I fish his phone out of his pocket and check the app. It's 102. Still, alcohol can be a problem for diabetics. I go back down to the kitchen, get a tall glass of orange juice, and put it on his bedside table in case he wakes up with low glucose. Then I sit at his desk and read some of his old baseball magazines for forty-five minutes, check his sugar again to make sure he's still normal, and get up to go.

I'm closing the door behind me when I hear Matt's voice. I had thought he was asleep, and in fact I think he may be. He sounds like he's talking from down in a deep hole, addressing no one in particular.

"I wish," he says, "I wish. I wish I knew."

I wait in his doorway for a moment, wondering if he's going to say anything more, wondering what it is he wishes he knew, but there's nothing else, and I quietly let myself out of the room and then out of his silent, empty house.

Twelve

— *Matt* —

I've been working on my stories. Chris said that they had to be true, and they are. They're just a little exaggerated is all.

I mean, I have only so many of them. It's not like Rosie and I were screwing every single day. I don't want to tell him about Sarah, but I've been stealing some of that material. Like, taking things Sarah and I have done and just replacing Sarah with Rosie and telling it like that. Technically a true story, just altered a little bit.

And Chris has come through in return, though not as much as I had hoped. He's let me into his house two more times, and we raided the supply in the bathroom and the medicine cabinet, but we take only a bit here and there so his parents won't notice. Still, the bag of pills at the top of my closet is getting more and more full.

I wish we could make things happen faster. I don't want to pressure Cole, but I keep on asking if he's seeing Viola, and he's been kind of cagey about it. I think maybe he's not. If things work out with his plan, it will be great, but then she'll leave for school right after. Maybe they can make something work long-distance or something. And if it doesn't work out . . . well, I don't want to think about that. I don't think I could go off to Bucknell leaving Cole in the state he's been in.

Chris doesn't say anything today when I walk up to him in his driveway; he doesn't even respond when I call his name. I start to reach out to shake him, and then I worry that would be the wrong thing to do, and I'm just about to run up to the house to get his mom when he finally speaks.

"Let's go."

I breathe a sigh of relief, glance up at his lopsided house—there's no sign of his mother—and get him into the van. He doesn't say a word as I secure his chair. "You all right today, Chris?" I ask. He doesn't answer. "Buddy, can you just say something so I know you're okay?"

"I'm fine."

"Okay." I get into the driver's seat, adjust the mirrors, and back out.

Five minutes into the drive, Chris still hasn't said anything, and I decide that I'm just going to jump in. I have sort of a mash-up, something Sarah and I did in her shower that I'm going to tell him about, except I'm going to set it with Rosie in the showers in the locker room at school. He's going to love it.

"All right," I say, breaking the silence. "You want to hear one you haven't heard? This is one I've been saving." No response.

"So," I continue, "so it was after practice one day, last spring, and, um, I'd stayed late. I thought I was the only one in the locker room—"

"Shut up."

"Sorry?"

"I said, shut up."

I twist the rearview mirror down so I can see his face. He's staring straight ahead, out the windshield at the road ahead of us. "What's the problem, Chris?" He doesn't say anything. The silence stretches on. "Dude . . ." I look back again, and I'm horrified to see that tears are pouring down his cheeks. "Shit, Chris . . ." I look around, spot a pharmacy, and start to pull into the lot.

"Not here!"

"Chris—"

"I said, not here! People here know me. Someone'll come knock on the window or something."

"All right, all right." I pull back onto the road, drive another two hundred yards, and pull as far as I can onto the shoulder with my blinker on. I put the van into park and twist around to look at him. "What's the matter, Chris?"

He's wiping at his face with his one usable hand. I look around for a box of tissues but don't see one. "I'm okay," he says. "But I don't want any more stories. And I can't get you any more meds."

I feel panic start to set in. "You don't have anything else?"

"I have tons; it's just that my mom noticed some were missing."

"Oh, shit . . ."

"It's okay. She convinced herself that she'd cleaned the old stuff out. But we're done."

"Okay, Chris, it's cool . . ." He's crying again, and I have no idea what to do. "It's cool, Chris; I said it's cool. You've kept up your end and all; we're good."

"It's not that."

"What is it, then?"

He doesn't answer. We sit in the van, traffic passing on our left, the air conditioning blowing. It's hot outside, almost a hundred degrees.

"Can we just go?" Chris finally asks.

"Yeah, sure." Not knowing what else to say or do, I turn away from him, put the car into drive, and pull back out onto the road. Five minutes later, we're at the PT clinic. I get out, open Chris's door, and look at him carefully. He's stopped crying, but his eyes are still red. "Are you okay, Chris?"

"I'm going to say this once. And I don't want you to tell anyone. And I don't want to talk about it again."

"Okay."

"I went to the doctor." His voice is shakier than usual.

"Yeah?"

"I always go to the doctors. Lots of them. But I went to see my physiatrist."

"What's that?"

"It's a rehab doctor."

"Okay."

"And, so, I'm eighteen now, and so I met with him without my mom."

"Right." I suddenly have a sinking feeling that I know where this is going.

"He asked me if I have any questions. Like, about . . . um, about the long, the longer term. We haven't really talked about some things."

"Yeah." I want to put my arms around this kid right now. I want to pick him up out of his chair and hold him. "I'm sorry, Chris."

"Don't."

"I am, man, I'm just—"

"I said, don't. Just get me out. I'm going to be late."

I get him out.

"No more stories," he says once we get through the process. "I don't need to know about that shit. It's just pretending. It's just a way of forgetting that it's never going to happen to me."

Without saying anything more, he drives down the sidewalk and in through the automatic door, leaving me alone in the parking lot. I lean against the front of the van and put my head back, closing my eyes, feeling the sun on my face.

I remember Chris from before the shooting. There was a day, not long before, a day when we got to go outside for recess for the first time after a long, cold stretch. I remember him running; there was still slush and ice all over the place, and we were all being careful about slipping, but he was fearless. He ran and ran, back and forth across the playground, like an animal that had just been let out of its cage, and he never once slipped. I remember the sun in his hair.

I wonder if he remembers it. I wonder if it was the last time he ran.

I want to go out to the lake, want to go back in and swim again, straight across, without Cole pulling me out this time. Just me and the water, deeper than anyone knows, and I'll make it across or I won't, one way or the other, no interference. There's even a moment when I think I should take the van and just go, leave Chris here and drive out and ignore whatever families are there with their kids this morning, but then I realize that I'm slipping into sleep and that the sun is burning my face, and I shake myself awake. I feel dried out. Twenty minutes have already passed.

I push off of the van and walk the perimeter of the parking lot until Chris comes out, and I walk back to meet him. I open the van back up and wish that I'd started it five minutes ago to run the AC. I get him in, and we drive back to his house.

"You all right?" I ask.

"Yeah."

"You want to talk at all? About that appointment? With the physicist?"

"Physiatrist."

"Right."

"Not really. I've had hundreds and hundreds of doctors' appointments. I didn't think there was anything new they could tell me. I guess it never ends, though. I guess there's always more shit."

"Yeah." He doesn't want to talk. I wouldn't either.

"You know, the bullet didn't hit me in the spinal cord," Chris says after a moment.

"What?"

"The bullet. It didn't hit my spine. It didn't hit any major organs. The surgeon told my parents it was the luckiest, most incredible thing she'd ever seen. Missed every single vital organ. Missed my spine. She said I should be dead, nine hundred and ninety-nine times out of a thousand I'd be dead."

"Then why . . . how'd it do this to you?"

"That gun was so powerful, the bullet was going at such a high velocity, that it just . . . it rippled. Imagine taking a bowl of Jell-O and slamming it down on the table. Imagine how the force would ripple through the Jell-O. Now, imagine that something really delicate was running through the Jell-O, something like a little kid's spinal cord. Those waves, those waves of force, could damage it, right? Well, that's what happened. That bullet hit me with such force, so much power, that even though it missed everything, it still shredded spine tissue. That's why I can move this hand, because some of the fibers weren't totally demolished."

"That's insane."

He nods. "It's beyond insane."

"Do they think the PT can make it better?"

"No. I have to do the PT just so my body doesn't rot underneath me."

I was home, I think. *I was home in bed when that happened. I was home reading a comic book when this kid's body was turned into slammed Jell-O. I was drinking chicken soup out of a big mug when Sam Keeley came into our classroom and Chris moved his legs for the last time in his life.*

"You know, Chris, crazy things happen," I say. "I saw this thing on TV with special cells, these, like, stem cells, and—"

"Yeah. I know."

Neither one of us says anything else.

I drive him home and get him out. He steers across his driveway, up toward his house, which still looks empty. I want to call something after him, want to tell him I'm sorry. Not just for trying to tell him the story. Not just for using him for the pills. For everything. Everything. For every time I've run out onto a baseball field. For every time I've touched a girl. For every moment that's gone by for the last eleven years. I'm sorry for all of it.

I don't say anything. I go home. My dad is waiting for me on the lawn.

"Matt. We need to talk."

Dad's wearing work clothes: his khakis and a shirt and tie that look like Easter-egg colors. He's holding a baseball in one hand.

"What's up?"

He tosses the ball up and catches it. "Where have you been?"

"PT. I took Chris to our PT."

"I just heard from PT. Following up on an invoice. For sessions missed without twenty-four-hour cancellation. All the sessions, actually."

When I was little, I thought my dad was the biggest guy in the world. All boys think that, I guess. I mean, I thought he was huge. Everything about him. His hands, his legs. And then I got older and he got smaller, and I started to realize something: my dad is the biggest fake, the biggest sellout in the world, and now I hear him talk on the phone to his clients and I want to knock him down, take the phone, and shout into it, "That's not really him, you know!"

Dad does pharmaceuticals. Not the science stuff. He's in legal. He tells insurance companies what they have to cover and what they don't. It's like a cost-benefit thing. If you don't cover something, there are people who are going to wind up in the hospital, people who are going to die, but it might cost less than paying for the drug in the first place.

So, think about that. And then think about it for a guy whose kid has type 1 diabetes, and you'll start to get some idea of what a fucked-up thing it is.

Dad tosses me the ball, underhand. I catch it.

"Throw it back to me."

I underhand it back.

"No." He tosses it to me again. "Throw hard."

"You're not wearing a glove."

"Just throw it."

I switch the ball to my right hand and flex my arm, bending it, touching the ball to my shoulder. Pain shoots into my fingertips. I shake my head.

"You can't, can you?"

"No."

"You haven't been going to PT."

"No."

"Don't the meds help?"

"I haven't been taking the meds."

"What the hell are you doing, then?"

I stare at the ball, the red stitching in the smooth white leather.

"I don't know."

I look up, and Dad's standing right in front of me. I don't know what I expect him to say; I'm basically expecting him to scream, and I realize at the very last minute that I'm actually bracing myself for him to hit me, even though that's something he's never done.

So I'm not ready for it—it's the last thing I'm ready for, really—when he does what he does, which is put his arms around me. He pulls me into him like he hasn't in years, in years and years, maybe not since I was a little kid, and he holds me tight and I feel something inside me starting to crack. I feel like it's going to come up out of me, through my chest and throat and come spilling out, and I can't allow that to happen, so I break away from him and try to say something and can't do it, and I go into the house, leaving him standing on the lawn with the baseball dropped at his feet.

I go up to my room and close the door and lock it, leave the lights off, and I wait, but he doesn't come after me. Then I go to my closet, open it, and dig through a pile of laundry, old magazines, and worn-out baseball gear until I get to the back.

It's been a long time since I've looked at my collection. It's in a big red metal box, and I dial the combination into the lock —the month and the day it happened—and I open it up and look inside.

There's the class photo, all of us looking at the camera, me standing in between Cole and Andy. Cole looks nervous, Andy's got his eyes closed, and I'm grinning like a madman. It was taken before and sent home at the end of the year, when all the other classes got theirs. Mom said they shouldn't have sent it but they couldn't *not* send it. She put it in a pile on her desk, and I took it when she wasn't looking.

There's the comic book I was reading that day, and there's the little stone I took from the playground the one time they let us go back before they tore the school down.

And there is Cole's little face staring out at me from the cover of the *New York Times,* and the *Washington Post,* and *Newsweek* magazine, and *People,* and from *Rolling Stone* eight years later, when they did a special on gun control after that shooting at the mall in Wyoming.

I reach into my pocket and dig out the item I've taken from Mrs. Ryan's house. A little thing, taken from the closet in a room she never goes into. She wouldn't care. I feel guilty anyway, though it's hard to notice, because it's a little bit of guilt dropped into an ocean of it.

I set the chipped chess piece, a pawn, down on top of one of the magazines, and I close the box, lock it, and carefully put it away. I have to go to work at Finn's. I have to go and check on Paul; it's been weeks since I've seen him. I have to call Cole and thank him for the other day, for the orange juice on my bedside table. I have to come up with a plan B on the drugs for Eddie. I have lots of things to do.

Still, I don't move. I wait, though I don't know what I'm waiting for, other than for this summer to be over, for life to move on, and for me to find out whether I'm supposed to be a part of it or not.

Thirteen

— Cole —

Very few things rhyme with "Viola," especially if you don't want to reference crayons in your poetry. Not that you have to use a simple rhyme scheme; I'm just saying that it's not so easy. Still, I wrote fourteen complete poems about Viola before I got up the guts to talk to her. Now it's eight months later, and I'm on my second Viola notebook.

I have it with me when I walk into the diner late on a particularly hot Thursday afternoon. It's just past four, and I'm hoping to get about an hour of writing in, but the place isn't empty. Two of the booths alongside the windows — right where I want to sit to keep an eye across the street — are filled with kids from school. No one I know well, but all kids I know well enough, so I go and sit with them, sliding onto a seat next to Hazel Marberry, who gives me a big, sad smile. It's a known fact that Hazel wanted to go to the prom with me. My not taking her had nothing to do with her bad case of acne and everything to do with the fact that I simply wasn't going at all. I wanted to go with one person, and she was going with someone else (which everyone knew was just as friends), so I stayed home. I wasn't Hazel's first choice anyway, so I don't feel too bad. I was a supposedly safe second.

Across from me sit two guys, a kid named David and one whose name I forget but I know I had science with; and also a girl, Alex something, who I thought was cute sophomore year. The waitress comes over, and I order coffee and mozzarella sticks, then sit fiddling with my mug and looking out the window, wishing the diner had been empty so I could have sat in this booth alone, writing. I'm nervous, all keyed up, and I need to calm down. I can't do it at home, where I'm alone, but I also can't do it when I'm talking to other people, pretending to be interested in what they're saying. For some reason I'm able to relax when I'm writing out in public, around people but not having to interact with them. That's what I was looking for.

Instead, I'm listening to David talk about a party he went to last weekend in painful detail, acting like I wish I had been there when that's the last thing I would have wanted. Some of the kids in the next booth turn around and are listening as he's getting into the story, building it up so that it sounds like the most epic experience anyone could have had when it was probably a few dozen kids sitting around a basement drinking warm beer out of plastic cups. Predictably, he gets to the part where some of them were going outside to smoke and then someone had some pills. One of the kids in the booth behind him asks where they got them, and David says from Eddie. That's not a huge surprise;

everyone's known Eddie's been using since sixth grade and selling at least since eighth. He gets it from his two older brothers. There have been rumors about them for years, all about how they're tied in to some hardcore gang in New York or the mafia or something, how they were involved in killing someone and how if you bought from Eddie, you had to get him his money right on time, or else. Typical high school.

Eddie. I've tied my hopes up in a guy who barely graduated, whose claim to fame is that he can get you weed and pills and (rumor has it) coke on demand, a guy who spends his days flying the family balloons around fairs all over New Jersey and eastern Pennsylvania. True, he did seem to know what he was doing on our practice ride. I would have liked to take Viola up right after that if I could have, but Eddie couldn't make that happen. There needed to be a day when he was free, when one of the balloons wasn't in use, and when the fairground was empty. Not many days lined up like that over the summer, but one did, and it's tomorrow.

It's tomorrow, and I still haven't figured out how to make up the difference between what we've promised Eddie and what I have. Matt said he had a plan, but he's disappeared on me, hasn't answered any of my messages for days. I've got one more card to play, later on tonight. If that doesn't work, I'm going to be at Eddie's mercy.

I'm bobbing my head and nodding along to the story, ignoring Hazel watching me out of the corner of her eye. The waitress brings me more coffee and looks disappointed when I tell her I don't want anything besides the mozzarella sticks. David's story finally seems to be over, and the kid whose name I don't remember crunches some ice from his drink and turns his attention to me.

"What's going on with your boy Matt?" he asks.

"He's working a lot this summer. We hang out sometimes."

"I heard he's got something going on with a much older woman."

I shrug. "I don't know."

He looks over at David, who replies, "Sarah Jessup. Her dad was on the force." David's father is a police officer, although I think he's on disability now.

"The famous one, right?" the kid asks.

David nods importantly into his drink. "The one in the picture."

The guy who asked about the drugs is twisted around in his booth again, listening. "Are you telling me that Matt Simpson's boning the daughter of the cop who's carrying you in the picture?" he says to me.

The girl next to him and Hazel break into a chorus of giggles. I smile weakly and shrug.

The boy smirks and turns back to his table. Hazel and the no-name guy at our table are getting into something having to do with the sugar packets; one of them dumped sugar in the other's coffee, and now they're throwing the little packets back and forth across the table at each other and laughing. I wonder if they're together, and for some reason, I feel a surge of desire for

Hazel and jealousy of this guy. I could've gone out with her, and now I almost wish I did. Not taking her to prom felt like a matter of principle at the time, like I wasn't going to settle for less than what I wanted, like I was going to stay loyal to my love for Viola, but the reality is that I was spooked. The only thing I was staying loyal to was my loneliness.

I turn from the window and look over at the counter. Almost all the stools are empty now; just one of the cooks from the back is taking a break and watching the TV that's nestled in the corner by the ceiling. It didn't used to be there. I scan the failed House and Senate bills covering the walls, looking for any new ones, letting the moments slip by . . .

One moment leads inexorably into another, and most of them go by unnoticed, but some of them hurt more than you'd think they could. They fall away just the same way, though, regardless of their significance. There wasn't any change in camera angle at the moment my father died. Nothing went into slow motion. There wasn't a close-up on anyone's face; there wasn't a soundtrack; there wasn't anything to set it apart. It was just a moment that we were in together, and then there was another, without him in it with me.

A sugar packet strikes me right between the eyes. "Hewitt," the nameless kid says. "Mission control, come in." Hazel giggles and kicks him under the table.

I put my cup down. "What's up?" I ask.

"I said, what're you doing with yourself this summer?"

"I'm working at Finn's and taking it easy. You know. Nothing much. Might go away or something."

"You deferred, right?"

I nod. There isn't much to say about it. I take another sip of coffee as the table lapses into an awkward silence. I look out the window, and there she is, coming out fifteen minutes earlier than I thought she would. I finish the coffee in one gulp and get up from the booth, grabbing my backpack. I take a twenty from my pocket and toss it on the table and say goodbye, and then I'm out the door and hustling across the street.

She's wearing a black skirt and a matching jacket, a white blouse, and carrying a leather briefcase.

"Viola!"

She spins around. "Cole! What are you doing here?"

The horrible thought crosses my mind that she's meeting someone else. I imagine Conrad pulling up in some uber-expensive German sports car.

"I was just over at the diner, trying to catch up on my writing. Getting off work?"

"I am."

"You want a ride home?"

She looks me up and down. "I haven't see you in a while."

"Yeah, I've been super busy. So . . ." I nod toward my car, parked at the curb. I have this all planned out; I'll drive her home, and when I pull up to her house, I'll turn to her and ask her to meet me at the fairgrounds tomorrow at sunset.

"I was looking forward to walking. I've been inside all day."

"I'll walk with you." I shoulder my backpack, and we set off down the street together.

"Where have you been?" she asks.

Where have I been? I've been writing. Reading and writing, writing and reading, barely stopping. Shut up in my room with a mountain of laundry, piles of dirty dishes, and about three dozen library books. That's why writing at the diner seemed like an appealing way to wait for her this afternoon.

"Sorry," I say. "I've been tied up. Lots of hours at Finn's."

"I'd say so."

I've wanted to see her, for sure. But I want this poem to be perfect, the poem I'm planning to recite in the balloon. I've been reading the Romantics, Keats and Byron and Shelley, and Shakespeare's sonnets. I was blocked for a while, totally stuck, but now I think I have something really good.

We walk on, leaving the downtown. The heat from earlier today has backed off a little bit, and the sidewalk here is covered in shade. Viola stops by a telephone pole and leans against it as she reaches down to adjust a shoe.

"Men are lucky, Cole. These things are killing me. I don't understand shoes that aren't made for walking." She slides them off and stretches her toes.

"Let me carry your bag," I say.

"It's fine."

"Are your feet okay? There are acorns. Here, wear mine." Without thinking, I kick my sneakers off and push them toward her.

"I'm not going to wear your shoes, Cole. Are you saying I have big feet?"

"No, they're too big — the shoes, I mean, not your feet — but, you know, they're better than nothing. There might be broken glass."

"I'm fine." She continues on in bare feet. I scoop my shoes up and hurry to catch her.

"I love summer nights," I say. "Have you ever been out in a boat on a summer night?"

"Not that I can think of. Well, I had a friend who had a boat. His family used to take us out on the Thames, and I guess sometimes it was in the summer."

"I mean a little boat. Without a motor. So it's quiet."

"A rowboat?"

"Yeah."

"I tried to row a boat in Hyde Park once, but the oars were so heavy. They don't look like they are when someone strong is using them. I got out on the lake and couldn't get back in. My father had to rent a second boat and row out himself and tow me in. It was embarrassing. He wasn't happy."

"Was this recent?"

"No, I must have been, I don't know, maybe eleven or twelve."

"My father used to row us. Out at the lake. There's only one lifeguard boat there now, but when I was younger, there were two, and they used to let him take one of them. I guess they figured that the chances of two emergencies at once were pretty slim. It was like the one that's there now, this big wooden thing, and we'd flip it and slide it into the water. He'd let me help, though I wasn't really doing anything; it was so heavy. Then he'd row us up and down the lake, out into the middle. The oars were too heavy for me, too."

"Hmm." We're into a residential area now. She speeds up without looking at me, a bit too fast to have a conversation. "How far are you going to walk, Cole? Your car is back in town."

"I don't know. It's a nice evening."

"It is indeed." She sighs and looks up at the sky. "It's supposed to stay nice for a few days. Not too hot. I wish I was going to be here."

"Where are you going?"

"Plans changed. My parents. They never think to tell me, you know? Conrad and his family came early. They came today. We're flying up to Nantucket tomorrow."

"Tomorrow? You're leaving tomorrow?"

"I'm leaving tomorrow."

I stop walking.

"Cole?" She's stopped and turned.

I realize that I'm scanning the ground alongside the sidewalk, looking for something I recognize, a name I know. Just a flower, a weed, anything.

"Cole? What's the matter?"

"Don't go."

"What?"

"Don't go to Nantucket."

"What are you talking about?"

"Don't go tomorrow, at least. I want you to . . . I want you to meet me."

A pause, then, "Where do you want me to meet you, Cole?"

"Meet me at the fairground. You know the state fairgrounds? Meet me out there. Meet me at six thirty tomorrow night, just inside the gates . . ."

"Is there a, a fair or a carnival or something?"

"No."

"Then . . ."

"Just meet me there. Please."

"Cole . . ."

"I know, I know, it's crazy. I know you're supposed to go to Nantucket. I know Conrad has his plane, and your parents . . . I just, please. I want to show you something."

"What am I supposed to do, Cole? Just, what, tell my parents to go without me?"

"Why not?"

"Why not? *Why not?*"

"Yeah, why not?"

"*Why*, Cole? How about that? You tell *me* that. Why should I?"

"Because I have a surprise for you."

"Jesus Christ. You have a surprise for me?"

"Yes."

"You know what would have been a surprise, Cole? If you'd returned one of my texts. That would have been a surprise. If you'd given me a ride home from Matt's party, that would have been a surprise. If you'd sat with me and drunk a whole glass of lemonade, and maybe even read a poem or two, what a surprise *that* would have been!"

I stare at her, speechless. She goes on.

"I *was* surprised, Cole. I was surprised when you disappeared after you had been coming around, when it had seemed like you enjoyed spending time with me."

"I did . . . I do enjoy spending time with you."

"Then where have you been?"

I've been retreating.

"I've been writing a poem."

"You've been writing a poem?"

"For you. It's for you."

She shakes her head wearily. "The summer's over, Cole. I don't want a poem. I think it's too late for poems."

"Don't say that."

"I don't understand you. I don't understand you at all. All summer long, you've been, I don't know. You've been . . . hesitant."

272

"I know."

"I don't know what you want."

"I know."

"And now . . . it's the end of August, Cole. It's time for me to go."

"I know. I know. Just, please, tomorrow night."

"You hurt me, Cole. I liked you. You're someone special. I wanted you to be someone special for me."

"I'm sorry."

"You're not like anyone I've ever met. You . . . you know about flowers. Do you know, now when I walk Winnie, we always go down to that little stream we discovered?"

"You do?"

"We go and we look at the water, look at the flowers. I never knew that stream was there. All the times I walked by it."

I nod.

She shakes her head and looks away. "Everyone else in my life is going somewhere. You were different, and I liked that."

"You liked that I'm not going anywhere?"

"I liked that you are where you are now. You're not someplace else."

"So stay here with me. One more day. Meet me tomorrow night."

She shakes her head again. "I don't know."

I'm not going to say "please" again.

"Please."

"How do I know you're even going to be there? How do I know you're not going to be off somewhere, writing your damn poem?"

"The poem's done."

"I don't believe you'll be there."

"I'll be there," I say. "Six thirty. No matter what. I'll be there."

"I don't know how to tell my parents that I'm not going with them so that I can . . . what? Be surprised? Hear a poem?"

"You can get on that plane," I tell her. "You can fly off to Nantucket and to the rest of your life, but I promise you, I promise you that I will be there tomorrow night. Even if you won't. I will be there."

"Fuck you, Cole. That's not fair."

"I will be there."

"So, I get to fly away and think about you out on the fairgrounds, all by yourself? Fuck you."

I shake my head. I've got nothing else. "I'll be there. You don't have to feel bad if you're not. But I'll be there."

She turns away and continues on down the sidewalk, pausing to slip her shoes back on. She doesn't look back. When she gets to the end of the block, she turns the corner and I lose sight of her.

I start back toward town, still in my socks. A breeze is picking up now, and I close my eyes and let it wash over my face and hair, realizing that I'm sweating. There's a hollow feeling in the pit of my stomach. I finally stop when I pass a bench and sit to put my shoes back on. I'm not hurrying. I turn down a side street. My phone rings, and I snatch it from my pocket, wondering whether it might be Viola. It's not.

"Cole, baby."

"Hi, Mom."

"Where are you?"

"Just out, walking. Are you all right?"

"Of course I'm all right. I was just checking in with you. I'm heading out for the evening with a friend and there's nothing in the fridge for dinner, so you should grab something, or order in."

"Sure. Sure I will. Who are you going out with?"

"I'll leave some cash."

"Okay. I'll be fine. You're doing all right?"

"I'm good, Cole. Love you, baby."

"Love you, too."

I hang up and keep walking. At least I won't have to worry about her being at home, worrying about me.

I haven't been down this way in a really long time. I recognize some of the houses, and then I pass one with a little garden in the corner of the yard. It has a small fountain, a statue of an angel holding a seashell with water rising out of it. I know what this is. It's Susie Edwards's old house, and that's the fountain her mom put in after she died. It's where she had those weird posthumous birthday parties. I study it, the water rising up and then arcing down, still caught in the basin perfectly after all these years.

I'm standing here in front of Susie's old house, and something's building up inside me, something I haven't felt before. I don't even have a word for it. It's an anger, and a bitterness, and a need that I don't know what to do with. *This is what people are going to do with all those pills I'm giving Eddie*, I think. *All these people out there, feeling something like this. They're going to use the pills to make this feeling go away.*

I kick a golf ball–size stone that was sitting on the edge of the sidewalk. I used to play soccer. I wasn't very good, but the stone sails straight and true, bending through the air, straight into the fountain. The angel's head shatters, and a piece breaks off the seashell. The water is still coming out, but now it's spraying at an angle, landing in the bushes alongside the garden. A dog in a nearby yard begins to bark. I look at the house, but the windows are dark. There's no car in the driveway.

I step onto the lawn and examine the ruined fountain. There's no way to set the head back on the angel. It barely matters, I think. This town sprouts memorials like mushrooms. Everywhere you look, there's something. Still, this was just for Susie. I remember her mother's face when she laid the cakes down here. I wonder whether she still comes out on Susie's birthdays, by herself. I retreat to the sidewalk and continue on my way, telling myself that I'll mail her some money or something, even though I know I won't.

I get back to town without realizing it. I take a deep breath. My mind is clearing. My car is across the street, and I make my way over. It's past six, things are mostly closed, but not the pharmacy over in Wynnewood. Maybe Viola will be there tomorrow night. Maybe she won't. Most likely she'll be up in the air with Conrad, flying along the coast, heading to Nantucket. The chances of everything lining up, Viola and Matt and Eddie, everything clicking into place, seem incredibly remote. Still, I know one thing: I'll be there. I can't stop now. I may fail, but it won't be because I didn't show up.

I start the car and pull away from the curb, into the evening traffic.

Fourteen

— *Matt* —

Sarah took me back after the argument at the ball field. We didn't talk about it at all, just went on with what we had been doing. Meeting at her house, though I haven't been spending the night, and I'm less and less careful about where I park and about sneaking in the back. This evening I walk to her house after work and go right in the front door.

"Sarah?"

"Down in a minute."

I stroll into her empty, generic, undecorated living room. A moment later she comes down the stairs. "I didn't know you were coming tonight."

I shrug. She studies me in that way she does, like she's weighing her options. She's wearing jeans and a V-necked men's undershirt. She looks great. We sit on the couch, close to each other but not touching. I feel like there's nothing to talk about.

"How's packing?" she asks.

"Okay." The truth is that I haven't packed a thing. My mom has stacked boxes in my room, but they're all empty.

"Are you taking everything? All your stuff?"

"Not really. I mean, I'll still have my room at home. I'm not going to take my stuff from when I was a kid. Like, all my baseball trophies." She nods but doesn't say anything. "Have you ever thought about going back to school?" I ask. "Going to college?"

"No. Yes. Yes, I did. When I was a lot younger."

"Why didn't you?"

"Money, I guess. For one. Not really that, though. Dad didn't think much of the idea."

"Of college?"

"Of me and college."

"I think you could go to college."

"I guess I could. I thought about it. Not college so much as just leaving New Jersey."

"Where would you go?"

"Nebraska."

"That's a strange place to want to go."

"No stranger than anywhere else, I guess. No stranger than here."

I think back to what Lucas had to say about Officer Jessup. "What kind of guy tells his kid not to go to college?" I ask.

Sarah doesn't respond for a moment.

"My dad loved me."

"Sure."

"And I loved him. And I hated him."

"What was he like?"

"He was a cop. He was always a cop. Did your dad do dad-stuff with you? Play catch?"

Only for about a hundred thousand hours. "Yeah, I guess he did."

"My dad took me to a carnival once. Just once. Out at the fairgrounds. He bought a bunch of tickets and let me go on rides. He didn't come on with me, just watched me go on them by myself. He said the tickets would last longer that way."

"That's nice, I guess."

"It was the day my mom was leaving. They didn't tell me. He took me out, and when we got back, she was gone. She was gone, and all her stuff was gone."

"You ever see her?"

"No."

"And then it was just the two of you?"

"Yeah. And he was hard to be around. Off-duty, he was okay. Not really warm, but okay. But when he was in uniform, he was 'Officer Jessup.' Not 'Dad.' Never 'Dad.'"

"Literally, you had to call him Officer?"

She nods. "And he worked a lot. And the shooting happened, and he was in the photo. Everyone thought he was a hero. He was on TV and everything. Do you know that people wanted him to sign copies of that picture?"

I shake my head.

"I watched it all and thought: *If only you really knew him. The real him, what he's really like. You wouldn't think he was such a great police officer. You wouldn't think he was a hero.*"

"He's gone now."

"He's gone," she says, "but I'm not. He's gone because a blood vessel burst in his head. I didn't leave. I didn't do anything. If that hadn't happened, I'd still be living with him. I didn't decide anything about it."

She suddenly seems restless, picking at a seam on the couch, pushing herself away when I reach out to put a hand on her knee. "You want to go somewhere?"

"Sure." We haven't been out of her house since the ball field. "Where?"

She's quiet for a moment, and then she looks at me. "Show me where you live."

"Where I live? You want to see my house?"

She nods.

"All right."

My truck is at home, so we take her car. Neither one of us talks much on the drive over, other than me giving her directions. I'm tired, and I can tell she is too. It's like a blanket lying over us both. I stare out the window and watch the houses getting bigger as we get closer to mine, the cars in the driveways getting nicer.

"That's it, over there."

She pulls over and rolls to a stop across the street and a few houses down, looking out her window, the back of her head to me.

"It's nice."

My parents are having some sort of a party. There are a bunch of cars in the driveway and in front of the house. All the lights are on inside, and I can hear noise from the pool out back.

"Have you always lived here?"

"All my life." I wonder if she's going to want to go inside, meet my parents. I wonder if I should invite her in. We sit quietly as she watches the house. Then I lean over and kiss the side of her neck. She stiffens and pulls back. "What's wrong?" I ask.

"I don't know."

"It's all right," I say, even though it's not. I want her. I want to feel the way I did the first time with her. I want to feel like there's a future. I want to feel something.

She turns and looks me full in the face. "You know what I liked about you, Matt? You were my decision. My first real decision."

"Do you still like me?"

Instead of answering, she asks me a different question.

"If I were still me but I were your age, if we'd gone to high school together, do you think you would have liked me? Do you think we'd have been a couple?"

I imagine it, imagine her, a pretty eighteen-year-old, not particularly interested in baseball, not headed to college. Would I have liked her? Would I have noticed her?

"Sure," I say. "Yeah, sure we would."

She looks at me for a long moment, then shakes her head and turns back toward my house. Her voice is low and quiet when she speaks. "That first night, I told you something. I told you that I liked it when you were honest."

I don't say anything.

"I'm going to go home. By myself."

We sit for another few seconds, and then I get out of the car. I lean down and look at her through the open window. "Why did you want to come over here?"

Sarah stares back at me, then shrugs. "I just wanted to know what world you came from. I wanted to know where you were when you weren't with me."

She shifts into drive, and I step back as she pulls away from the curb. I watch her taillights as she turns the corner at the end of my street and disappears. Then I look at my house, across the street. The world I come from.

I don't want to go inside, but a white Lexus has my truck boxed in. I study the situation. It's too close for me to get out, even if I drive over the lawn. I walk around the side of the house to the pool, the sound of the party louder now. There are a bunch of middle-aged people standing around, drinking and talking, all of them thick and pleasant, smiling and nodding along to whatever bullshit the person next to them is saying. No one's in the water, of course. *Please don't ever let me be like these people,* I think. *Please let me die first.*

"Matt!"

Dad's spotted me.

"What are you doing over there in the shadows? Come on over."

He's standing with three other guys. I don't recognize them.

"Dad," I say as I walk over, "I —"

"Matt, this is Ken Murphy, Mark Sutter, and Christian Forrest." All three nod and raise their glasses. "This is my son, Matt. Matt's off to Bucknell next week."

"Your dad says you're a hell of a ballplayer," Ken — or possibly Mark; I've already forgotten — says.

I shrug and nod, looking at the empty pool.

"He is," Dad says. "Second base. He —"

"Who has the white Lexus?" I ask.

All four of them stare at me.

"The white Lexus," I say again, looking up from the water and studying them. Two of the guys shake their heads. The third takes a drink from his glass and looks away.

"Where's Mom?" I ask.

"In the house," Dad says quietly.

I turn without another word and make my way through the crowd, toward the patio door. There are more people inside. Mom is in the kitchen, drinking wine with Chris Thayer's mother.

"Hello, Matt!"

"Hi, Mom. Hi, Mrs. Thayer. Do you know—"

"I was just talking about you," Mrs. Thayer says. "How great you've been about taking Chris to PT. He's going to miss you."

"What are his plans for the fall?" I ask.

"Oh, he's very excited, but it doesn't surprise me that he hasn't said anything. He can be so modest. If you asked, he'd tell you about it, though. He has an internship. He worked very hard to set it up. He actually deferred the start of classes until the spring because they wanted him full-time . . ."

Mrs. Thayer goes on about Chris's plans, but I look around the room and tune her out. I can't imagine what kind of an internship Chris could do, and I'm happy that he can maybe take some classes, but the walls are closing in, and I need to get out of here.

"It sounds great," I tell Mrs. Thayer. "He's going to do great." I turn to Mom. "I need to go somewhere, and there's a white Lexus boxing me in."

"Not mine," Mrs. Thayer says with a smile. Mom scans the room. "The Penningtons have a Toyota, I think . . . No, I don't think it's anyone in here."

"All right." I manage to nod to Mrs. Thayer, and then I go back outside.

There's a breeze, and I realize I'm sweating when it hits my face. Chris wasn't being modest. I'm sure that, whatever he's got set up, he's embarrassed. He's just one more broken person I'll be leaving behind when I go. Like Sarah. Like Mrs. Maiden. Like Cole.

It's hard to breathe.

"Does anyone here," I shout, addressing everyone in the yard, "own a motherfucking white Lexus?"

All conversation stops. The crowd goes completely still. Then a small man in a beige suit nervously raises his hand. "Do you need me to move it?"

"Please."

My father grabs me by the arm and pulls me away, to the side of the house.

"What was that?" he hisses. "What the hell is the matter with you?"

"I need to go out."

He holds his glass to his head as if he's icing a headache. "Matt—"

"Charlie? Matt?"

Mom comes around the side of the house.

"What's going on?"

"Matt's having some sort of an episode and acting like an ass."

"Matt? How's your sugar?"

"Great, Mom. Perfect."

"Let's do a finger prick so we can calibrate your sensor . . ." She reaches for the glucometer she still keeps on her belt after all these years.

I think about offering her my middle finger for the blood sample but decide that would be too immature, even for me.

"Hey, Mom, there's something I've been thinking about. There's something I need to ask you."

She waits, glucose meter in her hand.

"Was I really so sick that day?"

"What? What day are you talking about, Matt?"

"Christ, *the* day! The only fucking day that's ever mattered!"

"Are you asking me about . . ." She trails off.

"I'm asking you about the day Sam Keeley shot more than half my class."

They both stare at me, speechless.

"I'm asking you whether I was really all that sick. Whether I really had to stay home that day."

"Matt," she finally whispers, "your blood sugar . . . you were so young, and your sugar could be labile . . ."

I shake my head and look out at the driveway, where the guy in the beige suit is climbing into the Lexus.

"I could have gone that day. I could have gone to school."

"Thank God you didn't—" Dad says.

I cut him off. "Do you know what time Chris Thayer's dad gets up?"

"What?"

"His mom, she works at night. Not tonight, obviously . . ."

"We know what she does, Matt. She works at the hospital . . ."

"Yeah, and his dad works for you, right?"

"Well, I'm not his direct supervisor . . ."

"So, do you know that, to, like, do whatever they have to do to get Chris ready in the morning, he has to get him up crazy early because she's asleep? Do you know what kind of insane bills they have to pay?"

"Did Chris tell you about this, Matt?"

"Chris doesn't talk to me about anything. I didn't know that he had a goddamn internship. That's the point; nobody knows. You think everything's fine, that he's this brave kid who's going on with his life. And then you go inside his house, and . . . or Cole; do you know what it's like inside Cole's house? I think they still have his dad's hospital bed in their living room, for Christ's sake!"

"Matt," Mom says, "we know it's hard. We know how hard it is for the Thayers. And Cole's mother—"

"Everyone wants to think it's okay. They put out some black chairs at graduation and have a moment of silence, and then everyone moves on. Except that they don't. No one ever gets to move on."

We stand still, in silence, staring at one another like strangers.

"I'm going out. I may not come back tonight."

"And where exactly are you going to be?" Mom asks.

"Cole's."

"Not until—" She stops as Dad lays a hand on her arm.

"Matt," he says, "we just want—"

"I'm sorry," I say. "I am. Tell your friends I'm sorry." I turn and walk to my truck. They watch me go, but they don't try to stop me as I drive away.

I wake to the sound of a mother scolding her children just outside my window. My seat is reclined, and I have to crane my neck to look up. Sunlight is streaming in through the windows. The clock on the dashboard tells me it's 11:02.

I slowly raise my seat, wincing as I move. The mother is right outside my window; she's parked there to share the shade, obviously thinking my car was empty, and now she turns from her efforts to apply sunblock to two writhing children and sees me. I look back at her and nod. She shakes her head in disapproval and turns away, shooing the children toward the beach.

I tilt the rearview mirror so I can see myself. I'm unshaven, my eyes are bloodshot, and my hair is a mess. I try to run my fingers through it, give up, and look around. An empty bottle of vodka is on the floor on the passenger side. I stopped by Luther's house after I left my parents. He's always good for it, no questions asked. There are also three granola-bar wrappers and an empty bag of Skittles I'd been keeping in the glove box for an emergency. My sugar must have plunged at some point.

How much did I drink? How long did I sit here, trying to work up the nerve to go for another swim?

My mouth is dry, but I don't have any water. The Snack Shack should be open now, but I was due at Finn's an hour and a half ago, so I turn the car on and start driving. Finn is always understanding; he won't mind. Even though I'm late, I keep to the speed limit, scanning the sides of the road and the rearview mirror, looking for a cruiser, feeling like a pussy. I want to blow into town at eighty miles an hour and tell Lucas and the rest of the police force to go fuck themselves.

I pull into my space behind the store and slip in the back. It sounds quiet out front. It's always quiet. Finn should accept that the Stop & Shop's in town, sell for whatever he can get, and then get out. Go live on an island somewhere. He must be sixty, maybe sixty-five. I'm taking my apron down off the peg and looking forward to a drink of water when I hear his voice behind me.

"What the hell is this?"

I turn. Finn is standing in the doorway, a rolled-up newspaper in his hand. For a crazy moment, I think the old man is going to swat me with it.

"Where have you been?" he asks.

"I'm sorry Mr. Finn . . . I just, had a hard night."

"It's past eleven o'clock, and you're coming in here looking like this."

I look down. I'm in the same clothes I had on when I was in yesterday afternoon, a drink stain on the front of my shirt. "I'm sorry . . . This is the first time this has happened."

"First and last time, Matt. I'm running a business here. I understand that with your family you might not need the money, but this is how I put bread on my table. I've been running back and forth between the register and stocking the shelves. We have produce that's going to go bad back here."

That stings. I have the impulse to ask him exactly how many times he's had to dash to the register this morning. I'm guessing probably two, for geriatric customers who would have waited all day to be rung up.

"I'll get to work right now."

"Not looking like that, you won't. This store has an image to maintain. It's what sets us apart from that box out on Route 21. I'm not going to have you here looking and smelling like you spent the night in a dumpster. You have a sick day. Your only one. Go home; come back tomorrow cleaned up and on time. I'll call Cole; he wants extra hours." Finn turns and leaves the stockroom.

I hang the apron back up and go out to my truck. Five minutes later, I'm parking outside the Gerbers' house.

Mrs. Gerber answers the door. She looks flustered. "Matt, we weren't expecting you."

"I got the day off from the store. I thought Paul might want to do something."

She looks me up and down. "That's so sweet of you. I'm sure he would. He does. I'm just helping him out with something upstairs. He's having a hard moment."

"I can wait."

She grimaces. "Well—"

"Who's there?" Mr. Gerber's voice comes from deep within the house.

She pauses. "It's Matt Simpson, honey."

"Matt! Send that boy in here!"

Mrs. Gerber sighs and steps to the side. I enter the house and make my way into the den. Mr. Gerber is sitting in the same chair he had been in when I arrived on that first morning, early in the summer. Same robe, too, though now it's the middle of a workday rather than Saturday morning, and he has a day or possibly two days of beard on his face, and the newspaper sits to the side of his chair as he stares into the coffee cup on his lap. He fumbles to lower the feet on the recliner as I come in.

"Matt, my boy, come and sit down."

The room is less neat than when I was last here, and I have to sit at the end of a couch, closer to Mr. Gerber than I'd like. From here I can see that his eyes are red-rimmed, and I can smell that the drink in the mug isn't coffee.

"You're here to see Paul again?"

"Yes. I thought I would take him out."

"Hmm. He was out of sorts after the last time. But perhaps that's normal. I think you may remind him of his brother."

"I don't have to take him if you don't want me to."

"No, it's fine. It's good for him to go out. It's good for Ruth and me to have some time. We can't avoid these issues forever, can we?"

We sit quietly for a moment as Mr. Gerber sips from the mug.

I want to get up, get Paul, and leave the house, but before I move, he starts in again.

"Matt, there's something I've always wanted to ask you."

Don't ask me about the shooting, I think. *Please don't ask me a question I can't answer.*

"Do you mind? Do you have a moment?"

It's probably not about that. He probably wants to talk baseball. I nod.

"Matt, where were you sitting on the morning when it happened?"

Whatever limited air was available goes out of the room.

"I wasn't there, Mr. Gerber."

"What do you mean, you weren't there?"

"I was in that class, but I was home that day. I was home, sick."

"Sick? Sick with what?"

What a bizarre question. "It was my diabetes. My mom was worried about my sugars."

He shakes his head. "Unbelievable. I'd always thought . . . well. I suppose I must have known that once, mustn't I? It's funny what the mind remembers and what it forgets."

The smell. Not Mr. Gerber's liquor, something else. Something less familiar. I put a hand over my mouth and nose, but it doesn't help.

"Didn't you usually sit next to Andy, Matt?"

"Yes. Or Cole."

"Where do you think Andy would have been sitting?"

"It would have depended—it depended on the activity, on when it was . . ."

"Eleven thirty-two."

"I'm not sure, Mr. Gerber. I'm sorry."

Mr. Gerber leans back in his recliner and sips again. His eyes leave my face and unfocus, scanning the middle distance in front of him.

"Maybe I should go check on Paul?" I say.

Neither of us moves. Mrs. Gerber's voice rises from upstairs. It sounds like she's helping Paul in the bathroom.

"Do you know that Paul should have been in that class?" Mr. Gerber asks.

"No."

"Well, of course he should have been. He would have been there, but the school insisted on putting him into a special-needs classroom. We didn't want them to do it, but we finally gave in that winter and let them move him. He would have been sitting there, next to Andy."

Just like with Sarah, I don't know what to say. I never know what to say. What's the point of these fucking conversations, these memories that can't be changed, these things that can never be fixed?

"They had all these counselors around afterward," Mr. Gerber continues. "They did some groups that people went to, special ones for us parents who had lost a child. People wrote things, a few people were interviewed for the *Times,* and then later on, that asshole wrote his memoir. I didn't pay much attention, but I know what they said. They said, 'We didn't know. We didn't know that we had it so good. We didn't know how fragile it all was. We didn't know that it could come apart in an instant.'" He takes another sip from his mug, more of a gulp this time. "Can I tell you something, Matt?"

I nod because I can't think of what else to do.

"I knew." He leans in toward me, elbows on his knees. "Every moment I had those two little boys, I knew exactly how much I loved them and I knew exactly how fragile they were. And it bought me nothing. I had to suffer the loss along with all the ones who didn't know, who didn't appreciate what they had. I had to be taught a lesson that I already knew. Knowing didn't change anything. I had to live through that moment anyway, and I've had to live through every moment after."

He drains the rest of his mug, sets it down on the coffee table, and rises unsteadily to his feet. "Paulie!" he yells. "Get the hell down here! Matt's going to take you out! You want to sit around in your dirty underwear all day?" He burps and makes his way around the table and out of the room, fumbling to tie his bathrobe.

I sit alone, rubbing my face. I can't stand the smell. I sniff my own shirt and then look around. There's the mug, but it's not the smell of liquor. It's getting deep into my throat, almost burning me. I stand, turn one way and then the other, and make my way over to the window, pulling hard to open it and then stooping to stick my head all the way out. The breeze is a relief on my face, and I take it in deeply through my nose, afraid that I might vomit.

"Matt?"

I reluctantly duck back inside.

"What are you doing? Are you all right?" Mrs. Gerber asks.

"Do you smell that?"

"Smell what?" Her nostrils flare.

"That . . . I can't describe it." It's almost like pee. "Do you have a dog?"

She shakes her head. "Do you want to go home, Matt? You look like you could use some rest."

"I'm okay."

She seems to have her doubts, but she also looks desperate to get Paul out of the house, and so ten minutes later, we're driving away in the Explorer, and a few minutes after that, we are standing in a roadside park that I've driven by a thousand times without stopping at. It's on the way to the lake, but I don't want to go back there, and I can't think of anyplace else to go.

We wander, side by side, through rusted teeter-totters and swings with broken seats. It seems like the town has upgraded most of its playgrounds, but for some reason this one's been allowed to fall apart. I sit on the only working swing and push myself back, bracing my legs, looking down at a patch of dry dirt where who-knows-how-many kids dragged their feet when their mothers told them it was time to go home. I look around; the parking lot, my car the only one in it, lies across a small field, and on the other side are the woods and, somewhere beyond that, the river. Paul shuffles through a patch of dandelions. A car goes by on the road, and then it's quiet again. I close my eyes. It's better here; the air is cleaner. It's still. It has the feeling of a place whose time is past.

"Paul?"

Paul kicks at a dandelion head and doesn't respond.

"Do you remember what Andy used to say?" I ask. "That thing he used to say, whenever we went anywhere or did anything? He'd shout it like he was a superhero. It was from a movie."

Paul is standing still. He rarely makes eye contact, but he is coming close to it now, studying my lips.

"I had forgotten for a while, but I remembered last night. He used to shout, 'To infinity . . . and beyond!' Do you remember that?"

"To . . ." Paul trails off.

"That's right, 'To infinity . . . and beyond!'"

Paul frowns.

"I want you to say it," I tell him. "Try to say the whole thing." I repeat the phrase again, slowly, with emphasis.

"To . . . inf . . ." The four syllables aren't coming together in his mouth.

"Say it, Paul. I want to hear you say it one time. Shout it!"

He finally raises his eyes to mine and shakes his head no.

"Andy used to say it all the time. It was from an old movie.

We thought it was the funniest thing, the way he'd say it and then jump off his bed or run out of the room, pretending he had a cape on."

I don't know why I need to hear Paul say it, but I do. Maybe it's like Chris needing to hear my stories about Rosie. Maybe we're all stuck obsessing over the things we can't have, the experiences we can't go into, as though looking and hearing and thinking about them will help the pain of wanting.

There's a moment of silence as we stare at each other. I push myself farther back on the swing with one toe, gripping the chains with both hands.

This isn't going to help.

"I want to hear you say it, Paul. Say it like Andy said it."

"I can't."

I stare at him for a moment, and then I laugh. I don't mean to. I'm not laughing at him. I'm laughing at myself, at the situation, at the whole goddamned world around us, but looking at Paul, I know he thinks that I'm laughing at him, and that even if I try to explain it, he'll never understand, which is almost as bad as laughing in the first place.

He turns and walks away from me, and I let him go. I'll let him have his space for a minute. There's no one else here; he can't get into any trouble.

I lift my foot and allow myself to swing forward, bending my knees so that I don't hit the ground, up and then back and then forward again, swinging by myself in the late summer heat.

Fifteen

— Cole —

Last night was a busy one at the pharmacy, and there was a long line of people snaking all the way back through eyewear and family planning. I took my spot at the end of it, next to a colorful display of Trojans, which made me think about the still-unsolved mystery of the condoms under the couch. I looked past the people in front of me and spotted Kiernan, hustling behind the counter, along with another pharmacist. I didn't like the look of her; she looked like someone who took her job seriously and would phone in any irregularities just because she was supposed to.

I finally made it to the front of the line, and the woman waved me forward. I turned around and looked at the guy behind me, who was holding an obviously sick toddler in his arms. "Go ahead," I said with a smile.

"Oh, God, thank you," the man said as he carried the kid up to the counter, where the lady pharmacist looked back at me and smiled in appreciation as well. I felt awful. Doing good things for the wrong reason is worse than not doing them at all. Then Kiernan was free, and he beckoned me up to his window. I dug the remaining prescriptions out of my pocket as I approached.

"Hey," I said. "Listen, I was in a while ago with some prescriptions for my dad, and—"

"Yeah, I remember you." The guy's face and voice were both flat. He was staring right at me.

"Yeah. Right, so I was just wondering—"

"Are those more prescriptions?"

"Yeah."

"For your dad?"

"Yeah."

"Right. So, listen, I think that you ought to leave."

"Please, is there anything you can do?"

Kiernan's eyes darted to his left, down the counter toward the lady pharmacist, and he leaned close to me and whispered, "Listen, asshole, do you know how much trouble I was in over those pills I gave you? I could have lost my job."

"I'm really sorry, I just—"

"Are you some sort of a moron? Why would you come back here? There are, like, a dozen pharmacies in a ten-mile radius."

"Yeah, I just thought that you—"

"Me? You thought I would hook you up?" He was still whispering, but the lady leaned back and looked down the counter at us, and he shut up.

I should have just gone, but I was desperate. I knew it was my last chance.

"Is there anything I can do to make this happen?" I asked him.

He burst out laughing, no pretense of secrecy at all. Then he looked back over my shoulder at the growing line and called "Next!" I felt my face flush hot and bright as an elderly man made his way to my side. Kiernan looked at me one more time and leaned over the counter. "Dude," he said, "you are, honest to god, the world's worst dealer, second to none."

That was it, right there. Absolute truth. He was right; there are lots of other pharmacies around, but he was also right about me not knowing what I was doing.

So I went home. I hardly slept at all, though. I couldn't read, I couldn't write, though I tried. I lay in bed, thinking about Viola flying over the ocean, Conrad beside her, tall and handsome, one hand on the controls and the other on her knee. I thought about Matt, shacked up with Sarah Jessup somewhere, fucking her brains out. I lay in bed, rehearsing the poem I'd written for the thousandth time. I lay in bed, hating my best friend, hating my life, burning up inside.

I finally dozed off, fully dressed and on top of my covers, and now I'm waking up and it's already past noon. It takes me a moment to realize that my phone is ringing. I fumble for it and hold it to my ear.

"Cole?"

"Hi, Mrs. Simpson."

"How are you?"

"I'm fine."

"I was just calling to check in on Matt."

My eyes dart around the empty room. "He's . . . fine."

"He hasn't been answering his phone."

"Yeah. Uh, he's asleep. His phone must be on silent."

"Good. Good. I know he was having a hard time last night. How's his—"

"Fine. His phone says ninety-eight."

Silence for a second. "Thank you for being there for him, Cole."

"It's not a problem."

"Tell him to check in with us soon."

"I will."

I say goodbye and hang up. Then I call Matt, but it goes to his voicemail. I need to find him, find out if he has anything for me to give Eddie tonight, the way he said he would. The way he's been saying all summer, telling me not to worry about it, telling me to trust him.

I wash up, change, check on Mom—her door's closed—and then I go out, get in my car, and start driving. Matt's supposed to be at work. He probably spent the night with Sarah and let the battery on his phone run down.

I'm almost at the grocery store when my phone rings.

"Cole, it's Mr. Finn. How are you?"

"Fine . . ."

"Listen, Cole, Matt wasn't feeling well today and I sent him home. I have an appointment later on this afternoon and could really use the help. How do you feel about some extra hours?"

"Matt isn't there?" I pull the car over to the side of the road. I can see Finn's sign maybe a hundred yards farther on.

"It seemed like he'd had a long night. Cole? Are you there?"

"I'm here, Mr. Finn, but I'm sorry, I can't come in. I . . . have an appointment too."

"All right. Give me a call if anything changes. I may have to close the store early today."

"I'm sorry, Mr. Finn."

"That's all right. I'll see you tomorrow."

I hang up, make a U-turn, and drive back the way I came. I know where Sarah Jessup lives and I go by her house, but her driveway is empty. Maybe they went somewhere for the day? Could they be at the lake? I start to drive in that direction, but before I get there, I spot his truck in a parking lot off Route 21. I pull in beside it and there he is, swinging by himself across an empty field. I kill the engine and get out of the car.

He's all alone, looking up at the sky, pumping his legs to make himself go higher, like he's a little kid who was forgotten here by his parents but who isn't too worried about the situation. I stop in front of him, and he looks at me but doesn't stop.

It's very quiet; the only sound is the *squeak-squeak* of the chains on his swing.

"Do you know," I ask, "what a tremendous asshole you are?"

He keeps swinging and doesn't answer right away. "What's the matter, Cole?" he finally asks. He's infuriatingly calm.

"Do you know what time it is?"

"Yeah. So?"

"I have five hours. Five hours until I'm supposed to meet Eddie."

"I know."

"And?"

He grins. "And, I have something for you." Matt jumps off of the swing, lands in mid-stride, and is off toward the parking lot. "Come on!" I follow him to his truck. He opens the door, reaches into the glove compartment, and comes out with a bag that is full—and I mean full—of pills.

"Where did you get this?"

"Don't worry about it."

"What is it all?"

"It's the good stuff." He looks at me and laughs again. "You are one crazy son of a bitch, Cole. I thought you were going to hit me!"

"Well, I thought you'd—"

"What, you thought I'd forgotten about you?" He hands me the bag. I gently squeeze it, feeling the sheer mass. There are pills of all different shapes and sizes. Little square brown ones, and oval blue, and circular pink. It's beautiful. Put together with the bit I have left in the freezer, it's not quite enough to be half, given what we already turned over to Eddie, but it's a lot. It should be enough.

"You look disappointed," Matt says.

"Disappointed? No. Just . . ."

"You know what I think?" he asks.

"What?"

"I think you were kind of hoping that this was going to fall through."

I look at the bag and don't say anything. It's not the kind of psychological insight Matt is prone to, but I can't deny that it's true.

"She's probably not going to be there, anyway," I say. "She's probably already gone. Her family decided to leave for vacation early. She's probably, you know. Gone."

Matt shrugs. "Maybe," he says. "Maybe she is. And maybe she's going to be there tonight, you know? I mean, who the hell knows? Just do one thing. Do one thing for me."

"What's that?"

He puts one hand on my shoulder. "You gotta show up."

"Yeah. I know. I told her I'd be there, no matter what."

"No, promise me."

"I will. I just said it. I will."

"No, I mean: Show. The. Fuck. Up. Like, all the way."

I look back at him. His eyes are red all around the edges, like he hasn't slept much. "I'll be there. I'll show up."

"All the way."

"All the way," I say, half understanding what he means but wanting him to let go of my shoulder.

"Good." He seems pleased. He leans back against his truck and shuts his eyes. I look around the empty playground.

"You know, you probably shouldn't be calling me crazy," I say. "You're the one playing on the swings in an old park all by yourself."

"I'm not by myself. I've got Paul with me."

"Where?"

He opens his eyes and scans the field and the edge of the tree line, a confused look on his face. "I spaced out for a second. I thought he was just walking."

Paul is nowhere to be seen.

"He was going that way," Matt says, pointing toward the woods. "I didn't think he'd actually walk off."

"Christ, Matt, I don't think he can *be* off by himself—the river's that way."

Matt takes two steps toward the woods.

"We should call the police," I say. He spins back around.

"No. No, we—we can find him. He's probably just a few steps into the woods. And there's no reception out here anyway, and . . . come on."

Without saying anything else, we run side by side across the field and into the trees. There's a little trail, and we follow it. It's silent, and it's immediately cooler. I call Paul's name once, but I don't hear anything back. I'm not sure he would answer.

306

"When did he walk off?" I finally ask. I want to ask what the two of them were doing in the park to begin with, but that can wait until later. Matt stops walking and gets that confused look again.

"I don't know. What time is it?"

"Almost two."

"I'm losing track of time."

"You look like shit." He does. His shirt doesn't look clean; his hair is messed up; one of his shoes is untied. He smells of BO, too. "What time did you get here?"

"Maybe one?"

"So he could have been gone for an hour?"

"Not that much . . . maybe forty-five minutes, though."

"Jesus." I look around. There's more land here than I thought. The woods stretch as far as I can see to our right and to our left. The playground is behind us, and the river is not far ahead. We're near a fork in the path. "We'll split up. You go that way, and I'll go this. Yell if you find him." Matt nods and, without another word, takes the branch I'd indicated. I set off in the other direction.

I tried to be friends with Paul after the shooting. He didn't have anyone after Andy was gone. He was in a different classroom, but I'd see him at recess sometimes, walking the lines on the basketball court, sometimes wandering into other kids' games and getting yelled at. He didn't seem to fit in anywhere. He just seemed a little bit forgotten.

I tried to play with him. I remember doing it; I tried to get him to play foursquare once, but he couldn't. I told my parents we should have him over to play, but they kind of looked at each other funny, and it never happened.

So I walked with him. All around, at recess. We'd go up one side of the basketball court and down the other, and even when he'd want to walk down the line in the middle and I knew we'd get yelled at, I went with him. We never talked. He never even acted like he knew I was there. I just walked beside him, around and around, all recess long.

But we stopped having recess together in the third grade. I don't know why, we just saw less of the kids in that special class-room, and I don't want to say that I forgot about Paul, but time went on and other things happened, and by the time middle school came around, I hardly ever saw him. When his parents asked me to help him line up at graduation, I wasn't sure he even knew who I was.

The woods have grown in close to the path on either side of me now. I don't see any sign of him, anywhere. I stop for a moment and listen; I can't imagine that he's moving that quietly, but it's silent, barely any noise from the animals and the distant rush of water from the river.

And then I do hear something.

It's behind me. The snap of a twig, and somehow there's no question in my mind that it's a footstep. I spin around, but I don't see anyone.

"Paul?"

Silence. Nothing stirs.

"Matt?"

Nothing.

I take a few steps back the way I came, the hairs on my arms standing on end, scanning the trees and the bushes.

There's no sound, no movement, but something is telling me that I want to go in the other direction, an urge so strong that I've taken a few steps backwards before I know what I'm doing.

This is crazy; I'm stressed and sleep-deprived and acting like a baby. There's no one out here other than Matt and Paul and me. I turn and walk quickly away, glancing back over my shoulder, still seeing nothing.

The river grows louder, and after another minute, I come around a bend and am standing on the bank, looking out at the water. There are rocks but they're not too big, and I can see everything, the rocky shore and the far side with a weeping willow and more woods. I dimly remember that this is some sort of preserve that's attached to the land around the lake. I scan the water, imagining Paul floating there, drifting in the shallows, his hair fanned out around his head, and the police coming, and then someone having to go to the Gerbers' house and tell them that their other son is dead.

He's not here. I turn and go back into the woods.

It's not much farther along that I find him. There's a spot where the trees break on the side of the path and you can step off, almost into a tunnel, and I think it looks like just the sort of little path that someone looking to hide would want to go down. And I'm right. He's there, in a small clearing, sitting on a fallen tree trunk. He has his T-shirt off, and he's holding it in both hands, twisting it and untwisting it like a towel he's about to whip someone with. His naked torso is very white. He's crying.

I step into the clearing. "Hey, Paul," I say. "Are you . . . okay?"

He doesn't respond. I sit down on the log and let the minutes slip by. There are so many things I could tell him, questions I'd like to ask, but I don't know if it's the right thing to do. I don't know if it would make the situation worse. What is there to say, anyway? To him, to anyone? What's left, after all these years, after everything there is to be said has been said? I don't say anything.

Maybe just sitting together is enough, though. Paul slowly stops crying and clenching the shirt, and after a few minutes, we hear Matt calling for us.

"We should go," I tell him.

We both stand and make our way back down the little tunnel. I look back at him just before we come out onto the main path.

"I miss your brother."

Paul nods, so quickly that I almost don't see. He doesn't look at me, but as we walk toward the sound of Matt's voice, his shoulder presses against mine, just for a moment. He probably stumbled over a tree root or something, probably didn't mean to touch me. But I choose to believe that he did.

Sixteen

— Matt —

BLT, no mayo; caesar salad with dressing on the side; onion rings. I'm not an imaginative eater.

I'm standing in front of the counter at the steakhouse, waiting for the same takeout order I always get. They're busy, even though it's early, barely past five. I check the time again. Cole has less than an hour and a half until his date with destiny.

It took a while to get Paul settled and to get his shirt back on, and then we took him to the diner and bought him something to eat and tried to get him to wash up in the bathroom. He went in and came back out looking just as bad, so Cole went in and must have washed his face for him, because he did look a little better afterward. I wouldn't have done that, wash another person's face, but that sort of thing seems to come naturally for Cole.

I took Paul home by myself. By the time we got there, he was calm enough; his shirt was dirty, but I told Mrs. Gerber that we'd been to the park, and she didn't seem to mind. I didn't see Mr. Gerber there. His car wasn't outside, and it occurred to me that he probably wasn't in any shape to drive, but there were only so many things I could worry about at once, so I said goodbye to Paul and his mother. Then I went out and drove around until I finally got hungry and came here.

The restaurant is in an old, sprawling house. I'm just inside the front door; there's a dining area ahead of me, and off to the left, there's another room with a bar. I stare at the menu on the counter, looking at all the things I never order. Then there's a voice from right behind me, and I jump.

"Mr. Simpson."

It's Officer Lucas. I never heard him coming. He's out of uniform, wearing jeans and a plain red T-shirt that's incredibly free of wrinkles, like he actually ironed it. He's holding a glass of beer and he's smiling at me, though not with his eyes.

"Officer."

"It's nice to see you again," he says. I nod. "Picking up dinner?"

"Yes."

"For you and your friend?"

"No, just for . . . What friend?"

"The good Mr. Hewitt. Maybe you'd like me to deliver it for you? Save you the trip."

I study his face. His cheeks are flushed. This probably isn't the first drink he's had. "What are you talking about?" I finally ask him.

"I'm going to have to have a talk with Mr. Hewitt. A long talk.

He seems a little jumpy, though. I'm worried that it's going to be tough for him. He actually seemed more than a little jumpy today in the woods."

The words I'd been about to say get stuck in my throat, and I stare at him with my mouth wide open. He laughs without trying to hide it.

"That was quite a large bag of pills you gave him. I assume that Mr. Hewitt is still in possession of them, were he to be pulled over while driving this evening?"

"What . . . the . . . fuck are you talking about?" I finally manage.

"Watch your language, Matthew. You're speaking to a police officer, even if I am out of uniform."

"Listen, Lucas—"

"*Officer* Lucas."

"Listen to me, dammit—"

He shakes his head. "No, *you* listen to *me*. I warned you. Several times, I warned you. And still, I've seen you at her house. You don't seem to understand, but I think I know how to get your attention. Cole Hewitt and I are going to be spending some quality time together, very soon." He pats my shoulder. "Have a good night, Matthew. Keep your phone on. We'll let him make a call, as long as he behaves himself."

Lucas turns on his heel and retreats to the bar while the words crowd into my throat and stick there.

"Sir, your order is ready."

I don't turn toward the counter, just take one step and then another toward the doorway Lucas disappeared through.

"Sir?"

Every possible thought I could be having is blotted out of my brain by one image: Lucas, creeping through the woods, following Cole. Cole, defenseless, alone. Me, not there to protect him. Again.

I follow him into the bar.

There's about a half dozen of them, three in casual clothes and the rest in suits, some seated and some standing, all of them talking loudly with one another. Lucas is by far the youngest. Even though it's not a big room, there are two TVs above the rows of bottles on the far wall, playing two different ball games. The bartender looks up at me and frowns in disapproval. He knows that I'm not twenty-one.

I step to the center of the room and speak slowly and deliberately, loud enough for everyone to hear me over the sound of the TV.

"Did you really think that you were ever going to be the guy?"

A few of the other men stop talking and turn, following the bartender's gaze. Officer Lucas is seated on a stool in the center of it all, a fresh glass of beer in his hand.

"I'm talking to you, Lucas."

He looks up in surprise, sets his glass down on the bar, and stands up while keeping his eyes on me. He's not that big. I can handle him.

"You were never going to be the one," I continue, keeping my voice steady. "You were never going to be able to give her what she needs, so you try to scare off anybody who can. It's pathetic. How long have you been following her around, hoping she'll notice you?"

He takes a single step toward me, his eyes locked on mine.

"She does notice, Lucas. She notices that you're just like her dad. You're the opposite of what she needs, another cop who wants to tell her how to live her life. And she's way too smart to wind up with you."

Lucas laughs and shakes his head. "You're such a little cock-sucker, Simpson. Why don't you go on back to your daddy's house? Maybe take a dip in that big pool to cool yourself off."

One of the men behind Lucas steps forward, spreading his hands. He's older, with gray hair and a mustache, dressed in khakis and a starched button-down shirt and blazer. "Gentlemen . . ." he begins. I look right past him.

"You know about a lot of things," I say. "You know all about my house and my friend, and you know where I work and what I drive. But you want to hear about the one thing you don't know? The thing I know all about and you *never* will?"

The bar is completely silent except for the sound of the announcer, droning on about the Mets' September call-ups.

"You want me to tell you what it's like with her, Lucas? I know you think about it all the time. Because it's nuts, dude. I've seriously got scratch marks all up and down my back. You should fucking hear her." Even as I'm saying it, I know it's an incredibly shitty thing to do to Sarah, but I see his eyes widen and his face turn red, and I can't stop. "She always likes it on the living room floor, Lucas. You should get up on your tiptoes and peek in the window sometime when she's on top—"

I don't get to finish the sentence. Lucas is on me, moving incredibly quickly, too fast for me to even get a hand up. He cuts around the older guy, and I'm on the ground before I know it; he drives me down and I can feel the floorboards shudder as I hit them. My head snaps back, and there's a burst of light in front of my eyes. He's on top of me, his knee grinding into my groin, a flurry of punches to my chest and face.

There's shouting and the crash of barstools, a voice bellowing above the others, which I somehow know is the bartender. I don't know where my hands are, can't even begin to put together a defense, and I know it wouldn't do me any good even if I could, because I wouldn't be able to deploy it against this force of nature. I try to bend my neck and look up; Lucas is straddling me, and I catch a glimpse of his face, twisted in anger, a semicircle of people behind him, and the game on the TV screen above his head, the Mets coming up to bat. And then his fist drives into my nose and my head snaps back again, and the last thing I think is that I'm going to throw up here on my back and that I'll drown in my own vomit and that Cole would remind me, if he were here, that I'm nauseated, not nauseous.

And then everything turns to black.

I'm vaguely aware of someone pulling me to my feet and pushing me toward the door; an arm around my waist; leaning over onto whoever's supporting me; smelling cologne and hair gel. The night air, "Steady there" whispered in my ear, and then I'm stumbling down the steps. A hand on the back of my head, guiding me, and then I'm sitting, and slumping to one side, and my eyes close.

I open them, and I'm in the back of a car, lying on a bench seat. It's vinyl and smells of plastic and antiseptic spray, clean and anonymous, comforting somehow. Like if I bleed on it, which I already have, it will be all right.

I push myself to a sitting position, feel like I'm going to puke, and lie down again. My shirt is stained with blood, but it doesn't look like there is anything else, so maybe I didn't throw up after all.

I know about head injuries from our mandatory concussion training. They create a blank period when your brain stops making new memories, and the longer the blank, the worse your brain's been banged up. The trainer who gave the presentation said that he'd landed on his head coming off a ski jump; the last thing he remembered was breakfast, and then the next thing was two days later in the hospital. "An amnestic period of fifty-two hours," he'd said. He sounded proud, and we were all impressed.

I'm thinking that my brain is probably okay, because I remember everything: Lucas pulling his fist back for the final shot into my face, the men behind him, even who was coming up to bat on the TV. It's all crystal clear, right up until it goes black. And now here I am, in this car.

It's some sort of police vehicle. There's thick plastic and mesh between the back seat and the front, and grills in the side windows. I panic for a moment and wonder whether Lucas has me in his patrol car. No, that's ridiculous. The other cops wouldn't let him carry a bleeding, unconscious kid out of a bar and drive off with him. The car isn't moving, anyway.

Man, I correct myself. *I'm a man, not a kid.*

There's a knock on the glass above my head, and I look up. A man who is not Lucas is looking in the window. I sit up again and wipe my nose. He opens the door, studies the seat, and then gets in and pulls the door most of the way shut behind him. It's the older guy from the bar, the one with the mustache.

"Matthew."

I lean against the door on my right to steady myself. I look down. There's a handle, but of course it wouldn't open from the inside.

"I'm Jerry DeLong. I'm the chief of police."

I nod. I know the name, and now I recognize the face.

"How are you feeling?"

"I'm all right."

"Of course you are." The chief chuckles. He reaches into the inside pocket of his blazer and produces a pen-size flashlight. "Look at me." I do as he says. The chief shines the light into one eye and then the other, looking closely, and then nods and tucks the light away again. "To be young and headstrong. You feel like you're going to throw up?"

"No."

"Tell me if you do, and I'll let you out. I don't need that smell inside my car. The blood is bad enough."

I sniff; I can smell the blood, too, over the vinyl. Metallic, a strange but natural smell. It's familiar. "Am I under arrest?" I ask.

"For what?"

"Hitting a police officer?"

"Son, you couldn't have hit that man if I hung him up for you like a piñata."

"I started it."

"Well, you certainly did do that. Although last time I checked, walking into a bar and saying something stupid wasn't a crime. If it were, I'd never get any rest."

I cautiously breathe out through my nostrils. The punch must not have landed squarely; if it had, my nose would be broken. The chief continues.

"Even if I could take you in for something, Matt, I wouldn't be inclined to do it. Your dad and I, we go back."

"I don't want any special treatment."

The chief shrugs. "There's a difference between what we want and what we get." He looks at me steadily. "You're lucky I know your dad. Lucky you weren't hurt worse tonight. You've always been the lucky one, haven't you?"

"I don't feel lucky. I never have."

"No?" He sighs deeply and turns to the window. "I suppose the truly fortunate ones never do."

I know what he's thinking. People don't talk about it, but it's always just below the surface. He must have been there. He must have seen everything.

"You think I was lucky that day, don't you?" I ask.

He turns back to me. "I do. We all do. You were the one who wasn't there. The day Greg Jessup carried your friend out of that classroom, he left most of your classmates behind where they lay."

"I know that."

"And you don't look at that as good fortune on your part?"

"I look at it as my mother worrying too much about my diabetes. I missed a lot of school in those days." I look down, my own blood drying on my hands. "Were you there?"

"I was. For seventy-two hours straight. With seventeen families. Their children didn't come out for a day and a half. Coroner, state police, FBI. They all had to do their work."

"What was it like?"

He shakes his head. "I've never told a reporter what I saw inside that school, and I'm not going to—"

"No, the families. What was it like with them?"

He's silent for a long moment, and I don't think he's going to answer. And then he does.

"You know what they all told me? They told me that their kid was really good at hiding." He pauses, his eyes still searching my face. "You know? Hiding? They had heard we were having trouble making identifications. It was a comfort to them. They wanted to believe that their child wasn't in that room after all. That they'd escaped and were hiding somewhere in the school. A locker, the boiler room. They asked me if we'd checked every single closet."

The smell of blood is flooding my nostrils. He goes on.

"No one was hiding. They were all inside." The chief looks away for another moment, and then back at me. "You know how many stories I heard about kids being great at hide-and-seek during the thirty-six hours before the official notifications?"

I shake my head.

"Like I said, I know your father, Matt."

"Yeah, I think he knows everybody."

"I've known him for a long time, since before the shooting. He's a good man."

"Sure."

"You don't think so now. You think he's just another suburban dad, a corporate hack. You'll never be like him, right?"

"You've got me all figured out."

"I remember him in the days afterward. Most of the other parents, the ones who had survivors, they went into hibernation. Locked up their houses, turned off the lights. Christ, I'm a father, I would have done the same. I would have put my son in my bed and wrapped my arms around him and held him close for a week straight if he had been little at that time, if he had been in that school, in that classroom.

"Your dad, though, he was different. He was everywhere. Not on TV; he avoided all that. He was helping. I had officers who wouldn't go talk to the parents who had lost their kids, grown men whose job it was, and they couldn't handle it. But your dad went to each one and did everything he could to help. He fed people, literally fed them. He paid people's bills for months on end. He bought the Thayers that van. He's an old-fashioned man; he didn't want any credit and he didn't want any limelight. He just took care of people the best he could. I'll always remember that about him." He looks at me again. "You ever talk about it with him?"

I shake my head. I had no idea about the van. I had no idea about any of it. "I guess I want to leave it behind," I say. I know it's a lie. If it were true, I wouldn't ask all these questions. I wouldn't hound Cole for memories. I wouldn't have the box.

The chief nods, rubs his leg again and cracks his neck, and looks past me at the empty sidewalk. "Let me tell you something, Matt, that I've learned and I wish I'd been told. There are some things you can't leave behind. They cling to you like cobwebs. They leave you with empty spaces. And the only thing you can do is to keep on going, as well and as gracefully as you can, without your missing parts."

We sit together for another moment. I feel exhausted. I put

my head back on the seat and close my eyes. "I'll take you home," the chief says. He gets out of the car and closes the door and climbs into the front seat.

We drive through twilit streets, neither of us speaking, the silence occasionally punctuated by comments from the police radio on the dash. We pull into my driveway, and the chief gets out of the car and opens my door. He bends down and looks inside.

"Part of being the chief of police is telling people how things are going to be. So now I'm going to tell you. You were never in the bar tonight, you understand?"

"Yes."

"Yes?"

"Yes, sir."

"Good. You're going to go inside and ice your face. I'll call you father later—"

"But—"

"I'm going to call your father later. You're going to go inside and stick your face in some ice, and you're not coming out again tonight. Officer Lucas—who, as far as you're concerned, you've never seen before—is going on vacation to get his head in order, and he won't be back until after Labor Day, if ever, and at any rate by that time you will be shagging fly balls on a baseball field in Pennsylvania instead of shagging women who are far too old for you back here in Jersey." DeLong coughs and shakes his head. "You were right, by the way. I knew Jessup for years. The last thing his daughter will ever need is another cop like him in her life."

I don't say anything. The chief looks at me again, studying my face.

"Am I being clear enough, Mr. Simpson?"

"Yes, sir. But sir, my friend, Cole Hewitt—"

"I know. I had a chat with the cashier while you were resting, and she told me about your conversation with Officer Lucas. He won't be within one hundred yards of Mr. Hewitt; you have my word on that." The chief steps back and lets me climb out of the car. "Do I need to worry about what will happen when you come back home for Thanksgiving and see Officer Lucas on the street, in or out of uniform?" he asks.

"I don't see myself coming back much."

"You may not see it, but it will happen. If I were a betting man, I'd lay money on your being in partnership down at your dad's firm in ten years."

I laugh out loud and shake my head. "That's not going to happen."

"My father was a cop. So was his father, and his brother. You know what I said I was never going to be when I grew up?"

"A cop."

"A cop. Our fathers give us something, and it's not so easy to give it back."

I decide to let that go. I nod and thank the chief for the ride, and for everything else. DeLong nods back at me and leaves me standing in the driveway.

My truck is back in front of the restaurant, and I'll have to retrieve it tomorrow. I should go inside now and get cleaned up. There's blood on my shirt and on my face; I would be lucky to slip into the bathroom without being seen, and I should probably just throw my clothes away. But I'm not feeling tired anymore. I'm not sure whether I slept in the back of the chief's car or whether I just rested my eyes, but my head has cleared, and the inside of my house is the last place I want to be.

My father's car isn't in the driveway, but my mother's is, a Land Rover just slightly more up-to-date than my truck. She has the bad habit of leaving the doors unlocked, and there's a copy of the key tucked in the glove box. We've told her that she's just asking to have it stolen, and that's exactly what I do now. I open the door and get inside, smell the new-car smell, turn on the engine, and back out of the driveway.

I am gone.

Seventeen

— Cole —

The smell of weed overwhelms me as soon as I come in the front door. There's no time to use the trellis; I have to grab what's left of Dad's meds and get out to the fairground. I'd told Mom I was going to be at Matt's, and she'd said that she was going out with a friend anyway, but the lights are on, and there's music playing somewhere. And there's the weed.

I make my way through the front hall — it looks like she actually did some tidying up — and into the kitchen. There's an open bottle of wine near the sink, cork still mounted on the corkscrew next to it. I silently step to the counter, mind reeling, nose filled with the dank scent of Dad's pot, and I peer into the living room half expecting to see him reclining in bed, smoking, the hospice nurse next to him on the couch reading one of her magazines.

That's not what I see. The bed is empty, but there is someone on the couch. Two people, actually, and they're not just sitting there. One of them is my mother, and the other is a man with longish white hair. She's leaning back, and he's sort of half on

326

top of her, kissing her, and it occurs to me that I've seen that hair before, that it's a hairstyle for a younger guy and that now that he's gone white, he ought to cut it. There's a pipe on the table in front of them, and the package from the mini-fridge is open next to it. Neither one of them has any idea that I'm standing here, peering in at them from the kitchen, and I have absolutely no idea — none — what to do.

The problem solves itself when the smoke detector goes off. We always took the batteries out if it when Dad smoked. The guy with white hair — it takes my brain a moment to accept that it's Mr. Finn — jumps up and looks at the ceiling. He steps up on the coffee table and reaches for the detector. He's laughing. Mom sits up, wipes her mouth, sees me in the kitchen, and screams.

There's chaos for a few moments because Finn seems to think that she's screaming at him for almost stepping on the pipe. He jumps down off the table, moves it, gets back up again, gets the batteries out of the smoke detector, and then finally sees me. Mom is sitting on the couch, face in her hands, and he's standing on the table holding the batteries. I walk into the living room.

Mom takes her face out of her hands. "Cole, baby," she says, "sit down." She gestures to the recliner on the far side of the room. Mr. Finn has gotten down off the table and sits on the couch next to her. I don't know what else to do, so I go and sit. I'm trying to make sense of two things at once: one, what the hell is going on here; and two, how am I going to empty out the mini-fridge with the two of them sitting right in front of it?

I look at them looking at me. It's a weird tableau; I feel like I'm meeting a girlfriend's parents for the first time, waiting for her to come downstairs, everyone trying to think of something to talk about. Not that I've ever actually been in that situation.

"Cole, baby," Mom says again, "I didn't want you to find out like this. I thought you were at Matt's for the night."

"Find out what, Mom?"

"Well, about Mark. About Mark and me." It takes me a second to remember that Mr. Finn's first name is Mark.

"Look at you," I say. "You're sitting right next to the bed where Dad died."

She looks at the bed, and Mr. Finn looks down at his shoes. "Cole," she begins again, "you have to understand. Or no, you don't have to. You don't have to do anything. I know that someone your age won't understand it, but please—I'm trying to move on. I just want to—have some happiness. It's not that I don't miss your dad . . . oh, God, this is so awful. We have to get rid of this damn bed. I just thought it would upset you if it disappeared—"

"You're not well, Mom," I say. "You've got Complex Bereavement. I'm *not going to college* so that I can stay here and take care of you."

She looks at me in surprise. "Baby, you're not going to college because you weren't *ready* to go to college. Which I completely understood, and supported you on. What happened with your dad was terrible, and I want you to have as much time as you need. But you don't need to stay here for me." She pauses in midsentence, her mouth still open. She and Finn are both studying me like I'm some sort of rare specimen. "Is that what you thought?" she asks. "That you needed to stay here for me?"

No, no, no. That isn't right. What the fuck is she talking about? She's been in her room, in bed. She looks like shit ninety-nine percent of the time. Sometimes she starts crying for no reason at all. I've driven her to the doctor, to the therapist. She's why I'm staying; I'm staying to *take care of her.*

"Cole, love," she whispers. I look at her and can't see her clearly, and that's when I realize I'm crying.

I'm not going to do this, not in front of him. "I was ready, Mom," I say. My voice is too shaky. "You needed me. You needed me here."

She stares back at me, unwavering. "Cole, you need to hear this. This is important. Cole, I am all right. I'm okay. I will always miss your father. Always. And you're right, I've grieved for him. I didn't move ahead with things, cleaning this room out for one, although that was mainly because I thought it might upset you more if I did things too fast. I see that I was wrong. I see that we should have talked about it more. But Cole, you need to understand that I am all right. I will be all right. You can go, Cole, whenever you are ready."

This is bullshit. This isn't true. Finn looks embarrassed. "I should probably leave," he finally says.

"No," I tell him. "I'm going." I stand, turn away, and leave the

329

house without another word. I hear my mom calling. She sounds more disappointed than upset, and that makes it even worse. I get back in the car, turn on the engine, and gun it backwards down the driveway, sending up a cloud of dust.

Where is Finn's car? How did he get here? Is he parking down the street? Is everyone sneaking around and getting laid but me?

It's 6:09 when I get to the fairgrounds. I hate being late. The truck is in the middle of the field, but there's no balloon. Materials are spread out on the grass around the wicker basket. I get out of the car, and Eddie emerges from the back of the truck, covered in sweat.

"Motherfucker," he says. "Where have you been? You think I can get this all done by myself?"

"You were supposed to have someone with you."

"Well, I don't," he says. "He couldn't make it, and I've been hauling this all by myself."

It's all right. We set it up before. We can do it. We can get it up in fifteen minutes.

"Let's do it," I say. "We can make it."

"Where's your shit?"

I reach into my glove box, my hands shaking, hoping that Matt's contribution will be enough to satisfy Eddie. I pull out the packed ziplock and hand it to him.

"I know it doesn't look like much," I say, "but it's supposed to be really good, uh, quality. Good stuff. Good, uh, shit."

Eddie marches to the hood of his truck and throws the bag

330

down, opening it up and taking out one pill and then another, squinting at them carefully, brow furrowed. I shift from one foot to another and stare at the gear. Seconds are passing.

"Cole," Eddie finally says. His voice is ominous. "Cole, come here and look at this."

I go and stand next to him. He's pinching one of the pills between his thumb and his index figure. It's an oval, sort of sea green.

"Cole, do you know what this is?"

I shake my head.

He holds it right in front of my face. "Take a close look."

"Eddie, I'm not the expert—"

"So let me tell you. This is a generic erectile dysfunction drug that was discontinued three years ago because it put guys in the hospital with boners that wouldn't go away."

"Oh."

"And it looks like someone used a pin or a needle to scratch the markings off of it. And this"—he holds up another pill—"is ibuprofen. Also scratched. It's crap. Half the stuff in this bag is crap."

"Oh."

"Yeah. 'Oh.' So, let me ask you something else, Cole. Do you think I'm a fucking idiot?"

I do. Although I may have underestimated him, given the knowledge of pharmacology he's demonstrating here. That's not what I'm thinking when I smile, though. I smile because it's dawning on me exactly what happened. Whatever Matt's source was for the pills must have dried up, and instead of telling me, instead of calling the plan off, he took old bottles from his parents' medicine cabinet and sat in his room for hours, scratching at them with a safety pin, putting them into this bag one at a time, pill after pill after pill.

Smiling turns out to be a mistake. I never see Eddie's fist coming; it catches me on my lower lip, and then I'm on my back in the grass, looking up at him, dazed. "I can get you more later," I manage.

"There is no 'later,' Cole," Eddie says. "There is a bigger picture here. That package is expected tonight. There is going to be a shit storm, and I am going to be right in the middle of it, you fucking asshole." With that, he turns his back to me, surveys the scene in front of him — the wicker basket, coils of rope, and the deflated balloon spread out on the grass — then shakes his head, spits on the ground — barely missing my outstretched feet — and gets into his truck.

"Now I have to clean up all kinds of shit," he calls from the open window. "You fucking stay here and watch this gear until someone comes to get it." He starts the engine. "Asshole!" he calls once more as he tears a tight U-turn, and roars across the field in a cloud of exhaust.

I finally get to my feet when the sound of his engine fades. There's blood in my mouth, and I spit into the grass. There's a patch of clover at my feet, but I can't think of its name. There has to be a way to do this. There has to be a way to adapt. It's

6:18, but Viola might be late, if she comes at all. I have done this before. I saw Eddie do it. I took notes. I grope for my notebook and flip to the right page. She's probably not coming, anyway.

The jottings don't mean a thing to me right now. I'd made a diagram that looks like spaghetti. There are at least three different kinds of rope on the ground at my feet, and I can't remember what the differences are or what any of them are for.

And then I hear a car behind me. Not the loud truck engine. Not Matt's Explorer.

The motor shuts off, a door opens and closes, and then there is silence. I don't turn around. I wish I were someplace else, anyplace else. There is literally nothing in this world that I can't mess up.

You're stronger than people think you are.

"Is this my surprise?"

I suck at my lower lip and bleed more into my mouth. "This was the surprise. It didn't work out the way I planned."

She steps to my side and studies my damaged face, then walks past me and approaches the balloon. She is wearing jeans and a sleeveless purple T-shirt, her hair up in a ponytail. It hurts me to look at her. She stops by the basket and turns back to me. "What exactly *was* the plan, Cole?"

The plan suddenly seems incredibly stupid. It always was, of course. Juvenile, stupid, an impotent attempt at winning the affection of someone whose mind is already a thousand miles away on the West Coast. I walk over to her. "The plan," I say, because it doesn't matter anymore, "was to go for a balloon ride."

"A balloon ride?"

"A tethered ride. I don't actually know how to fly a balloon."

"That's comforting."

"We'd just go up and down. On a rope." She looks doubtful. "Don't worry, it's not going to happen."

Viola hops up onto the edge of the basket, swivels, and drops inside.

I have two choices. I can stand here in the field, watching her. I can watch her examine the remnants of my plan. I can watch her drive away. I can watch her leave for college, leave my life, leave me here.

Or I can get in the fucking basket.

Promise me: All the way.

Matt would already be in the basket.

The awful daring of a moment's surrender / Which an age of prudence can never retract / By this, and this only, we have existed.

Holy fucking Christ, I love Eliot.

I swing up and over, into the basket with her. She leans against the far side, looking at me. I look at the sky, imagining the sunset I was planning on.

"Your mouth is bleeding," she says.

"I know."

Neither one of us speaks.

"Well?" she finally asks.

This is it. The piece I've been working on for three weeks is on the tip of my tongue. I've labored over every line, every image.

I've spent afternoons debating commas. I can say it in my sleep.
It's good. It's very good.

"I'm not going to recite my poem," I say.

"No? After all that?"

"No."

I step toward her. She crosses her arms over her chest.

"You disappeared on me to go and write a poem, and now I
don't even get to hear it?"

I take another step. My eyes don't leave hers. My face hurts. I
haven't done anything right all summer, but standing in this basket in the middle of a silent, empty field, I don't care about any
of it. I don't care about my mom and Mr. Finn and I don't care
about Eddie or about Paul and, for a sliver of time, I don't even
care about Matt. I care about this moment that's never going to
come again, and I care that I'll never forgive myself for missing it.

"You don't get to hear it. Not right now."

By this, and this only, we have existed.

I take the final step, and before I have time to think about
the blood in my mouth or about any of the other reasons that
this is an unreasonable thing to do, I kiss her.

This, and this only.

I kiss her with my broken lip, and when I stop and step back,
her eyes are closed. She keeps them closed for what feels like a
very long time.

Then she opens them.

She looks surprised.

Eighteen

— *Matt* —

How long have I been here?

It could have been an hour. Two. It could have been five minutes.

No, that's not right. Longer. On the longer side. When I got here, they were still closing, the last families packing up and heading home, closing up the Snack Shack for the night. And now it's dark. Mostly dark. There's still a tiny bit of pink in the sky, off to the west, beyond the Monument.

The smell is back, stronger than ever, unbearable. I wonder if my nose is bleeding on the inside somehow, or if I'm hemorrhaging into my sinuses from the beating I took, because when I focus on it, I think the smell of blood seems to be coming from inside of my head. But when I try to blow my nostrils out onto the sand, nothing comes.

It isn't just blood that I'm smelling. There are other things. There's something chemical mixed in, sharp, biting at the inside of my face. I try to scrape it out of my throat with a deep hock into the sand, and then I lie back.

When did I last eat?

When did I last check my blood sugar?

I can't remember. My granola bars are in my truck, parked downtown by the restaurant.

I shut my eyes. I think of Cole, floating out there somewhere at the end of a rope in a basket with Viola. I smile. I might doze a little.

When I open my eyes, I'm standing up and shedding my clothes.

There's a thin breeze coming in off the water, and I'm sweating.

I'm thinking of Cole's face, staring out of the newspaper. Of his eyes.

I'm thinking of Chris Thayer's little body, like Jell-O.

I'm thinking of eighteen empty chairs.

I'm thinking that maybe there were meant to be nineteen.

I'm not thinking anything at all.

The wind isn't blowing away the smell, and in the moment before I step into the water, I finally know what it is. It's familiar, but I've never smelled it before. It's the thing Cole told me about when I saw him for the first time afterward. Out in Vine Cottage, he told me the one thing he remembered, because I asked, and maybe he doesn't remember it now, maybe his brain scrubbed it just like mine seems to have, but that's what this is. Sent from his seven-year-old brain to mine in whatever words he used that day, it hid deep down, wherever you put the memories that you don't want, the ones that aren't even memories at all but are terrible things that you imagine because you don't have any choice. And now it's drifting up again.

It is the smell of blood, and gunpowder, and urine, all mixed together, lingering in the air in the long, terrifying minutes before Officer Jessup took Cole out of the classroom.

I'm in the water. I'm up to my knees, then my hips, then my waist, and now I bend and push off into the deep.

I hear a voice calling, somewhere in the distance, maybe back on the main road. Maybe some kids, heading to the Monument. It doesn't matter.

I don't pull too hard. I aim straight out to the center of the lake, straight toward the farthest bank, and whether I get there or not won't be my choice or anyone else's choice. The dice weren't thrown that day, but now they finally, finally are. I'll know the answer. I'll know whether I am meant to have a life.

One arm over another, churning the water behind me with my feet, I reach the center of the lake and stop. My arms and legs are shaking with the effort and with a lack of sugar.

I turn in a slow circle, gauging the distance from the shore. Finally, I raise my head. I'm dizzy, like I can feel the planet spinning around me. It's supposed to be infinitely deep here; it's supposed to keep on going and going. No one's been to the bottom.

I lean back in the water and float, letting my arms and legs rest, letting the lake hold me up. I imagine myself as I would look from above, a naked white speck in a great circle of darkness.

What would I find if I dove all the way down? What things that no one besides me has ever seen? I wonder about it for a moment, and then I turn myself in the water. I take a deep breath and let it out, feeling the air fill my lungs, and then I take another and I flip, driving myself downward.

I open my eyes, but there's nothing to see. It's black all around me, and I think you could really lose track of which way is up and which is down in a place like this. I kick, driving myself deeper, and I see something ahead of me. It's a burst of color, red then green. My legs are starting to shake, and I feel a hollowness in my stomach. I blow bubbles out of my nose, almost the last of my air, and I feel them trace the side of my face as they rise. I'm still descending.

The lights are exploding in front of me now, and I can hear them, their voices and their names.

Steven Abrams. Patrick Clemson.

They seem to be coming from somewhere ahead of me, though there can't be that much farther to go.

Susan Edwards.

I kick harder, reaching out with both hands and pulling at the water. No one else knows what is down here, but I do. I do now. I kick as hard as I can. I'm reaching the last of my strength.

Andrew Gerber.

The last of the air is gone from my lungs, and I stop, because I know I'm never going to get there. I stop descending and turn in the water, hanging suspended in space, and my last clear thought is that while I do remember the way back to the surface, I may have come too far to reach it on my own.

Nineteen

— *Cole* —

I'm looking out at the water. I'm listening.

I pulled into the lot just in time for the sweep of my headlights to catch something moving, a flash of white out on the water. I got out of my car and called Matt's name, but nothing came back to me.

His mother's Land Rover is on the far side of the lot, tucked in the trees. She called me and said that both he and her car were missing and that he wasn't answering his phone. I told her I knew where he was, because I knew he wouldn't want her to call the police.

Viola and I had sat by the basket for a long while, sometimes talking and sometimes not. No one ever came to get the balloon, and after the call came, we left it lying in the dark field. She went home, and I came here.

I might have again assumed that Matt was with Sarah, or at the gym, or out driving somewhere, but I didn't. I knew where he was. At least, I thought I did.

341

I stand in the stillness. He wouldn't be in the water alone; that can't have been him — it would be too crazy. He brought me with him when he tried to swim the lake; he at least had the good sense to do that. I walk around to the car and peer inside. Then I turn and make my way across the lot.

There is a moment, as I reach the boundary between the asphalt and the sand, when I think I hear something splash out on the water, and I stop and listen. There's nothing.

I continue on, past the locked-up Snack Shack, toward the boat. There had been a bit of moonlight, but now it is covered by a cloud, and I can't see much of the water.

I round the inverted hull of the rowboat. I see the pile of familiar clothes in the sand. I hear a splash again, far out on the water, farther than it should be. That's when I know, and I break into a run, reaching the waterside and calling my friend's name. There's no response. I hurry back to the clothes, dig into the pocket of his shorts and take out his cell phone, swipe the screen, enter the password, and tap on the icon for the app, cursing as it takes moments to appear.

Forty-six. The arrow pointing straight down.

I should call the police, but there's no cell signal, and it would take time for them to come. It would take time for them to bring a boat and get it in the water. It would take time for them to set up their searchlights. An image comes to me: dawn, here, on this beach. Cops. Divers trudging into the water. Men with dogs walking along the shore.

I'm not going to let that happen.

I run back and plant my hands on the wooden hull of the lifeguard boat, pushing as hard as I can. It hardly budges. I crouch and wiggle my fingers between the wood and the sand, and I lift. My feet scrabble, seeking traction, and I cry out to the sky as my legs and arms and back all strain.

My father had done this; my father, who stood six foot four inches tall and before the cancer weighed two hundred and twenty-five pounds, all of it muscle. I'm not my father, but I keep straining, keep lifting, and the boat begins to turn, rolling over reluctantly, the center of gravity hovering between earth and sky and then shifting, leaving me on my knees as it flips right-side up.

I leap to my feet, seize the oars that had been under the boat, and throw them inside; then I run around to the stern. I plant my feet again and push. It takes a moment, but the craft begins to move down the beach, the hiss of passing sand mingling with my panting in the silence. The momentum builds, and then suddenly the bow strikes the water and I plow directly into the solid wood, the wind knocked out of me, and then I'm pushing again and leaping in, seating myself in the center and seizing the oars, positioning them on each side, pulling as hard as I can.

Dad was always the one to row, even when I was old enough to try. I would sit behind him in the bow, but when we came to an interesting place to stop, he would turn around so that we were facing each other, and we would talk. We talked about biology, mostly, about the flora and fauna of the lake and the shore around it, the birds above us in the sky. It seemed like he could see whole universes in a little patch of water, or under a boulder by the shore. He could answer any question I asked, all the way up until the last one, when there had been nothing he could offer other than holding my hand and whispering that this, too, like all things, would pass.

The oars are heavier than I thought they would be. My muscles ache as I try to lift them simultaneously and make the long, sweeping movements that Dad had made. I lean back, looking up at the night sky, and propel myself out onto the lake, and when I've come some way, I turn and scan the water around me.

I have no idea where to look. The sound I had heard seemed like it was far out in the water, but this is a big lake, bigger when you're looking for someone in it. I spin in a complete circle on the seat, straining my eyes, and then I scream Matt's name out over the water. Again, there is no reply.

I resume my rowing. I'll position myself in the center of the lake so that I have the best chance of spotting something in any direction. I will stay out here for as long as I need to, all night. I will row in concentric circles until I have covered every square foot of water. I will not leave without him.

I reach what I think is the middle, and as I rest the oars, the moon emerges and the light spills down over the water and there he is, floating just a few feet off of the bow. He is face-down, and as I watch, he waves his arms slowly and turns his head to the side, gasping for air. I seize the oars, my hands burning and blistering, but I'm able to maneuver the boat close to him, managing to guide it near Matt's shoulders without striking his head, and I lurch over to grab him and I pull him in, tipping and nearly capsizing.

He lies naked in the bottom of the boat. He doesn't respond to his name. He is breathing, shallowly and quickly, and he is shaking. I turn us toward the beach, and even though I think I have nothing left to give, I get us to land. As the bow grinds into the sand, I vault out and pull the boat up onto the beach, and then I turn back to Matt, who is not moving.

The first time Matt slept over at my house, well over a decade ago, his mother gave my parents a lecture on diabetic shock. I listened to it too. I was fascinated by the idea that all the strength could drain out of a person if he took a bit too much insulin or was too active without eating enough. I'd carefully memorized the symptoms, and when Matt came over, I always made sure that there was some orange juice in the fridge. I don't have any orange juice now, though.

I leave him in the boat and run up the beach. The door to the Snack Shack is locked. I step back and kick it as hard as I can, but it doesn't budge. I try again, and a pain explodes in my hip. I hobble around to the front, but the order window has a board over it with a heavy padlock. I continue up the beach, my hip screaming, my shoulders and back still aching to the point of numbness from rowing. I reach the parking lot and then my car. I back up my old Volvo in a wide U-turn, pause for a moment to fasten my seat belt, and then I step down hard on the gas.

The station wagon lurches across the parking lot with the screech of rubber, the rear fishtailing back and forth as I pull hard on the wheel, and then I'm in the sand. My tires fight for traction and I keep my foot down, urging it to go faster, bracing my arms against the wheel until at the last moment I remember that's not what you're supposed to do, and instead I throw myself behind the dashboard, across the passenger seat.

The car crashes into the Snack Shack like a battering ram. Wood buckles, the door is knocked off its hinges, and an entire corner of the structure crashes down onto my hood. For a moment, everything is silent. I slowly sit back up and look out at dust settling in the glow of the headlights. Then I unbuckle, open the door, and stumble from the car, bruised and dazed, crawling over the fender and through the wreckage, forcing my way into the building. I finally reach the fridge and pull it open, grab a bottle of juice, and then crawl out and run down the beach. I climb back into the boat.

Matt is shaking badly now. His entire body is secreting a thick, unhealthy sweat. His breathing is even more rapid than before. I open the bottle and hold it to his mouth, trying to pour a small amount inside, but he doesn't respond. A stronger breeze is coming in from the water, and it reaches us in the bottom of the boat. Matt's shaking intensifies. I stretch out beside him and get him to turn, trying to shield him from the wind. I coax his mouth open and pour more juice inside, and this time Matt takes some of it in.

I continue on, just like that, sheltering Matt with my body, pouring small amounts of juice into his mouth, feeling his heart hammering and listening to him breathe. There are moments when he whimpers, but he doesn't open his eyes. I don't know what happens if you can't get someone out of shock, but in time he stops shaking, and his breathing becomes more regular. Most of the bottle is gone. Now I have to get him warm.

I climb back out and retrieve a wool blanket my father left rolled up in the back of the station wagon, and I spread it over him. I shine the light from my phone on his face; Matt's color is coming back, though he seems to have a bunch of bruises, and his nose looks damaged. I finger my own split lip and trot back over to his pile of clothes in the sand, picking up his cell and checking the app. Sixty-eight and rising. Good.

I climb up to the bow of the boat and perch there, looking out over the lake, which is now illuminated by the unobstructed moon. There are too many things to think about, so I don't think about anything. Minutes pass by.

"Cole."

I look down. He's pushed himself up onto one arm and is looking around.

"You're an idiot," I tell him.

He nods. I slide back down into the boat and onto the seat

in the center. Neither one of us says anything more. He's looking down, and his wet hair is plastered to his face, falling over his eyes. He doesn't brush it away, and it's irritating me as I stare at him, waiting for him to say something. Without thinking, I reach out to swipe at it. It's only when my fingers brush his face that I realize the water on it is warm and he is crying.

"I'm sorry," he says. His voice is low and raspy.

"No worries. I was feeling like going for a row."

He shakes his head. "I'm sorry I wasn't there with you. I'm sorry I wasn't with Andy."

"I'm not sorry," I say. "That was the luckiest thing about that day. It was the luckiest thing that's ever happened to me. That you weren't there. That I didn't lose both of you."

"*That* was the luckiest thing?"

"That was the luckiest thing."

It was.

"What the hell were you doing out here?" I ask him.

"I wanted to know."

"Know what? If you could swim it? You already swam it!"

"I wanted to know if I was meant to live."

"Well, you're alive."

"I'm alive because you saved me."

"Maybe I was meant to save you. Maybe we were meant to save each other."

He looks at me for the first time, but he doesn't say anything.

He looks down at the empty bottle of juice in the bottom of the boat.

"Cole?"

"Ycah."

"I'm buck-fucking naked."

"You are." We look at each other. We both laugh.

I tell him it's time to go home, and he agrees. But still, we sit in the boat for a little while longer.

Twenty

— *Matt* —

I figured she'd want to meet at her house, or maybe out at the lake. She didn't. And now we're sitting in the diner, cups of coffee in front of us, and I'm imagining a dozen pairs of eyes on me.

This must be what Cole feels like. It doesn't feel good.

Kathy listens to our orders without writing them down. She looks at Sarah for just a moment too long, and then she walks away. I study the Senate bill hanging over the saltshaker.

"You leave tomorrow?" she finally asks.

I look at her and nod. She's not wearing any makeup. I didn't realize that she always was when I was with her, but I can see it in its absence. She's dressed for work; this is her lunch break. She has the white ribbon in her hair. She smiles.

"You must be excited."

"I am."

"Does the season start right away?"

"Yeah, first practice is in a few days."

I'll be starting the season on the disabled list, but I'll be playing soon. I've taken the meds for the last three days running, and they help. My arm is still weak, but the team has a trainer who's going to work with me. I'll be throwing soon.

"What about you?" I ask. I imagine her, here, alone in her father's empty house. She smiles.

"Well, if a guy like you can make it to college, I might be able to get there too."

"Yeah?"

"Maybe."

"You should. You really should. I mean, you wouldn't have to go, like, full-time. I know someone who went to Rutgers part-time—"

She shakes her head. "Not here. I'm leaving New Jersey. I was thinking of the University of Nebraska."

"Oh."

She peels the wrapper off a straw and twists it around her fingers. "You'll miss me when you come home to visit."

"I guess I will."

"You were hoping you could drop in from time to time, hmm?"

"No. That wasn't what I was thinking."

Kathy brings our food and sets it down, but neither one of us eats. Sarah looks at the nearest posting. "What do you think of that?" she asks.

I look at it. It's a newer one. High-capacity clips. "I don't know."

"Dad hated that stuff. The gun-control people. We never came in here to eat."

"I think . . . I think it'd have to help, wouldn't it? The thing in Texas, that office complex—"

"How many people? Eight?"

"Eight for now, but they say it might wind up being nine or ten."

She nods. "It would have to help."

I study the bill. "Who writes this stuff?" I ask. "Who can even read it?"

"Lawyers."

"Yeah. My dad's a lawyer."

"You could go to law school," she says.

"I guess." I remember what the chief said, about winding up at Dad's firm.

"You could do something about this." She nods toward the failed bill. I wonder what the vote was. I wonder if it was close.

"You think I'd make a good lawyer?" I ask.

"I think you'd make a good senator." She takes a bite of her sandwich. I wait for her to finish chewing and laugh, but she doesn't. "What about me?" she finally asks. "What do you think I should do?"

"I think you should be a teacher." I hadn't thought about it, but as I say it, I know it's right.

"You think? A teacher?"

"A teacher," I say. "Ms. Jessup, fifth-grade teacher."

"I like younger kids. Ms. Jessup, first-grade teacher."

"That's better," I agree.

We eat in silence for a few minutes. I know that this is the last time we'll ever see each other. When her plate is clear, she pushes it to one side, reaches across the table, and takes my hand.

"When I think of you," she says, "I'll think of you on a baseball field, diving for the ball. I'll think of you in a college classroom, studying to be a lawyer."

I nod. I don't know what to say.

"How will you think of me?" she asks. "How will you remember me?"

I look out the window and see movement reflected behind me, my best and oldest friend wearing a baseball cap, sitting on a stool at the counter, swiveling halfway toward us and then pausing and turning back to his food. His back is straight. He's listening. I wish I could pause time and ask him what I should say. I wish I had his mind for making images out of words. I'd like to tell her something that she can remember, that she can take with her to Nebraska, that she'll have when she walks into a classroom as a teacher for the first time, because I know she'll be so scared.

There is an image in my mind, but I don't know if I have the words.

I turn back to Sarah, and I tell her. Probably not as well as he could, but the best I can.

She smiles.

Twenty-One

— *Cole* —

This is the first morning to hint at autumn. Everything is still green, and the day will turn hot later, but at this moment, there's a chill promising that summer is eventually going to end.

Matt is leaving today. I pull up to his house in my scraped and dented car. My bruises are beginning to fade, and I can walk without limping now. It looks like he's almost done packing; his dad's truck is stuffed.

I'm not the only one here. A van is pulled up to the curb, and as I walk up the driveway, Chris Thayer comes out the side door of the house and rolls toward me. I haven't seen him since graduation.

"How are you, Cole?" he asks.

"I'm good, Chris. How are you doing?"

"Good." He stops next to me. "Just came to say goodbye."

"Yeah. Me too." I hesitate. "What are you doing this fall?" I finally ask, afraid that the answer is nothing, although I thought I heard he had some sort of job.

"Internship," he replies. "Declanell Industries." He looks at my blank face. "They're a pretty big company. They're actually one of the biggest biomed firms on the East Coast."

"Oh. What are you—"

"Engineering, dude. Biomedical engineering. I'm putting in a half year at DI, and then I'm going to Princeton."

"You're going to Princeton? That's . . . amazing, Chris. That's amazing. I didn't know you were doing that."

He looks embarrassed. "Well, I didn't talk about it much."

"Why not?"

"I just . . . I don't want to be a poster boy, you know? The kid who triumphs in spite of his disability. That's what it was like, being class president. I don't like everyone watching me all the time. I mean, people already stare at me, but I don't need to symbolize something."

"Yeah, I get that. I know something about being a poster boy."

"I guess you do. Any words of wisdom for when all eyes turn to you?"

I don't have any of my own, but I remember a little kid on the night of his holiday concert, terrified to go onstage. I remember his best friend, holding his hand and whispering in his ear. "You don't have to do it all at once," I tell Chris. "You just have to get through one breath at a time. One moment at a time."

"Decent advice."

"Also, screw all of 'em."

He laughs. "I like that better. What about you? What are you going to do?"

"I'm working at Finn's, taking a couple of online classes, and then I'm also heading to school in the spring."

"Cool."

Matt emerges from the house carrying a plastic container, and he shoves it into the back.

"Anything I can do to help?" I ask.

"Perfect timing," he says, slamming the tailgate with effort against the overflowing baggage. He grins at me. He's been busy packing, and I haven't seen him since the diner.

Matt asked me to come to breakfast with them. I didn't know what to expect, but I told him I would because he seemed so nervous. He'd been with this woman all summer, but something about sitting down with her in public freaked him out, and he wanted me there. He'd told me the story of how his face got banged up, and I asked if he was afraid of the cop, but he shook his head. "I just don't know what to say," he told me. "I'm scared I'm not going to know what to say."

I wore one of his old baseball caps and got there early. I sat at the counter, nursing a cup of coffee and a plate of pancakes. I noticed that being exposed like that didn't bother me quite the way it used to. When they came in, he steered her to the booth right behind me, where I could hear every word they said.

He did well. When she asked him her question, at the end, I almost had to turn and look. I wanted to jump into the booth next to him and take my best shot at it. But I didn't have to; he did a good job on his own.

"I'm going to remember you on the beach at nighttime," he told her. "I'm going to remember you looking up at the stars. I'm going to remember you looking lonely but not afraid."

Pretty good.

Maybe he *would* make a good senator. I can see it. I'd probably vote for him.

Matt's mother comes out of the house. She's crying. Chris's mom is with her, an arm around her shoulder, and they're followed by Matt's dad. He's going to drive Matt out to Bucknell and then bring the truck back. He looks sad but calm. He's a good guy. When Dad was first diagnosed, Mr. Simpson came out to the house and spent a whole weekend with him and Mom, figuring out everything with the insurance, making sure it would all be covered, and when anything came up with any of the treatments, they called him and he made the problem go away. Mom told Matt the story a few days ago, when he came over for dinner, the first time he'd been over in a long time. We ate, and then we sat in the living room, bed and mini-fridge gone, and Mom told him all about what his dad had done for us.

It's weird to say goodbye in front of people. Matt shakes Chris's hand and then gives me his car keys. "Promise me," he says, "first time it snows, drive the truck instead of your wagon."

"Sure."

"I mean, the Volvo's built like a tank, but you get no traction."

"Yeah, I know. Thanks."

"You remember how you skidded across the school lot last winter?"

"I missed Mr. Kelly's BMW by an inch."

"I was rooting for you to at least nick it."

"I know you were."

I pause, searching for something to say, and in the space of that moment, Matt grabs me in a bear hug and lifts me off my feet. "Cole," he says into my ear, "I love you."

"Yeah," I say. "Me too."

He looks at me and laughs. "I'll see you at Thanksgiving," he says, and then he goes and hugs his mother and gets into the passenger side of the truck. His dad gives his mom a hug and a kiss, gives me a big wink, gets in on the driver's side, and backs them out of the driveway. I see my friend through the glass, looking out at me, looking at the home he is leaving, and I wave to him and make myself smile, and then he is gone.

I leave the Simpsons' house behind and drive toward the center of town. It's the unofficial end: the last day of the last summer that we'll all be children. It's Independence Day. Some people, like Viola, have already left. I have a ticket out to Berkeley for the first weekend in October. I'm not trying to make it a surprise; I asked her if she wanted me to come out, and she said she did. Who knows what will happen? For now, it's enough that the ticket is sitting there in my desk, a date on the calendar to look forward to. A possibility. Something to show up for.

I pass the street where Sarah Jessup lives, and I step on the brakes and lean over the empty passenger seat, peering down toward her house. There's a FOR SALE sign hanging there. I speed back up again.

Most people leave, in one way or another. Some people leave home. Some people's bodies fail them, and they sleep under the ground in the cemetery on the edge of town, in a spot where the field full of gravestones gives way to forest, where the light of the sun strikes my father's name at dawn but where the shade falls at midday, when I sometimes sit with him now. His favorite quotation is inscribed below his name. It's from Charles Darwin, and it reads: A MAN WHO DARES TO WASTE ONE HOUR OF TIME HAS NOT DISCOVERED THE VALUE OF LIFE.

Someday, when I publish my first book, I plan to dedicate it to my father and to place that quote below his name so that they can live on next to each other somewhere besides on a tombstone.

I reach the center of town and pass Finn's Grocery, already open for business. My mother's boyfriend is out front hanging a sign, his white hair tied back. I honk and slow down and he turns, sees me, and waves. I wave back and drive on.

Most people leave, but there are a few who never will. I come out the other side of the downtown, turn, and stop in front of the Gerbers' house. There's a carnival today at the fairground, and Paul wants to go. It's going to be the last one of the year. I think we're mainly going for the food, although his mother also told me that he likes some of the rides, the merry-go-round and the Ferris wheel. I'll take him, and I'll go on with him as many times as he wants.

I turn the car off and get out. It's quiet here, for the most part. There's no one else in sight.

And then there is. A little boy in one of the front yards across the street. He bolts across the lawn wearing nothing but shorts and a pair of swim goggles. He grabs a coiled hose and turns it on, and when he straightens up, he notices me for the first time, watching him from beside my car. He might be five years old, or maybe six. He has bright red hair sticking out in all directions, and pale skin, and he's smiling like whatever he's up to with the hose is the best idea in the world.

We stare at each other for a moment, and then he turns and continues on about his business. He drags the hose toward the backyard and disappears around the side of the house, and seconds later I hear the screams and squeals of other children.

For a moment, I can believe that the sounds are coming from the other direction, that they are the echoes of three young boys, best friends who love one another more than anything, playing and tumbling and wrestling on a late-summer morning many years ago. But the house behind me is silent.

I turn, and I go inside.

Twenty-Two

— *Matt* —

You never have to pay to get into New Jersey, only to get out. It's an observation that Dad never gets tired of making, but this time, I laugh along.

We're fourth in line in the only toll lane for the Phillipsburg Bridge. Most highways don't even have these lanes anymore, I don't think, but this old bridge does, and Dad seems to love it. He has a roll of tokens in the cup holder and patiently waits to pull up to the little basket where he can throw one in and turn the light green, while cars stream through the transponder lanes on each side.

One of the cars goes through, and we edge up in the line. I settle back in my seat and close my eyes. I was up early this morning. It took forever to pack and the truck is stuffed, filled with clothes and baseball gear. There are two boxes of vitamins and low-carb snacks that Mom insisted I bring along. There's a coat for when it turns cold, since I may not be back before then.

Boxes and bags, all the things that, for one reason or another,

I couldn't leave behind. Not too much memorabilia, just enough from my box to remind me of where I'm from. And, deep within it all, an old book that belonged to a girl I hardly knew; a girl who might have grown to be, among many other things, my friend.

The truck has reached the front of the line. I open my eyes. Dad rolls down the window and tosses a token into the center of the basket. The light in front of us turns green, and we accelerate out of the booth and onto the bridge.

— *Acknowledgments* —

I am deeply grateful to my agent, Adam Schear, who was an early and constant supporter of this book, and to Margaret Raymo and the wonderful professionals at HMH, who have been generous with their insight and publishing wisdom. Thanks as well to my friends and fellow writers Allison Freeman, Mark Cecil, and Christian Douglass for their editorial contributions and support.

I would not have been able to write this book had I not been surrounded by a wonderful family: Anna, Abigail, and David, who survived siblinghood and became my friends; Jacob, Nora, Nathan, and Charlotte, who are the lights of my life; my mother, Rebecca, a tireless and insightful reader who manages to combine unconditional support with a keen editorial pen; and my father, Jonathan, who cultivated my love for books and went back to read my first favorite story from the beginning the very same night he finished it.

My gratitude for my wife, Leah, is beyond words. She is my trusted editor and first reader, my partner and collaborator in this and all things, my best friend, and the love of my life.